Abuse Cocaine &

Abuse Cocaine & Soft Furnishings

Andrew Sparke

Abuse Cocaine & Soft Furnishings

ISBN 978 0 9576211 2 1

Cover by Noxiousdesign based on an image taken from the 2002 Turkish film 'Uzak' (released in the US as 'Distant') used by kind permission of Nuri Bilge Ceylan and NBC Films.

APS Publications, 4 Oakleigh Road, Stourbridge,West Midlands, DY8 2JX

Chapter I Now: November

Leave Istanbul in the rain. I'd like to think the city is crying for my leaving. But it isn't. It's just a wet, dull, late November day. Common enough. But for me distinctly abnormal.

The car edges along in heavy traffic. Past the Inonu Stadium, home to Besiktas, The Hilton up near Taksim Square, high above, as a backdrop. Staying there long ago I'd seen a home game, looking down from the comfort of my hotel room watching tiny footballers scurrying around, not then appreciating the atmosphere I was missing. But that was before a woman changed me from one of life's spectators into a painfully real participant. It always takes a woman to change those of us who grow too much armour too young.

No obvious road numbers on the gantry signs. Chockfull lanes take us over the suspension bridge from Ortakoy to Beylerbeyi, the waters of the Bosphorus as grey as the air. Toll points in this direction but with our electronic tags we sail through, picking up speed as traffic thins. Heading faster now for Sabiha Gokcen Airport. Expecting to fly. The city pushing me away. Go home. Except it's not home anymore. I want to cry. By an effort of will I don't.

***

Luton Airport in the chill darkness of an autumn evening is one of the least welcoming ways to enter Britain. Particularly when there's no prospect of anyone you care about being there to meet you. Not that travelling further tonight feels any more appealing. Weary and not thinking straight, I haven't phoned ahead to get my car out of its long-term rented garage so the sanest thing seems to be to take a room at the Holiday Inn Express, eat a cardboard cheese sandwich, drink an expensively cheap scotch and go to bed. Note I don't say sleep which comes eventually but not in the most refreshing of shapes.

Morning is a marginally better time to turn over the contents of my massive, red pack. Not much chance of losing that on any arrival lounge's luggage carousel. Change of clothes and discard most of what I'm carrying. Henceforth my pockets will contain familiar objects which feel foreign with disuse. My keys with their shop loyalty fob. A wallet containing sterling. A few coins. An AA card long expired. An auto-booth photo, passport sized, of an ordinary girl but the flaw rests with the camera's inability to capture her lovely face as I know only too well. I never managed it. Her picture's been put away these long months as well as all the rest of my English life. Time to take the whole bloody lot out of cold storage.

I don't bother to shave. I know I'd feel better if I did but I don't want that. Stubble suits the grimness of my mood. Phone my pet mechanic and discuss delivery of wheels to my home. Catch a train. Spend more time in motion. Dozing. I don't remember eating anything but I think I must have had something in addition to copious disposable cups of coffee. East Coast Mainline coffee proves surprisingly alright actually and I catch myself smiling. Something to be stamped on before it becomes an epidemic of happiness. One thing I can't afford. Stay focused on why I'm here. To help someone who needs it. To hurt another who deserves it.

***

Lincoln Station is right in the middle of town. This inevitably means a spell of waiting behind the level crossing gates that sever the high street if you need to visit a shop on whichever happens to be the wrong side of the tracks from your own starting point. On alighting from the rear portion of a two carriage train, I come close to falling over, a mishap underlining the urgency of getting my shoes re-heeled. And where's the menders? You've got it.

I get to stand there for several minutes as the arrival of the next Nottingham Sprinter clashes with an engine pulling a prodigious quantity of filthy, rust-coloured oil tanks. I don't have to be on foot of course. I could have taken a taxi but a masochistic streak holds sway today and I want the aching arms from lugging my own baggage around. If I had engaged my brain, I would have realised just how conspicuous a long-haired, muscular man with a limp, carrying brightly coloured luggage, would be in a place as compact and insular as this city. Perhaps sub-consciously I don't care and want to be noticed. It’s certainly true I'm sick of hiding out.

The crossing gates swing open in a grating series of judders and I move through, part of a shoal of impatient pedestrians, cyclists and motorists each careless of the wellbeing of any of the other road users. My route takes me past shops and bars, each more nondescript than the last, across the main road, up past the sprawling wings at the rear of City Hall. On West Parade I reach my first port of call.

I'm outside an ugly, concrete sixties structure. I consider the flight of steps up to the plate glass doors. A zigzagging ramp off to the side offers a concession to disability. My old ankle injury can be a bit problematic at times but I think I'll opt for the stairs. I take up my bag and walk. A large sign on the grass catches my eye. Surprisingly, given the on-going discussions about disposal and probable demolition, it's not a For Sale sign. It simply states 'Lincolnshire Police'.

The counter with its glazed, floor-to-ceiling, security screening is far too extensive for the single civilian staffing it. She's busy being harassed by an angry old man, seemingly engaged in lengthy repetition. I take stock. Peeling institutional green paint, supposedly calming, but the few utilitarian chairs are bolted to the floor. Nothing would encourage anyone to linger. I examine the woman in command of this depressing reception area instead. Mid thirties maybe, a red-head power-dressed in a sharp grey suit and paler blouse. She fits my prejudices perfectly. The only places you find these creatures nowadays are in cop shops and fire brigade offices where most of the service personnel are smartly uniformed men and female support staff feel it's incumbent upon them to wear more make-up than the average bank cashier. I make a bet with myself that the lower half of her suit below counter level will be a skirt rather than trousers and her feet will be wedged into court shoes, plain but high-heeled.

I don't get to find out. A voice at my elbow reveals the noiseless arrival behind the security glass of another agent of law and order. "Can I help you, sir?" The soft Lincolnshire burr and the sergeant's stripes could almost convince me that he really does want to be of assistance.

“I'd like to see Chief Superintendent James.”

“Is she expecting you, sir?”

She might be if she's clairvoyant. “I don’t know.” This is an old game. It's called evasion.

“Do you have an appointment?”

When your girlfriend sends texts without the normal quota of Xs you can be pretty certain she's irritated or upset with you. I think it's the same with police officers who stop saying 'Sir'.

“Not as such.”

“Well you need to make one and come back then.” His mask of politeness is definitely slipping. There's steel in his voice.

“Except. I was told to come here the moment I got back.”

“And who told you to do that?”

“She did.” Game, set and match to me.

It takes five more minutes before I find myself being escorted to Clare James' office to receive exactly the sort of greeting I'd anticipated.

“What the bloody hell are you doing here?” She doesn't mean why am I in her office or even her professional domain. Her ambit is far broader. She means anywhere other than Turkey.

“Nice to see you too. You're looking particularly lovely today. Being in charge obviously suits you.”

“Don't soft-soap me. This is dangerous and stupid! Even by your standards.”

And then she gets really angry. I don't even get a cup of coffee before leaving. I do get one clear message though. “You're on your own now.”

“You don’t mean that.”

“I bloody well do.”

That’s telling me.

***

My next stop is the corner shop. Don't recognise anyone. It looks like it's changed hands again. It has been awhile since I was last in here. The stock's much the same though and I fill a bag with the bare essentials; rolls, butter, milk, apples, cheese and ham. You can get by on that lot for several days in my experience.

Finally to the front door my keys happen to fit. One of the tall, Edwardian houses fronting West Common. The paintwork seems to be holding up to everything the weather can fling at it but I suspect I'll have to do something with it in the spring.

The hall smells slightly fusty but not as bad as I'd feared. My incompetent cleaner may have been doing a better job of keeping it aired than I give her credit for. Don't suppose her actual cleaning's improved but I can't sack her. Jaki's my niece and she needs the money. She's in the second year of an environmental sciences course at the university. One day she's going to make the world a better place. Just not necessarily a cleaner one.

My bag hits the floorboards with a thud. The groceries need more tender care and take priority when I decide to recognize my arms have given out. I make it to the kitchen before all hell breaks loose. The din is indescribable. Imagine an old-fashioned alarm clock magnified several times over. Or picture the actual truth. For no reason that's obvious to me, Jaki has parked the telephone on the kitchen table inside the large biscuit tin with the lid loosely resting on top. It stops ringing before my heart has dealt with the shock and I've found the damn thing. When it's out of the tin and still in my hand, it rings again.

I grab the receiver and don't wait to find out who's on the other end. Knowing the object of your rudeness can really blunt the impact. “Did you just ring?”

“Yes. I've tried a few times."

“Oh Mum. I'm sorry. How did you know I'd be here?”

"Your sister..."

My mother hates other family members being better informed than she is. And I do try to be a good son and take her feelings into account. Which is why I told my sister not to tell her. A useful maxim to remember is 'Once a grass, always a grass'. But I must be confused. I thought it was my younger brother who used to snitch when we were kids.

“Yep. But I'm not likely to be here long. I came to...”

Might as well try to stop a hurricane by voice command. She just talks over me. "I hope you're not going to pick up with that woman again. It's not that I don't like her; I mean I've never actually met her, but I'm worried about you. You see..." I give her a few minutes to express her concerns but ultimately take the only course of action open to me. I hang up. Then with the receiver off, put the phone back in the tin and put the lid back on. Firmly this time. Bingo. No more calls. The line must have developed a fault.

***

Need a plan of action. Running around like a bull in a china shop isn't a tactic for long term success. I definitely need to see 'that woman' again. Which isn't likely to be easy. A lot of difficult ground to cover. Explanations and so on. But just finding a safe way to reach her is the first problem. This isn't thirteenth century Verona and there isn't a balcony-climbing solution for avoiding armed guards, assuming there are any lurking around. But her mobile number will have long since changed and the nature of my return home is pretty well guaranteed to be brought to her husband's attention.

Actually there are multiple reasons for organising protection and Clare doesn't look like the failsafe fall-back I'd been counting on. Back in Istanbul I'd be calling in the friends made learning kick-boxing before my ankle started protesting too vigorously. Here it may need to be hardware rather than bodies. Reminder to call Patrick or somebody else. Or everybody I know.

And will I stay here or bury myself in a safe lair to evade confrontation until I've seen how the land lies and I'm sure I'm ready? I wish I'd thought this through instead of taking the first available flight out of Istanbul. But the messages were compelling and I won't beat myself up about my need to respond. Hefty sigh of resignation, retrieve the phone, call a taxi and book into The White Hart. Without using my own name.

***

My niece has one of the new student flats with a view over the river. It means a short morning walk to lectures, down to the Brayford Pool, the old Roman port, and into the glass building with the red-wood cladding, the design of which still splits local opinion right down the middle. Even all these years after the planners gave it the thumbs-up of bureaucratic approval.

The residences are far more traditional. Red brick and tile construction. The only controversy they caused was whether they needed to be there at all. Talk to West Enders and far too many of them still deny that building the first brand new British university in thirty years could ever benefit the city. Which is why Lincolnshire tradition is sometimes seen as a euphemism for myopia.

Jaki flings her front door open with all the coiled-spring enthusiasm of her twenty years on the planet. An ear-splitting squeal accompanies a massive hug. “Unc! You're back. I've got so much to tell you.” She doesn't believe in reticence or ambivalence. What you get is full-on and genuine. Always.

There's one development in her life, I don't need explained to me. Lurking behind her in the hallway is a tall, athletic young man with a shock of dark straw for a hairstyle. Based on physique alone, Jaki could do a lot worse in the boyfriend stakes. Even better that, in his case, appearances are far from deceptive.

“Hi Rory.”

“Hi Coach.”

Jaki lets go of me and there's more than a hint of exasperation when she says, “Do you know everybody?”

Laugh at the idea. “Not entirely. Just the ones I trained. How goes the season, Rory?”

He nods thoughtfully. “Okay.” A quiet, self-contained youngster our Rory. Self-disciplined and possessed of both massive talent and a great work ethic. Accepting my authority as his coach is for him an on-going if quiet form of rebellion against a less than wonderful father. At nineteen he's earned everything they're beginning to say about him and he certainly won't be playing lower division football at Sincil Bank much longer. Where the talent comes from, who can say? Perhaps from his Italian mother’s side of the family. But I’ve never met her which makes me guilty of idle speculation.

Jaki pulls me through into the lounge. “Grab a seat, Unc.” I'm almost pushed onto the cheap slab of foam wrapped in brown fabric which passes itself off as a settee. “Tea? Coffee? Cake? Biscuits?”

“Tea. Strong. No sugar, please. And you've just reminded me. Why on earth would I find my telephone stashed in my biscuit tin?”

“So I can hear it ring when I'm cleaning upstairs of course.” Logical in its way I suppose although why she'd want to answer calls for me is another matter entirely.

“And how long have you and Rory...” I don't want to mis-label this fledgling relationship. And I'm asking her not him. The answer will come much quicker and in far more detail.

Except it doesn't. “Ages.” She tosses the one word over her shoulder as she moves into the kitchen leaving Rory to add the most salient fact.

“I finally moved in last week. She's pretty special isn't she?”

Pretty headstrong and periodically daft I'd say but then it's all in the eye of the besotted. And Rory certainly seems that.

“Yes. She is.” Change tack. Not making idle conversation. But because of his text to me in Turkey I want to know. “How's your brother doing?” I don’t know his brother. As far as I recall I’ve never even met him. All I know is he doesn’t play football. And doesn’t need a coach.

Rory doesn't immediately reply. “Your brother. You remember?” I was aiming for the light-hearted touch. I should have known better.

A longer pause while Rory weighs up the right words to use. “He's okay. He and Dad don't see eye to eye on anything nowadays. But he's alright. He's a good kid really. But that's not what I needed to talk to you about.”

Perhaps I misunderstood but his message definitely mentioned his brother and trouble in the same sentence. That alone would have spurred me to pack my bags even if I hadn't already booked my flight in the immediate wake of Megan’s communication less than twenty four hours earlier. “You made things sound pretty serious.”

A nod. “They are. I wouldn't have called otherwise. I didn't mean you to come back. I thought if we could talk, you'd put me in touch with someone who could help me. When you didn't pick up, I sort of panicked.”

“What have you done? What's wrong?”

“Nothing. I haven’t done anything. The problem is there's nothing much I can do.”

“Alright. Look Rory, whatever it is, you know I'll help. You're one of the few people who have any idea why I had to go in the first place. I haven't any of my own kids. Just nephews and nieces. So send me a message like that and of course I’d come straight back. You must’ve known that.”

“I suppose I did. It's just so difficult. I can't talk to my father. And Mum mustn't know...”

“So what's going on?”

No direct response. “It's a normal Thursday tomorrow.” He means there's a long session on fitness and tactics ahead of Saturday's match. “I'll be free by four. If I pick you up, would you come somewhere with me? It'd be much easier to show you.”

“Okay.”

“And then you'd see my new wheels.” Suddenly the smiling boy is back in place of the anguished young man. It's like the sun coming out.

“Good. The only thing is, I'm not at home. It's too risky. I'm at The White Hart. Ask for Mr Jackson.”

A glance in my direction. Contemplation of what he knows. Says nothing.

I get up. And Jaki barges back into the room. She's been inside the kitchen door hanging on every word. She knew Rory would handle a one-to-one better. The seriousness of whatever's looming has penetrated even her relentless cheerfulness. She doesn't make so much as a token protest when I say I have to go. Just as well really. I ought to get a taxi. And some sleep.

Rory offers to drive me but I think she needs him more than I do. Lincoln's not exactly a large conurbation and I should be able to manage to walk as far as the hotel. I think.

***

The White Hart is another aspect of traditional Lincoln. A comfortable, sprawling old coaching hotel near the castle. So much more soul to it than the concrete monstrosity on the far side of the cathedral. That would never have got planning consent from me in a month of Sundays if I'd had any say in it. Drop the conspiracy and corruption theories. Probably just poor Sixties taste. The White Hart on the other hand...home from home.

And it has a well-stocked bar to its credit. Tonight I ignore it. I've done enough damage of late to my biorhythms.

I am going to sleep. I do.

Chapter II Then: May

I'm not widely travelled. Not really. Save by comparison with my parents. In their sixties they made their first test flight. It took them to the Isles of Scilly as a precursor and preparation for their once-in-a-lifetime journey to see my younger brother and his ever expanding brood, then numbering four with a fifth on the way, at Oamaru. That's in New Zealand for the uninitiated. Drive from Christchurch to Dunedin, blink, and you miss it.

My tally of countries, outside Europe and short business trips to the USA, is limited to the Antipodes but at least the New Zealand end is South Island rather than the usual tourist destinations.

The one place I've visited repeatedly is Turkey and I just keep going back. A mark of how much I like it. Feel equally at home in the city fug of spices, diesel oil and fish and in the empty spaces in the mountains. I'm a poor linguist, a slow learner and it must say something that I've persevered to gain a three or four hundred word Turkish vocabulary. I'm certain my grammar's pretty shocking but the Turks are a friendly and forgiving race and my fixation with the place, its people and its history has so far outlasted a marriage and a career so I think it's here to stay. I could reel off a long list of places I've stopped but the best was renting a jeep and driving into the hills inland from Fethiye to find a little village where I spent a fortnight losing a stone in weight but gaining a prize-winning photo essay. I captured it all. Bustling market days. The women slaving over their crops or sitting by the well, drawing intricate henna patterns on their daughters' hands. Their men idling in conversation in the village square. The wine bottles on the rooftops of each home with a marriageable daughter, broken on the day of betrothal and only removed on their wedding day. Magical simplicity. Even if a western upbringing's made it impossible for me to ever contemplate living like that for more than a few weeks.

So if I want culture or just a break, it's Turkey I head for. I'm no skier but they say there are fledgling resorts near Istanbul for that now too. Probably serviced by second-hand chairlifts condemned for replacement by zealous Austrian resort inspectors.

Alanya. Cheap. Cheerful. Far enough South to come with as near a guarantee of sun from May to October as anywhere can give. And decent hotels. For this fortnight I'm back at the Alaiye Kleopatra. Comfortable room with a balcony overlooking the pool. One hundred yards from the beach. And full board includes all drinks, which needs treating with caution if you don't want to lose the holiday in an alcoholic daze.

There is one problem and it's with the pool. Or rather with the positioning of the hotel buildings around it. As the sun moves across the sky, a shadow expands over the serried ranks of sunbeds and by late afternoon only the corner nearest the road is unaffected.

My first day comprises leisurely breakfast, beach, an apple and a coke in the bar for lunch before a casual stroll round the local shops. So it's about four o'clock before I want a brisk swim and to crash out. Now I could grab a cushion and lay my new towel on the concrete but there is one apparently free lounger in the sunshine, sandwiched between two others with barely enough room to climb onto it. One of the abutting loungers bears a mound of somnolent flesh, snorting gently in sleep. The woman on the other side might be awake behind her sunglasses, unless she's mastered the feat of keeping a paperback aloft while dozing.

"Is this one taken?" It may be neither physically occupied nor reserved with a towel but you never know. The woman pushes her sunglasses down her nose a fraction. "It's all yours." Her voice is pleasantly melodic. A slight trace of a regional accent. Unaffected. And English. Most of the other guests are German.

Another voice comes from behind her. "Isn't Ellie coming back down?"

"I don't think so." Turning back to me, "You can have it."

"Thank you."

Prop up the back of the sunbed to a comfortable angle. Lay out the green towel with the gold advertising logo. Extract suntan lotion and reading material from canvas tote. Kick bag under lounger. Squeeze into gap. Sit down. Swivel legs round. Relax. And steal another look at the woman in her yellow bikini. Her sunglasses and book are back in place but something about the way she's holding herself reminds me women supposedly have better peripheral vision than men and that she's probably only too aware I'm looking. And liking what I see.

Don't stare. Recap salient points. Neatly cut raven hair. Henna-rinsed. Fortyish. Younger than me. Good cheekbones. If her nose and chin were a fraction smaller she'd be very pretty. The imperfections give her something closer to lasting beauty. Olive skin. Wonderful hands. Not small but lent delicacy by her long fingers and neatly painted nails. Quite tall. Full figure.

Something rising to the surface of my memory brings a soft laugh to my lips.

"What?" Said gently. Not in irritation. She's gazing at me with the sunglasses lowered again. Her eyes are staggeringly dark. Almost black.

Not long after my scabrous divorce, the bluntly spoken Yorkshire-woman who until recently happened to be my friend Patrick's wife, was questioning me about my latest transient girlfriend. I carefully described her by colouring, height and personality and Annie snorted and said, "No. I mean has she got breasts? Once you've found one with real breasts you'll never look back!" Annie would approve of this one.

Shake my head. "I'll tell you when I know you better." Already it's when and not if.

"All right." A flick puts her sunglasses back in place.

We sit and read in companionable silence. She seems to be reading anyway. Her pages turn at regular intervals but I can't take in anything. My heart's racing but I don't know how to get her attention and re-start the conversation naturally.

She solves things by getting up and putting her stuff together to go in. Have to say something before she's gone. "See you at dinner then." I don't even phrase it as a question. Kick myself for not coming up with anything better. Or at least vaguely original.

She pauses. Smiles. Says, “Of course”. Walks away. I don't take my eyes off her until she disappears from view.

I'd forgotten her brunette friend. I find her watching me in turn, amused. “She's married,” she says.

Take a deep breath. “The best one’s always are.”

“No. I mean be very careful. Gail's dangerously married. And easily hurt.” Guaranteed to intrigue.

Next steps are pretty obvious. Exchange names and offer to buy Megan a drink at the poolside bar. Not quite accurate because the drinks are free. Sit on half-submerged stools, our warm legs water-soothed and pump her for as much information as I can get. Find out they all come from Lincoln and booked through the same travel agent as I did. And they were on the same flight and transfer coach as me. What I don’t learn is much about Gail.

The sub-species I belong to are strange creatures. I can sit beside a lovely, entertaining and obviously single woman, making conversation as she touches my arm for emphasis, her interest broadcasting loud and clear but all I want is the other one. The one with all the quiet mystery.

Sod it. In trouble again.

***

Dinnertime at The Alaiye. Not the ideal place to get to know someone. Too much activity. Self-service by and for all with milling waiters replenishing serving trays and fetching wine and beer. No sense of privacy. Not least because I'm sharing Gail with the slim brunette and a chunkier blonde. That's Megan and Ellie respectively. Oddly it doesn't matter that I'm getting besieged by questions from the others because Gail's clearly engaged by the answers, asking quiet points of clarification, laughing periodically at something one of us has said and never, it seems to me, looking away from me for long.

Turkish coffee and brandy out on the poolside terrace afterwards. A different matter entirely. Comfortable chairs. Cooling breeze. Sitting beside her rather than across from her now. My knee just brushing hers. No retracting movement from her. And having her to myself. Her friends are across on barstools chatting up the staff. Abdi's grinning with them and trying out his English.

And something's beginning here. We both know it. An ease between us. And no rush to take it anywhere quickly. A long haul ahead. I have a sense it won't matter if it takes a whole lifetime to find out where we're going to end up. When she rises to leave, she touches the back of my hand lightly, trailing her fingers across it. I look up at her, thinking about standing too and before I can, she bends, kisses my cheek, says, "Good night," and is halfway to the door before I can do anything. High on style. Totally in control of herself.

***

I'm at breakfast before any of them. Actually I doubt Megan and Ellie will appear at all. Last seen very drunkenly carousing long after midnight. I thought about tossing a paper dart or a handful of sweets at them from my balcony but resisted temptation.

I'm by the window. Watching a black and white cat stalking birds on the corrugated metal roof of an unfinished house across the alley. He's making good use of the water tanks as cover. The first I know of Gail's arrival is a hand stroking my neck. It's the most erotic thing I've felt in years. Look up. And she's smiling fit to bust. Brightly patterned silk top. Loose over white pedal pusher Capri pants. Matching white sandals. Ugly enough to be really expensive. Not ugly on her feet at all. And nail varnish picking up one of the colours in her top. Now I'm the one who's smiling. My lucky day.

"Hi you. Sleep well?"

"Umm."

"And what are we going to do today?" Not that I'm assuming anything.

"What have you got in mind?"

"Ever had a morning in a Turkish bath?"

"No. Would you recommend it?"

"I would. Set us up for lying on the beach."

"Okay then."

"I'll get some transport organised after breakfast. What will you have?"

"I don't usually have much. Bit of fruit. A coffee."

"I'll get you sorted." And I do.

Thanks to the Thomas Cook rep, we share a minibus on a tour of half a dozen hotel pick-ups working our way northwards along the coast. I don't care how long it takes. Gail's sitting beside me and her hand rests coolly in mine, fingers intertwined. Feeling like they belong there.

Actually I have a thing about hands. Faces, looks and intelligence are all important to me but if I don't like a woman's voice or her hands don't please me, it's not going to happen. Gail's hands are just lovely. Her fingers make me want to stroke them. To use the soft pull of a massage grip, holding and stretching each finger gently between my thumb and forefinger. Linking thumb webs in an easy caressing motion. Rolling her hand between mine, stretching and flattening the palm. I've stopped just thinking about it and I'm doing it. And she's not watching the movements but the concentration of my gaze. And she murmurs something which doesn't quite register, except that its soft and approving. And when I'm done, I bring her hand up to my mouth and kiss the back of it and put it down. She re-grips mine tightly and doesn't let it go until the bus pulls up at its destination.

We start with the salt room. White crystals scrunch under the soles of our bare feet, absorbing the moisture in the air. So it's a dry heat. Invigoratingly different. Sucking at you until you have to go and laze in the rock pool in the atrium. Or do the ice-cold plunge. Or visit the steam room where you can hardly see six inches in front of your face for the misting droplets filling your lungs and coating your skin. And then you go back to the salt room and start again.

There's a party of Russian women keeping pace with us today. They present more like a mixed group of co-workers than a family but what do I know? We don't speak a word of Russian. Or precious little of anything else really. So we don't know what they're yacking on about. Only that their laughter is infectious. One tall and stunning young woman in her early twenties is strutting - no other word for it - in her polka dot bikini and she's telling a story to her companions sitting near us on the hot pine benches. Maybe it's based in truth but she's using exaggerated hand movements over her body and the filthiest of chortles, bending towards them, volume rising. She pulls her hair up on end, cups her body for them and almost spits something more out. And I look at Gail and she looks back at me. And neither of us can help it. She has us spellbound too. Not understanding a word of it but roaring with the rest. And it's only because we're in the salt room that there are no tears running down our cheeks. An exclamation, a burst of applause from her fellows, a wave of the hand, a twisting turn and she's gone. I can see her outside the glass sliding door, shucking her feet into the obligatory plastic mules. The oldest woman says something sounding like an instruction and as one they follow her out. Leaving Gail and I clutching each other, in the weakened state of near hysteria.

"Oh God! I need a swim now."

Gail agrees. "Me too."

"What on earth do you think she was on about?"

"No idea. But I'll tell you this. I bet it was about a man."

"Is that the sort of thing you'll be saying about me to Megan and Ellie?"

"No. I'm keeping you to myself."

"Thank God for that!"

***

Exfoliating scrub from a masseur wearing rough cotton mittens. Lying head to toe on a great marble slab, our bodies, swimsuits and all, covered in dense white foam. Allowed to lie drowsily for a few minutes. Then hauled around and rinsed off with cool water poured onto us from shallow metal pannikins. Handed towels and sent off to loungers outside in the sun, our faces caked in green mud-pack treatments, cracking in the heat as they dry out. Grinning at how bizarre each of us looks to the other. Washed off and taken upstairs for a short massage. Relaxing up to a point but, compared to the rest of the morning, perfunctory and ineffective. But then I'm judging it from the standpoint of the fact that my back and legs would handle mauling for rather longer than the fifteen minutes allocated.

Gail seems very contented though and we're dressed and out to the minibus before most of the other passengers.

She looks delicious. There's colour in her cheeks and a lingering smile. I know what I want and so I do it. Put an arm around her waist and pull her in so her head's tucked into my shoulder and her whole body is leaning on me, absolutely no resistance or tension in her at all. I kiss her forehead and her arms tighten around me. This is one possible definition of heaven.

***

We manage a light lunch. A shared sandwich. Collect beach tickets from the hotel. Walk past the ice cream stall. The grinning Turkish teenager has varieties of Cornetto we've never seen before. We try the ones with a molten caramel core.

By the sea, a massive Somalian allocates us loungers and an umbrella. His teeth are pearl white and his skin so dark it contains hints of purple. The contrasts you find everywhere in the world these days. Not for us the culture shocks of inward migration our parents had to deal with. We're immune. Taking it all for granted. Believing that we all want the same things. Money, happiness, tolerance, joy. Don't we? He shows us where we can sit. Plenty of room right by this impossibly blue sea. It's too hot and most of the sun worshippers are in the bars lunching or drinking. We set up the umbrella, lie down, the chairs as close together as we can get them, and talk. Quickly find ourselves into serious stuff.

"You don't seem married. Are you?" She gives the question an air of importance.

I'm glad the answer is no. "Not any more. I started following Rod Stewart's advice."

"Which is what?"

"He told the press he'd been married too many times and if he got the urge again, he'd just walk out on the street, find a woman he didn't like and buy her a house."

Gail's unamused. Puzzled if anything. "But he is married. And hasn't he got young children?"

“Yeah. He obviously stopped listening to his own advice.”

"But you won't get married again?"

"I didn't say that. I'm through the post-divorce, anti-marriage phase. I learned more about myself and why I shouldn't have married Julie in the first place. Always an edge to us. Never comfortable. Lots of arguments. Power games. Anyway she got a house out of it. Took most of the money I made out of professional football. But who cares? It doesn't matter anymore. I'm okay and I don't rule out being married again. To the right person this time. What about you?"

She ducks the question. Tells me only what I already know from Megan. "Yes I'm married." Unflustered but uninformative.

"You're not wearing a ring."

"It came off at the airport."

Consider the next question. "What does he do?"

"He's a businessman. Buys and sells. You know how it is."

I don't of course. Haven't a clue. My businesses are sport in various forms. Even the computer game which really made me money. And the photography's just a hobby and I'm not that good at it.

"Do you have any kids? What do you want to do with your life?"

"I've got my boys. They're my life." A calm but very strong statement. What do I make of that? "What about you? Do you have any children?" The questions keep being turned back on me.

Pause to consider. "We did have one. Very premature. He didn't live very long."

Her hand is on my arm, squeezing hard. "I'm so, so sorry."

"It was a long time ago."

"But you don't get over it do you?"

"No you don't. You just get used to it."

"I suppose you have to. I don't know if you really can. I couldn't."

The plaintively sympathetic note in her voice unstitches me. Part of the armour cracks and I can't stop a teardrop running down, across the bridge of my nose and other cheek, onto the towel beneath my head. In the merest second, she scissors herself across her lounger and is wiping it away with an outstretched forefinger. I feel oddly light-headed. I want to hold her. So I do it. She strokes my hair. I don't want to let her go. I suppose I have to.

Sit up. "I'm okay about it really." Vaguely true.

***

Swimming. Floating on our backs in silent accord, our bodies touching with the ebb and flow of the waves. Complete peace. It seems ridiculous given how little I know of Gail but there's no room for doubt about how I feel.

The Greeks have a legend. That all our souls wander the world unknowingly looking for their true other half, severed by the gods for their own meddlesome purposes. Perhaps because the power of two humans in complete unity challenges even their dominance of this world. Forget talk of lovers and soul mates. Ignore the gaps in what I know of her. Put aside the brutal inconvenience of her being married. Consider only the certainty of my conviction that she is the missing half of me and my life. And I don't know how I've managed to live the last half century without her. It no longer seems remotely possible.

The sun is low towards the horizon when we gather our things and walk off the beach, hand in hand, cross the main road and enter the Alaiye.

The first person we see coming across the foyer is Megan, blue sarong over reddening skin. She looks at us sharply, exclaims something loudly and her rush takes her full tilt across the tiles into a three way hug. She's jigging up and down in sheer excitement. "I don't believe you two. You're like cats who've had the cream. This is real isn't it? Oh my God!"

Gail gently detaches her. Drops my hand too. "What are you on about? Nothing's happened..."

"Of course it has. I can see it has. You've only got to look at you. You lucky cow..."

"Shush. Keep it to yourself. It's so complicated." And to me. "I'm going to sort myself out. See you at dinner?"

Assenting gestures. Words won't come. Watch her move across to the lifts. Something wrong with my focus. My eyes won't do anything other than follow her while she's in sight. As the elevator door opens, she half turns, checking to see I'm looking, gives me a little wave and is whisked away.

Megan shakes her head, regards me a moment and punches me hard on the bicep.

"What's that for?"

"You know why."

"Perhaps I do."

"My Dad used to say don't try to kid the kid who kidded Billy the Kid."

"Obviously a strange man, your Dad. See you in an hour or so." My turn to leave.

***

More post-prandial coffee and brandy. Different location. Push aside the drying rack's cargo of beach towels and slouch on plastic chairs, our feet up on the lowest rail of my balcony. Leaning forward would afford us a view of Megan and Ellie, five floors below at the terrace bar. Occasional bursts of laughter drift up to us. We're not looking at any of the sights available from here. The only thing intriguing us tonight is each other.

Darkness falls and we don't bother to turn on the wall light. An easy silence for a while. Hopefully both thinking along the same lines.

"Gail. Will you stay here tonight?"

The response is immediate so I know she's worked out in advance exactly what she wants to say. "I will. If you promise just to hold me."

Take her hand. Lead her inside. Gently bring her down beside me on the bed. She lies along my body in the curve of my left arm. Feels natural. Right. Comfortable.

After a while another suggestion. This one hers. "We could lose some of these clothes."

"We could. But I'm not starting it."

Gail leans up on an elbow and unbuttons my shirt. Tugs at it. Sit up to help and she peals it off my arms. Now it's my turn. A moment or two and we're back lying as we were. Now in just underwear. The night's warm and in what little light there is Gail looks gorgeous and her skin, thanks to the Turkish bath, is silky smooth. I know I won't sleep. I'll lie here so I can enjoy and remember every minute of it. She snuggles closer. Snuffles a little. My arm tightens around her. And I'm asleep.

Wake groggily. Something's wrong. I'm face down, head scrunched deeply into the pillow. The sheet is tucked around me. And Gail's gone.

***

She's not in the dining room for breakfast. I get coffee and a plate of croissants and cheese. Probably the choice of a Philistine but I like what I like. The problem is what to do. I don't want to chase after her but absolutely can't conceive of spending today without her.

A hand on my shoulder. Look up in desperate hope. The disappointment probably shows only too clearly.

"Can I join you?" The broad, open face looming over me belongs to Ellie. She's holding her coffee and sits down before I have a chance to reply.

"Gail and Megan have agreed we're all going to the beach together this morning."

"Ah."

"No. You too, silly. Assuming you want to spend the day with us."

Give her the look. The one that sneaks past sceptically raised eyebrows.

"I mean assuming you want to see Gail."

Now I'm smiling. "Course I do." Simple as that.

***

Oddly, doing the beach with Megan and Ellie along for the ride takes some of the pressure off. Information can be divulged obliquely and conversations held which might prove too bluntly difficult for one-to-one. The other women ask questions Gail might not and tell me stuff I might not have thought to ask. And there's something about swimming in a group. Laughing. Chasing and splashing each other. Natural ways to touch each other. Not least re-applying suntan lotion at shortening intervals. Spells dozing on the loungers under our big sunshades or just talking. Breaks for an ice cream or to fetch coffee or water. Not to mention lunch.

By sundown I know a good deal more about the woman in the blue and white paisley swimsuit; the woman well on the way to turning a wonderful golden-brown colour; the woman who's hardly hidden behind the sunglasses at all today. Or I think I do.

***

Tonight she doesn't disappear. Nor does she protest when I leave the curtains open to let in the pale moonlight. She does mutter something about hoping I'm not going to be disappointed. "I'm a bit saggy in places."

"I'll let you into a secret. Men don't want perfection. Most of us are scared by it. Dealing with the flaws tells us we really love you. Gives us such a sense of tenderness. And this ..." My finger traces its path along the faded silvery web of stretch marks. "Honourable battle wounds." I can't stop myself leaning across her and planting a neat row of little kisses across her stomach.

We both know where this is likely to end up. And it does. Beautifully.

***

Our first Saturday coincides with a major footballing event. The climax of the Turkish season. The play-off between the first and second placed sides. Never mind the points difference. The title goes to the winner of this one match. An alien concept to us but the way it's done here. Galatasaray v Fenerbache. The hotel is awash with soccer strips. Red and yellow for Galatasaray. Yellow and dark blue alternating stripes for Fenerbache. Like a civil war. The game is screened of course. Everybody crammed into the lounge bar. Even non-football fans like the girls are caught up in the excitement. Urged on by the bar staff to support Galatasaray.

If this was just about football, you'd have to say it's a fairly ordinary match, hinging on a single goal. But the atmosphere has an alcohol-fuelled electricity, pulling everyone to their feet at the final whistle. Gail and Megan are dancing with one of the waiters. Ellie slumps exhausted in her chair, as though she's played ninety minutes herself. And I seem to be singing with an arm round the shoulders of a large Turkish man. The party moves out onto the terrace. A grief-stricken fan who's been wearing his Fenerbache shirt around the hotel all week appears on his third floor balcony. Tears off the shirt and hurls it down into the swimming pool. The hotel manager, with the same affiliation, is no longer around. Gone somewhere to drown his sorrows no doubt. The first celebrant leaps into the pool and soon there are several others in with him. Fully dressed.

By now a constant procession of cars is driving up and down the parade outside the hotel. A cacophony of horns, shouts, cheers, the periodic crackle of firecrackers and the crash of exploding skyrockets form the rest of the evening's soundtrack. Complete strangers pass us glasses of wine or local brandy. Things become exceptionally hazy as the night wears on.

Wake hung-over, Gail's groans echoes of my own. Use the bathroom. Paracetemol and water. Breakfast in any shape or form now vital. Coffee. Pastries. Filler. Anything. Carry cups and a plate from the buffet to a window seat. Sit and look down on the poolside chaos. A single employee is working to restore order down there. Picking up overturned loungers and clearing away debris. Raise my gaze towards the sea, visible in the gaps between the adjacent hotels. And can't help laughing. A very pointed and personal message is in place to our disconsolate manager from the owners of the nearest rival hotel. A sixty foot long Galatasary flag, two red bars enclosing a yellow centre stripe, is draped right down their hotel-front. Passionate or what? Love this place.

***

The next ten days settle into a glorious pattern. But fly past far too quickly. We're a gang on holiday together during sunlight hours. Ellie, Gail and I get browner and Megan survives the sorest phase of sunburn by staying in the shade as much as possible. I discover just how many bikinis three women need to pack for a fortnight. In turn I get teased for the one change of beach shorts I've brought. If today is the white ones with the purple flowers then tomorrow it can only be the red pair.

One overcast day, we manage a walk around the old harbour. A longer expedition up the hill to the castle is mooted but rejected. Can't say we do much else of note. But it doesn't matter.

Every evening it's Gail and I, two people discovering each others' bodies, strengths and weaknesses. One night she comes out with the loveliest thing anybody's ever said to me. "Is this how it's supposed to be? It's never felt like this for me. Never!"

"Me neither, darling girl."

I like coming in from the beach and riding the lift up to our floor when keeping our hands off each other is problematic in the extreme. I love that we gently rub noses like Eskimos do before we kiss. A new one on me. I love how our mouths, our hands, our whole bodies seem to fit. And I love how she makes me feel.

What I hate is the thought of going home. Of not having her with me. That's the crap bit about falling in love.

***

It's an early morning flight to Birmingham; 5 a.m. from Antalya. Meaning a late evening coach out of Alanya. Cuddling with a degree of desperation in a double seat with the central divider folded back out of the way. A tea-stop half way. A quarter of an hour sipping apple chi and not knowing what to say to reassure each other. On to an empty, mostly closed, airport. More sitting. More hugs. More coffee. Book in together to get adjacent seats. Flying. Four hours or so. Not long enough.

Landing. Baggage reclaim. Customs. Let Gail's hand fall away. Green channel. Out into arrivals. Spot their driver immediately. Want one last kiss. Too late now. Don't look at her. Walk away, battered red bag over my shoulder. Across to Medium Term Car Park Number 3. My reliable old Mitsubishi four-by-four starts first time. M42 East. Estimated time of arrival? Don't care.

***

Pull in at Tamworth Services. Slow walk from car. No rush. Running footsteps behind me. Turn and she's in my arms. Not very circumspect. Tell her so.

"It's alright. They've gone ahead with the driver. Ellie'll distract him. I said I needed some air. This was a good plan to meet up here wasn't it?"

"A great one. The very best."

Pull her into my car and kiss her roundly for as long as I can get away with. But nothing’s long enough any more. And she has to go.

Chapter III Now: November to December

The midday tolling of the cathedral bells wakes me. Nothing else could. Disorientation in the gloom of my hotel room is, for a moment, total. I neither know where I am nor what I'm doing here. A few minutes meditation, a drowsy refusal to start the thought processes which could make sense of the day. Then force a reluctant body out of bed and straight into the shower. Drastic but it works. Enough to get me to appreciate I'm starving hungry. Not literally perhaps but in dire need of sustenance. Brunch calls, not to be ignored.

Eat. Wait. Rory phones. Wait some more. This time in the lobby. A dark BMW pulls up on the granite setts out front. A less flashy motor than most young footballers might choose but it's Rory we're talking about here. Greetings. Car admiration. And a short drive onto the St Giles' estate.

***

Rory leans on the bell. No immediate response. Tries again. Holds a finger on the button. It delivers a continuous whine incompatible with long battery life. Shouts. "Sandrine! Open up!"

The vaguely familiar young woman who opens the door is two separate stories severed at the waist. Her lower half, framed by a short red tartan skirt and black patent leather boots, comprises long and exceptionally attractive legs sheathed in black opaque tights. In contrast, her hair is lank, her face pallid and bloated and her clashing purple cardigan bears stains of indeterminate and differing origins. This is not somebody enjoying the bloom of good mental health.

She nods to Rory. Ignores me. Stands aside and lets us in. Smells, lingering faintly on the doorstep, become more apparent inside the flat. Spoilt food and unclean carpets mesh with other odours. None of them speak of anything except all-embracing hopelessness.

"Daniel! It's me." The call elicits hesitant footsteps and the emergence of a young child. Perhaps five years old. Pale and skinny. Stick-thin arms protruding from an overlarge

Black Sabbath t-shirt. Bony wrists and fingers which are all knuckles. The most shocking thing is that his features and the matching colour of his hair tell me the exact nature of Rory's problem and that it's going to change his life completely.

Turn round to ask Sandrine something and she's not there. Push on the semi-closed door behind us. A bedroom. Dingy and dark. Sandrine's lying on top of the bedcovers, her eyes closed, already asleep. There's a dirty green blanket draped on a chair. Put it over her and pull the door to. Leave whatever afflicts her to wear off. She's not in any fit state to consent or oppose Daniel coming with us. Write out a note for her. Put my mobile phone number on it. Leave it on the kitchen table in a patch cleared of breakfast debris.

Rory ushers Daniel out ahead of him, hands on his shoulders. He's got a black coat on over the t-shirt, jeans and scruffy trainers. Surprisingly it's an expensive one. He sees my look of curiosity. "My Dad bought it for me," he says.

Check my watch. Nearly five. "Would you like to get something to eat?"

Daniel doesn't respond. His gaze is watchful. Careful. Distrustful.

Rory intervenes. "How about McDonalds?"

A flicker of enthusiasm. A nod. "Please."

"Hope the gaffer doesn't spot us. He won't see burgers as an acceptable mid-season diet."

Daniel proves he can eat. He manages his own and half of mine and would have stolen a chunk of Rory's if he'd been allowed. As the food goes down he visibly thaws, the tension leaving his little body. He watches me over the burger clamped in both his hands. When his eyes catch mine his head lowers but there's a little smile there. It feels like a breakthrough of sorts.

"We have to take him back now. Wish we didn't have to."

"We need thinking time. Look, Rory. Give me all the facts and we'll work out what's possible."

Nobody talks much in the car. Daniel is solemn again. Back in his shell. Rory concentrates on driving. I'm deep in my own thoughts. A career's about to be mucked up or even sacrificed. A little boy needing his father, however young and unprepared for the task. And what of Jaki? She and Rory are much too new to deal with this together. In love or in lust they might be but that's hardly enough to carry them through this at their age. Daniel's existence will necessarily drive a wedge between them. Dark thoughts. No answers.

Sandrine is up and about when we drop Daniel off. Dull-eyed but functioning well enough to offer to make us a cup of tea. I look to Rory and to my relief he says, "No thanks." The risk of consuming anything in this household is too great. I suspect Rory's also worried about the security of his car. St Giles' isn't the sort of place you leave an expensive vehicle unattended for very long. Not if you want to find it with a full complement of wheels on your return.

The trip back to my hotel is going to take no more than minutes so the grilling won't wait.

"When did you find out about Daniel?"

"A couple of months back. Sandrine brought him to the training ground. She wanted money."

"And you gave it to her?"

"Some. I don't think much of it went on Daniel though."

"Are you ready to be his Dad? It's a tough call."

Rory looks at me askance. Like I've lost the plot. Finally I get it. And don't need the proffered explanation. "He's not mine. He's my brother. My half brother. He's my Dad's."

I don't do speechless. Or lost for words. Normally. But the only words which come are expletives. The sort used between team mates and opponents in my playing days. The ones I've spent years schooling myself never to use in front of the kids, however much they aggravate you. The extremes of frustrated language Rory's never heard me use. But he lets me curse. Even better than I do, he knows how much more problematic his own father's involvement makes things.

And part of me stays in shocked disbelief. Rory's Mediterranean good looks I'd presumed to come from his mother. Daniel in turn the very spit of him. But the true shared genetic heritage at work here is that of Tony Lenahan. A sociopath with a few too many reasons to dislike me than is strictly good for my long-term well being.

"Nix the hotel. Take us to Jaki's. This is a hell of a mess. And it'll get worse when he knows I'm involved."

"He won't be best pleased with me either."

"Selfish sod! He won't be trying to tear your head off."

"Maybe not. But he will take it out on Mum...and Sandrine."

An exceptionally bleak assessment. But probably the truth. With one last sting in the tail. "And he doesn't know its your niece I'm seeing yet."

***

Jaki's not in. Note for Rory on the dining table. Conversation postponed. Might as well take the opportunity to sleep on it. Mind turning to the issue of self-protection. Need to see Patrick. Phone him. He says "Come to the office." It's gone seven o'clock. Does he never go home?

The brass plate says MacFarlane & Co, Solicitors and a short list of partners. Two names in fact and one of them's semi-retired. Probably can't cope with working alongside Patrick. A lovely man. Do anything for anybody. But probably unliveable with. Make that definitely. The ex-wives attest to that.

The street door's unlocked. Just walk in. Call and a voice shouts back. "Through here."

Here is a large office designed around a traditional and massive desk, covered, as is normal for Patrick, in towering piles of paperwork. He may know where everything is but it's a hard claim to believe in the face of such apparent untidiness. A hand ruffles through his red hair and he laughs.

"You're back then. The jungle drums speak the truth."

"I am. And I've got a bit of a problem."

"I bet you have. Coffee?"

"Love one. Black. Lots of sugar, please."

Slump down into the comfort of the old green leather Chesterfield in the bay window. Recent days on the edge are catching up with me. Patrick peers over the top of his half-moon reading glasses and moves the biscuit barrel within my reach. "Looks like you need sustenance. So what's going on? And why are you back?"

"Those are really tricky questions."

"Thought they might be. Well give me enough to satisfy my curiosity anyway."

"Where to start? Time to sort things out with Gail. And ongoing issues with Tony Lenahan for starters. You've still got the papers I left in your safe. I think you can open them and read them now. Going away hasn't worked out too well as a tactic so I need to find a way to permanently disarm him. And you remember Tony's son, Rory? Now shacked up with my niece. A long-lost, abused half-brother's come to light. Perhaps more accurately we're talking neglect. He's got a mother with a serious drug habit. Then there are some vicious sods who may shortly get clearance from Tony to break my legs. And probably more problems still where that lot came from."

"You like living dangerously, don't you?"

"Not at all. Quiet and calm would suit me fine." Persuade Gail to forgive me and run away with me. Go anywhere we want to. Make a new life. But that's not happening anytime soon.

"So what do you want from me by way of legal services? Your stock's doing well so money's not a problem."

"I don't want anything legal. Can we talk safely here?"

"Un-bugged you mean? Safe as anywhere. I do take certain precautions."

"I need to take some precautions too. Around my personal safety."

"Ah! You're talking about guns."

"Yes. Something small I suppose."

"Ever even fired a pistol?"

"No. But you can show me."

"There's no way I'm doing that. If you ever had to use it, the odds are you'd freeze and end up having it taken off you and getting shot with it yourself. I'm not being responsible for that. I'd have to be off my head to give you a gun. And I'm as sane as they come."

The last bit's debateable but he sounds like he's made his mind up. Arguing with Patrick over anything significant is usually a futile exercise and will have no effect on the outcome at all. Except we'll both lose our Celtic tempers.

"What do you suggest I do?"

"Get yourself a minder and a driver. I'll get somebody across to you by lunchtime tomorrow. It'll cost a bit but you can afford it. Where are you staying? You're not at home are you?"

"I'm at The White Hart."

"Sound move. Don't leave the hotel tomorrow until they turn up. Let's take this seriously. Okay?"

"I am doing. Thanks. I may have to go out first thing but I'll be back by midday." No need to tell him I'm intending to breakfast with the enemy in the morning.

Handshakes. Crisp. Business-like. Hard to accept this is the norm for me and my oldest friend. Real men don't hug. It's all bollocks.

***

One more taxi ride before I can go back to The White Hart. One place I can still walk in uninvited and be sure of scotch, coffee, assistance, whatever. Down Cross O' Cliff to talk to one of the longest serving members of the council. Peter Ross comes to the door without any undue delay, despite his angina and worsening arthritis. A stooping, white-haired man of indeterminate years, scorning use of the stick which might make things easier. Living on his own, he's always appreciative of company. His wife died over twenty years ago and his only daughter inherited a house, re-married, this time to the cathedral's praecentor, and moved up into a rarefied world not well suited to acceptance of his blunt Yorkshire common sense. So he sees far less of his own flesh and blood than of his former son-in-law. And it's not like he sees him that much.

Get settled into cosy armchairs with a beer apiece before his curiosity spills over. "What're you doing here tonight then?"

"Can you get me in to see the new chief?"

"What?"

"There's a new Chief Executive isn't there? He has started, hasn't he?"

"Two weeks ago. I suppose I can ask him to see you. What do you want to talk to him about?"

"Will you believe me if I say it's better you don't know at the moment? It's not unconnected with what you were telling me about when you were in hospital a few months back."

"I suppose I'll have to trust you then."

"When will you be able to ask him?"

"I've got to go in tomorrow night for a committee meeting. So I'll head in a bit earlier and have a word with him. Better yet I'll ring his secretary in the morning to let her know I need to see him. Jane's a good girl. She'll sort me out a slot. And I'll ring when the committee's finished."

"Ring my mobile. I'm not likely to be near the landline at home much in the next few days."

"Right you are. I will. Are you okay though? I've not seen you in far too long."

"You mean you'd not noticed I've been missing the last few months."

"We'll you've not been bothering me for favours lately. So I suppose I was aware you'd not been about. I meant it when I asked though. How are you?"

"I'm fine. Getting things sorted."

I'll never be likely to tell him the whole truth about my current existence. A City Councillor he may be but he'll always be, first and foremost, my ex-father-in-law.

***

Times are changing. Lincoln's reputation remains that of a city with a dearth of black faces. Yet one of Tony Lenahan's principal enforcers is far removed from the white norm. Brawn and brains in an unlikely combination. Sudhir's a Jain by upbringing. Supposedly living a life of non-violence and truthfulness without possessions. Extracting money from those who don't want to repay, or can't, not the obvious career choice for him. Suspect his Indian parents aren't brimming over with parental pride. Sudhir used to drive Rory to and from training when he was younger and he's essentially a talkative outgoing type, as big men can be.

Sudhir favours a greasy spoon behind the market hall, taking his tea with the stall holders and porters. It takes an hour or so before he walks in, spots me immediately and plants himself on a chair directly across the table.

"You have got balls, man. Likely you'll lose them anytime soon." He may have seen too many Tarantino films.

"Hello Sudhir. Can you tell him I'm not here to cause trouble." Lie number one. "Got some personal business to sort out and then I'll be gone again. I won't cross him." Lies two to four inclusive. I could get to be way too good at this.

Sudhir sniffs. Buying himself time to think.

"Not up to me of course. I'd say you might get forty-eight hours. But then you're through. Can't promise though. He don't like you very much." A colossal understatement in all probability. No. Make that in all certainty.

"Can I buy you a tea?"

A shake of his head. "Can't drink with you man. You no friend o' mine."

"Appreciate that. I'll be off then. How's the family?"

A great grin breaks out. His Achilles heel. A boy and a girl and a stay-at-home wife who probably hasn't a clue how he provides for them.

"They're good, thanks. Very good. Now you be gone."

Obedience to instruction called for at this point. Head for the door. Think over having the last word. Check my smart-arse tendencies. Leave intact. That's good enough.

***

One thing I can do now I've seen Sudhir. Change my appearance. I was never a Robbie Savage but my hair remains fairly long. More grey in it now of course. Time to be radical. Have the whole lot clipped tight to the scalp.

Waiting in the barbers, considering my reflection. Wonder if I'm doing a sane thing. Not seen the true unvarnished shape of my head in more years than I care to think about. Tough. Can always re-grow it if I find I hate it. Or Gail does. When and if she ever sees it.

My turn. Seems to be an awful lot of hair on the floor. The alteration is significant. Grimace and a Chechen mafioso grins back at me in the mirror, the hairline receding and the stubble silver-streaked. Not much left of the young auburn Celt I used to be. The jawline's sharper too. More determined. Could be because I've lost a bit of weight. Decide I can tolerate the look. Pay the man. Take my coat. Hit the street.

***

Patrick is as good as his word. A few minutes into the afternoon and I'm the reassured employer of a couple of bodyguards. The bigger one, Jimmy, drives. His accent a harsh giveaway. From Belfast. His colleague is Ethan, another kick-boxer so we'll have something to talk about. From Boston. That's the South Lincolnshire town not the place that held the tea party.

They want me to predict my likely movements. Unpredictability seems a safer strategy to me. But there is one visit I can't put off any longer. Stellar Public Relations. Off Steep Hill. Aptly named. It's a hill and it's very steep. From the bottom to the very top. You have to admire that sort of consistency in a hill. Fortunately a meandering alternative route makes it possible for Jimmy to drop us off quite close to the office. The road up takes us right past Gail's home. A tall modern shell with far too much glass on a site hacked out of the hillside. Can't help looking to see if she's at one of the windows or getting into her little red hatchback. She isn't. No sign of her.

Jimmy stays with the car. Ethan sticks with me but grudgingly accepts an instruction to wait in the small ante-room laughingly signed as the reception so I can have a private conversation. With Megan.

No warm greeting. No hug. No pleasantries. Straight to the business in hand. Her Welsh intonation takes nothing away from her obvious impatience. "You took your time."

Where do women learn that tone? The one which without a single rude word calmly delivers the stiletto thrust of ironic rebuke and makes you feel a complete jerk. I think they take it in with their mother's milk. My niece could certainly do it almost as soon as she could talk. Long before she went to school anyway.

"I texted to say I was coming back."

"Well you're here now. At last. I'm really worried about Gail. She needs you more than ever. But she won't tell you that. So I thought I'd better get hold of you."

"Only one problem. I doubt she'll even agree to see me. She thinks I ran out on her."

"Of course she does. I've tried to persuade her there's a good reason. But it's hard to accept anything when you don't know why."

"And I can't tell you."

"Do you still love her?"

"More and more. Miss her every hour of every day."

"You went away to protect her?"

"In a very round-about sort of way. No; not really, to be honest. It was nasty stuff I couldn't expect her to deal with. Or understand. I was sort of looking after somebody else. And myself."

"Well, you not being here just made things worse for her. She had nowhere to go." And she tells me a story with two versions. The official one as told her by Gail. And the one pieced together from Megan's own suspicions.

My blood runs cold. And then I get angry.

Chapter IV Then: May to June

Text Gail even before I leave Tamworth services. "Missing you already xx."

Reply nearly instantaneous. "You really are crazy xx."

Get home to Trescombe. An old family name. The house just had a number until my mother commissioned a hand-painted sign. White lettering on Welsh slate. The least I could do was put it up beside the front door.

Scoop up the pile of post gathering dust on the ornate tiling of the hall floor. Ought to get a cleaner really. Could ask Jaki I suppose. Students are always skint. Take my correspondence through to the kitchen. Boil the whistling kettle on the gas ring. Make a mug of strong builder's tea. Pull out one of the light oak carver chairs made by the mouse-man. Nobody remembers his real name. Only that every piece of furniture made in his Yorkshire workshop carries a small, smiling rodent carved into it somewhere. Usually climbing one of the legs. A solid yet comfortable seat anyway.

Leaf through the letters, separating out circulars and adverts for the recycling bin. Examine the rest but nothing looks that interesting. So far as you can tell from the franking on each manila envelope.

Pick up the mobile and text Gail again. "Hi sweet girl. How are things? Any idea when we might get to see each other? Feels too long already xx."

Wait for a reply which doesn't come.

***

A new day. Another text from me. Still silence in the ether.

***

Two more days without reply. So now I know the score.

Over the last few years I've got pretty good at looking after myself. Couple of women were in and out of my life at one time but nothing serious and nobody's shared the expensive and wonderfully comfortable king-size bed I bought myself a while back. The dynamics of relationships in your forties can be quite odd. The baggage we all carry gets in the way. Friendships tend to fall into two types. There's the fairly cool companionship which works fine for taking in a film or a play but lacks any lasting appeal when you really need to share emotions or just talk about anything which matters. The other sort starts out pretending to want just friendship but sooner rather than later a raft of need comes pouring out and if you don't care enough to become their rock in a difficult world then you can't pretend and walking away is the only thing to do.

So I don't get surprised much these days. Except in Alanya I thought I'd found something very different. Something vitally real. Mutually so. Only it's now being made plain to me that for Gail it couldn't be any more than a holiday fling. She's had to put it away in the box marked 'Turkey.' Label it as lovely while it lasted but not to be continued in an English summer. I shouldn't feel this devastated. But I do.

There are no choices of course. Save one. Go back to work.

Current clients. Rory Lenahan. A real talent. Then there's a fifteen year old prospect Lincoln City FC think might turn out as good as Rory. I doubt it but Ben's likeable and biddable and applies himself so I'll do what I can for him. Away from coaching, I'm treating a married couple. Both distance runners. In need of remedial work. Davina's got hip problems and Bill's back and knees are going to push him into retirement one of these days. Keep telling them they should take up cycling instead but they're not persuaded. Yet.

Today is football. Rory and Ben and me messing about on the training pitch. They've already done a full morning with the first team and fuelled up with pasta for lunch. Now a session on skills. Dribbling and step-overs to be followed by shooting practice, hence the large net of balls I deposit by the goalpost.

In my time I was a right half. Attacking midfielder they call it now. Broke a leg. Lost a yard or two of pace. Moved into central defence. Football brain re-tuned. Got good at it. Messed up my ankle. Career over. Learned a few things to teach the youngsters though. Like you can't afford to show too much of the ball to a good defender. Or it won't be at your feet anymore. It'll have been hacked twenty yards away.

Shooting's the real fun bit. Got a wall of plywood figures to block off large chunks of the goalmouth. The lads have to find the gaps. Accurately. Time after time. Or bend the ball up, over and into the corner of the net. How many hours must Beckham and Zola and all the other dead-ball specialists have spent perfecting their cunning art? And I do quote Frank Lampard too often. He always says he made it by working harder and longer than the more naturally talented teenagers he was sent to soccer camps with.

Anyway hard work beats the blues. You go home exhausted. And you sleep. No time to ponder the demons of despair. So we work. Eventually send Ben in. His physical development isn't up to doing any more today. Whereas Rory, nearly three years older, can cope with much more. He gets another half hour and we play knocking the coke can off the crossbar. From twenty feet away. With the left foot. We're both naturally right-footed so let's make things more difficult for ourselves.

Gathering up the footballs together, I ask Rory how he's been doing while I've been away on holiday. He's fairly non-committal. "Yeah. Okay." That's the extent of his revelations. But he does surprise me in another direction. "It's my eighteenth soon. June the twentieth. I'm having a party. At Bentley's." It's a hotel out on the ring road, South of Lincoln. The former owners used to have the Station Hotel in the city centre before it was flattened. They had a good reputation. Well earned. The Bentley's now a Best Western Hotel. No comment. "It's the Saturday after my actual birthday. I wondered if you'd come. You can bring somebody. Obviously my family'll be there but if you can tolerate that...I'd really like you to come."

"Does your father know you're inviting me?" Tony Lenahan and I went to school together. The seeds of our enmity go a long way back.

"Not yet. But he'll be alright. It's my party after all. He's pretty grudging in what he says about you altogether but even he knows how much your coaching's done for me."

"Then I'll put in an appearance. If it's sticky I won't stay long."

"Good."

"Anybody else I know going?"

"Half the club for starters."

"I'll look forward to it."

Subject dropped. We gather up the rest of the balls. Shower and dress. Rory gets collected by one of his father's people, Sudhir, the Jain. I drive myself home.

***

Exhaustion therapy is fine while you work and sleep. The difficulties arise with the weekend. Unless you go away. And I'm not going away. Ring Jaki and offer to buy her lunch at the Pyewipe by the river. Not far from her flat. Intend to make her the offer of paid employment.

Now a couple of hours to fill. The temptation's too strong. I need to know something. Want some certainty. Pick up the phone. Call Megan. Don't get much joy from the conversation. When Megan realises it's me, her attitude is kind but bluntly unhelpful.

"Look I'm really sorry. Gail's a very private person and her life's...difficult. She wouldn't want me telling you anything she can't tell you herself. I wondered how things would be when we got back home. This isn't quite what I thought would happen. And I really feel for you. But there's nothing I can say or do. Just don't give up on her. Things may change."

Easy for her to say. Almost impossible to believe.

Try to persuade her to say more. She won't. Gently but firmly she brings the conversation to a close. And hangs up.

Useless.

***

A Friday evening at The Lawn. A former bedlam converted into a conference centre and concert venue by the council. Somewhere in the building there's still an original Victorian padded cell. A relic of the bad old days, pre-psychiatry. Now we're in a more enlightened age where everybody's in touch with their feelings and can express them. Like hell!

A decent local band playing tonight to a partisan home crowd. Here on stage tonight. Think about buying another copy of their live album and getting it autographed for Gail. Don't. What's the point?

Patrick's with me. I don't mind not reminding him that he owes me a tenner for his ticket. My treat. After all times are hard for jobbing solicitors and there's precious little sympathy coming his way from any other direction. It's what friends are for.

Walking down into the West End he starts in on me.

"What's the matter with you? You've not been yourself since you got back from Alanya." Unusually astute of him to notice.

"Nothing's quite working out as I hoped."

"A woman?"

"Naturally. Isn't it always?"

"Not with you. You've been pretty hard-nosed since Julie left. And how many years is that now? What's this one like?"

"Use the past tense."

"That's a shame. Plenty more fish in the sea though."

And I lose my temper at the fatuous cruelty of a thoughtless tongue. We're good at rows, Patrick and me. Our voices rise in volume until we're shouting and the original stimulus is long forgotten. Just releasing tension. Degenerating into laughter. And pints in the Queen In the West. No grudges held. Especially if Patrick's buying. Which he does.

***

Snapshots of a month.

You can stay home or be out in a crowd and the quality of loneliness feels much the same. There is a difference though. With other people around, pride and self-consciousness can stop you weeping. So go out and mingle.

First up an out of season friendly match to raise funds for a community football trust. Some of our players have done voluntary work for them in the past. Lot of arm-twisting of the directors to make it happen. But the special relationship we've had with Bradford since that awful fire means they're always up for anything like this. So in the main stand at Sincil Bank to watch the home team throw away a two goal lead. Rory scores both of ours. Suffice it to say our goalkeeper doesn't win Man of the Match.

A softer summer regime of training sessions. Then a break. Rory goes off to Spain on holiday with some of his team mates. God knows what they'll get up to.

Jaki starts as my cleaner. Can't detect much immediate difference but its nice having her around more. And it's a way of slipping her a few quid without breaking my sister's stricture that she has to earn any extra cash she needs.

Spend too long at the cinema taking in any film on the bill. For lack of anything else meaningful to do.

Bill's knee implodes. Not much I can do for him except recommend he sees a consultant surgeon. I know a good one and pass across the details. It does mean he and Davina are necessarily now retired from road racing. I point out once again the merits of investing in bikes. They may even be listening this time.

BBC Radio Lincolnshire persuades John Inverdale to revisit his roots and he comes to host a general knowledge quiz in aid of another charity who for whatever reason can't get past the Dean and Chapter of Lincoln Cathedral to hold one of their unique services for grieving parents. Currently a local controversy. Why Exeter, Birmingham, Manchester, anywhere but not us? Patrick's sextet comes fourth against stiff competition. We're really pleased with ourselves.

Sit in the kitchen with a spiral bound notebook and my fountain pen making a list of all the things I don't and would like to know about Gail and her life. It's a long list.

***

They say frustration is good for the development of the soul. If it were true, I'd be the healthiest man in the country. Psychologically speaking. I suppose knowing where you need to get to is an advantage but the lack of any way to get there is killing. Simply put, I want Gail in my life, in my house, in my bed and wherever I am. An endless litany of spaces I didn't even realise were empty before Alanya.

The worst thing is having nobody to talk to who knows her. Who can comment meaningfully on why she broke off contact. Who can tell me where she is physically and emotionally and when it might be possible to see her again.

Try to walk it off. Alone with my thoughts. No sort of solution.

***

Sudhir and another large man are guarding the door at Bentley's. I get a half-way grin and a casual wave through from him. Into the party. Stand and look around the crowded bar. Knots of sportsmen and giggling young women. Isolated islands of older people. I spot LCFC's Chairman and Treasurer with their well-groomed wives. And a couple of City Councillors. My former father-in-law doesn't seem to be among them. Can't see Rory either but he has to be here somewhere.

A strong hand takes my elbow and steers me round. I'm face to face with Rory's father. I've not seen Tony Lenahan in a long time. I'd like to be able to describe him in wholly derogatory terms. 'Pig face' for example. But I'd be lying. Well-built and hatchet-faced. Male pattern baldness is advancing and he's put on some weight but I'm sure women still see him as handsome. Just not the pretty boy he used to be once upon a time.

"Hello Anthony." Me being placatory. I know he likes the use of his proper name. It's a status thing. Actually he really prefers 'Mr Lenahan' but I've known him and ignored his existence too long to go there.

"Have a drink. Just one. Wish Rory a happy birthday. Then leave. I don't want you at this party."

"Rory invited me."

Yeah. I'd have had you chucked straight out if he hadn't. But he only knows you as a football coach. He doesn't really know what you are. Or what you did to my brother."

"He was a sadistic bully, Tony. And very lucky. When I bottled him I was aiming for his eye."

"You scarred him for life."

"Not a long life though."

I know I'm twisting the knife. Goading a rattlesnake. But I can't help it. I've never managed to stop hating the fourteen year old Mickey Lenahan. The passage of years and his demise haven't changed those feelings one jot. Of course it doesn't help that Tony bears a strong facial resemblance to his deceased older brother.

"He died a hero."

"A hero? The army was the only place that would have him. He was a homicidal maniac. He fitted right in perfectly. And then he got himself blown up. Game over."

Tony's controlled outrage leaks out only in his contemptuous tone. "You are scum. Insulting him to my face."

Shake my head. "No. Mickey deserved everything that came his way. After what he did." Correct myself. "Tried to do."

"And what exactly do you say he did?"

"You know the answer to that one."

No denial. "And you stuck a broken beer bottle in his face."

"As I said, I wasn't aiming at his chin. I missed. Of course if I'd been the one who was older and stronger I'd have half blinded him. The army wouldn't have taken him and he'd still be alive now. Ever consider that? I nearly saved his life. By accident."

Tony shakes his head. Doing a valiant job of reining in his temper.

"Right. I'll go. You can thank Rory for me."

"Don't let me see you around. Keep looking over your shoulder. One of these days I'll be there."

"You've been promising that more years than I care to remember."

"One day..."

Turn sharply to walk away. Barge into someone coming up behind me. The impact isn't what causes the colour to drain from my features. It's the shock on Gail's face.

Chapter V Now: November to December

Waking early. A nagging ache in my ankle. It seems to have stiffened in the night. All the walking I've been doing of late. Can't put my full weight on it at first. Need to flex and loosen it before I can get dressed.

Still there is one normal thing to start enjoying again. Getting to eat a meal at a table instead of from a room service tray. Thanks to Ethan and Jimmy it's safe to breakfast in the dining room.

Breakfast ends abruptly with a call from Megan. "They're going earlier than they said. You've got to get down here right away."

"Ok. I'm coming. Be there in ten minutes."

In the car. Across to Greetwell Road.

Lincoln County Hospital. Not exactly unfamiliar territory thanks to periodic trips to Casualty with trainees who've sustained broken bones in their feet and legs or occasionally a broken arm. Then there were the painful weeks spent in SCBU acting as though Oliver might make it if we prayed over him enough but always fearing the worst. Remember the reddened crying faces of other premature babies born with foetal alcohol or heroin issues. A shockingly common phenomenon. Or Irene, the lovely young girl kicked into early delivery by her irate so-called boyfriend. Other stories I've worked hard on forgetting. Not a happy place. Mostly. A repository of broken dreams. Ollie's brain bleed and slow decline just another little tragedy among so many.

Coming here is plain depressing. Usually. Today more mixed emotions. Churning fear that nothing good will come of this mixed with real hope that it could.

Down long corridors into a waiting area serving the operating suites. Megan sitting beside a trolley. The woman lying on it is Gail. A couple of staff wearing scrubs are leaning over her.

"This is cutting it fine. She's going under right now. Gail! Look who's here."

I reach her. One of the staff moves aside.

"Hello, sweet girl. Are you alright? What are they doing with you?"

Unless I imagine it, she squeezes my fingers. Slips away. And is wheeled into theatre.

Can't sit here. Find the cafe. The first coffee of a long wait. Megan chooses a doughnut. I insist on paying but can't face anything other than the drink. I can tell myself this isn't too serious but I'm paralysed with selfish concerns. Nothing requiring general anaesthesia is devoid of risk. And I want her back so much more than I can ever remember wanting anything else in my life.

Talking. Just for the sake of it. "Could it have actually happened the way she told you?"

"You'll have to ask her yourself. I'm still very suspicious."

"She's covering up for him?"

"Could well be."

"And today is corrective?"

"Re-breaking and re-setting. Pinning? A couple of small bones in her wrist which aren't healing properly."

"And she'll be in a cast? For how long?"

"How should I know? I'm not a doctor. So no comment."

"Thought 'No comment' was what you advised your clients never to say."

"There's an exception to every rule."

"Are you good at what you do?"

"No false modesty. I am. Need some representation?"

"Me? Why would I need...?"

"Maybe some image consultancy. New clothes to go with your hair for example."

"What about my hair."

"You've had it cut."

"Yes? What's wrong with that?"

"Nothing. It was too long for your age. You look better with it shorter."

"Is that what Gail thinks?"

"Yes."

"You discussed my hair with Gail?"

"Yes. In Turkey. But we covered your good points as well."

And so on. It passes the time. More coffee. Sitting. Standing.

My mobile goes off, the double tone vibration of a text landing. Grab it. An unrecognised number.

"Back finn theatre. Are toy close? Xx." Post-anaesthesia scrambling of the synapses.

Interpret as 'Get your arse over here, you selfish git. I need to see you.' But Gail wouldn't stoop to using language like that.

First we have to track her down. Takes a little while. Mainly to find a member of staff who can use the computer system well enough to locate her allocated ward. Before we can, there's another text. "Pls come o can't talk tho xx."

She has a bed. She's in it. Apparently asleep. Her left arm outside the sheets bears a plaster cast. So they seem to have operated in the right general area. Let's hope they honed in on the correct limb.

Megan whispers. "I'll leave you to it and come back later. I'll lurk down the corridor and make sure you're not ambushed by jealous husbands. Not that there's much risk of that. If he bothers to come at all, it'll be for half an hour this evening." She flounces off. At least the target of her righteous indignation isn't me.

The moment I sit down, Gail's eyes flicker open. I take her hand. The one without the cast. It feels oddly naked, as hands go, without benefit of nail varnish, rings, or bracelets. She wriggles luxuriously and goes back to sleep.

The bed has side rails to stop her falling out. Awkward damn things. If they didn't exist, I'd kick my shoes off and climb aboard to cradle her properly until she wakes. As it is I'm holding onto her hand for grim life as my wrist and shoulder go slowly but surely numb.

***

Gail wakes, grimacing with pain. Frees her hand. Gropes for the self-regulator. Gives herself a hit of painkillers. Turns to look me full in the face.

"You cut your hair." Croaking but clear enunciation.

"Yes. Thought it was time for a change." No need to tell her what else was on my mind at the time.

"I like it."

An opinion guaranteed to make me grin. "I was afraid you wouldn't recognise me."

She reaches to touch my face. Gently. "Well I do." Clears her throat. Runs her tongue over her lips. I can see how dry they are. Prop her head up and hold a glass of water to her mouth so she can take a sip or two. She swallows with some difficulty. "Hard to talk."

"Then don't. Would you like something else to drink?"

"Squash. Maybe."

"I'll get some."

"Later. Don't leave now."

Take her hand again. Manipulate her knuckles. Stroke the soft skin of her wrist. "I've missed you so much."

"I thought you'd stopped caring."

"Then you don't know me as well as you're going to."

"Talk about it later. Can't now. So glad you're here."

"Me too."

***

Megan drags me out late in the afternoon, worried about possible confrontations. Lean over and give Gail a kiss. "I'll be here again in the morning. Anything you need?"

"Just you." The right answer.

***

Up and in early. Text Gail from the main entrance to ensure the coast is clear. It is. She's sitting on the bed. Dressed. Looking much brighter. The remains of breakfast are on a bedside tray. I have magazines, peach cordial and her favourite mints. Make myself comfortable to ask the one thing I want to know today. Straight out. The direct approach.

"Did he...your husband? Did he break your wrist?" That's strange. Realise she has never used his given name. Not to me.

"No." Almost indignant.

"How did you do it then?"

"Just an accident. Having a silly argument and I stepped back and fell over Boo."

"Who's Boo?"

"Bootalicious, my new dog. A rescue. Got her from a friend's farm. She's really soft but very bouncy. Typical Springer. She wasn't working out as a gun dog. She was a bit nervy. Then she started chasing sheep when she got the chance. So they couldn't keep her. I've had her a few weeks now. I love her. She's this lovely mix of brown and white fur..."

Too much detail. Intended to distract. I don't want to be distracted. Get her back to the central issue. "What about your wrist?"

"I must have put my hand back as I fell to try to save myself and I landed with all my weight on it. It hurt something rotten but I didn't realise I'd broken anything. It was a Saturday night so I didn't want to be up at Accident and Emergency with all the drunks. So I left it. It swelled up overnight. Didn't sleep much cause it was so painful. Anyway Megan brought me to the hospital for x-rays and a young doctor set it. But he didn't do it right. Which is why I'm back here."

Don't say anything. It sounds too carefully rehearsed an explanation. And I know it's said that all manner of people cover up domestic violence when it's happening. Or perhaps it's just that I want him to have done it because then she might leave him.

"Don't you believe me?"

Interesting this should be the concern uppermost in her mind.

"Yes I do. Mainly because I don't want to think I've put you in a position where you need to lie to me. So if you say it's so, then it is. How long will you have to wear the cast?"

"They tell me about ten to twelve weeks. But they should send me home today. If the registrar says I can go." She anticipates my next question. "Megan will take me home. I can't let you do it."

I know that's true. Unfortunately.

***

Lunchtime. Megan arrives. Let her sit with Gail for a bit while I make some phone calls. When Megan's ready to go back to work she texts me and we meet up in the hospital shop. I go over Gail's account of the accident with her. Megan says it correlates closely with what she was told.

"But I still think she may have been pushed over. There's the other stuff since Alanya. Too many unexplained bruises. Things she's agreed to do with me or Ellie and then cancelled at the last moment. She's not herself. I mean, to me she seems really low too much of the time. What do you think?"

"I've only got yesterday and this morning to go on. So I don't know. I'll keep my eyes and ears open. Assuming I can see her once she's back home."

"We've got Christmas and New Year coming. She's got to get though the holiday period. That's stressful at the best of times. We'll have to see."

"Yeah, we will. I gather you're picking her up when she's allowed out. You will look out for her for me won't you?"

"You know I will."

Back to pass the time with Gail. Read chunks of the newspaper to her which seems to amuse her. We do the quick crossword. Ask if she wants to complete the Sudoku. She doesn't so I do it. Finish it inside twelve minutes. Look up. She's watching me. Smiling.

"How will we meet once you're home again?"

"I'll phone you. I promise. Don't look at me in that tone of voice. I will. Really I will!"

"Like you did when you got back from Alanya." I don't know why I bring that up. I didn't mean to go there.

"No. You know why I couldn't contact you then. It's different now."

"Gail, listen to me. This is may still be too early for us to be certain of each other. But I am sure how I feel about you. And anytime you need to, you can come to stay at my home. Permanently. Or as a temporary measure if that's what you need. Whatever you want, I'll do."

"Thank you. That's good to know. It's just ..."

"The boys? I know. They come as a part of the package. So of course them too."

"Alright. I'll bear it in mind. But you haven't met my monsters yet. I think I need to sleep a bit now."

Not quite the response I wanted to hear but at least I've told her.

So I watch her sleep. She neither snores nor dribbles. She looks peaceful. And gorgeous.

***

Once Gail's been discharged and carted away by Megan, I call Jaki to see if she's home from lectures. Then get Jimmy to drive me down to her flat. Even before Rory gets there it's a bit crowded with both minders coming in. Mugs of tea all round. And a council of war. About Sandrine and Daniel.

Define the problems. A five year old not being properly cared for. Is he being fed regularly? Is he going to school? Has he already been notified to social services? A young mother with a drug habit? Where's her supply coming from. What will get her to stop? The threat of losing Daniel? Does she even want to be a mother? Is Tony still involved with her and Daniel? How will he react to what he's bound to see as unwelcome interference with them? And St Giles'?. What a place for a boy like Daniel to have to grow up. Can't do much about the rest of the estate but could we tackle Sandrine's seeming inability to keep her home in a decent state? Perhaps this is where we could start. Talk this lot over anyway.

Jaki's wondering about official intervention to get round the obstacles Rory's Dad may pose. "Should we talk to a social worker right away? Get some proper advice."

"If we do, the risk is we'll lose control of the situation. They might just take Daniel away. They'd put him with a foster family. Mightn't be the best thing for him. And how would

Sandrine cope if that happened?" None of us can guess. Even Rory.

"Mind if I say something?" The mild-mannered approach is Ethan's. "Things probably haven't changed that much since I was in care. I wouldn't want to see a five year old in a home unless there's no other option. Even foster families can be pot luck."

Astonished. That's the most I've ever heard Ethan say. On any subject.

"How long were you in care?"

"I was taken in when I was eight. Left at seventeen. Two care homes. Five foster families. I don't recommend it."

"So we don't want to get the authorities involved unless we have to."

Ethan solemnly shakes his head. He knows what he's talking about so it'd be churlish to disagree with him.

"Hang on. We could make it clear we'd have to report this unless Sandrine gets her act together. Tell her she's at real risk of losing Daniel. You could phone her, Rory. See how she reacts."

"Not my idea of fun. But I suppose I could."

"It can't be just threats though. We need to convince her we're on her side. Supposing we offer to help clean up the flat in case social services are already investigating."

We all think it's worth a try. Gives us the opportunity to find out more from the inside about what's going on. Particularly about the drugs. It's Friday tomorrow. No training for Rory and Jaki can skip a couple of lectures.

"Okay. Rory, ring her now. Tell her you'd like to see her in the morning and you'll be bringing a couple of friends."

The call is made. Rory's not sure she's taken it in. But we have a plan of sorts.

***

The Chief Executive's office in City Hall is a decent size but not particularly grand. The new incumbent is younger and taller than me. Has a full head of hair and has still got plenty to smile about, as evidenced by the friendliness of his greeting. This a man not yet over-exposed to cynicism and frustration. A sharp contrast to his time-served predecessor.

We get settled across one corner of the room's large conference table and tea is ordered. The ubiquitous brew which most outsiders like me believe to be the true fuel on which public service runs.

"Councillor Ross asked me to do him a favour. To see you."

"Yes. Thank you. I should explain. I used to be married to his daughter. But my real link comes from the football club. I'm a freelance coach. I get paid to stretch and mould their best prospects. I beat them into shape I suppose."

"And that's what you wanted to talk to me about?"

"Not at all. It's more about the council's relationship with the club. I need to emphasise that I'm here in a personal capacity. I have no official status in this conversation apart from being a shareholder myself. I don't speak for the club. But I suspect many of those who could do would share my concerns. But they're not free to express their fears. Have you been briefed on this yet? What have they told you about the current situation with the club?"

"You mean do I know that the council has a stake in the club. That it owns the ground. That it has use of some club facilities. That we co-manage a health club under one of the stands. The answer is yes, I do. It's not an unusual situation. Something similar was the case in Leeds several years ago when I worked there."

"But you're not from Yorkshire originally are you? My former father-in-law would have made more of a fuss about your appointment if you'd come from God's Own Country."

"No. I'm from the wrong side of the Pennines. Mancunian by birth and upbringing."

"Not much of the accent left."

"True. Now. The football club?"

"This is all about realisation of assets. Things've been happening with residential developments on former club-owned land while I've been away."

"Where have you been?"

And I thought I was the only one who was easily side-tracked in conversation. "Istanbul for a few months. But that's not relevant. I'm concerned about possible fraud or corruption and I'm raising it with you only because your very newness means you're not likely to be involved in it already or to have any incentive to be part of a cover-up."

"You think members or officers are involved in some dodgy development?"

"Possibly. Make that probably. I know this isn't the easiest thing to dump on your desk in your third working week."

"No. But you'd better tell me about it."

So I do.

***

Friday. The actual first step is for Rory to run Jaki up Bailgate to the hardware shop armed with a list of essential supplies. No point in assuming Sandrine has anything of what's needed. My list covers plastic buckets, rubber gloves, disposable aprons and all manner of cleaning products. Plus tea, coffee, sugar and milk from the neighbouring newsagents. I offer her some cash but Jaki won't take it. "Rory can sort this." Don't know if he'll appreciate her stance on his behalf but that's their problem.

Rendezvous outside the flat. Jimmy can look after the cars. Ethan comes in with us.

The doorbell's given up the ghost. As I predicted. It takes time and repeated knocking to get Sandrine to let us in. She looks marginally less out of things than the last time I saw her but she's only half-dressed. Jaki steers her back into the bedroom to help her to sort herself out.

"Rory, open the windows and let's get some mugs sterilised for starters and we'll get the kettle on.

Ethan surprises me. "I'll do it." I thought he might stand on his professional dignity and insist on guarding the front door.

Rory and I clear all the rubbish off the kitchen table and dump everything disposable into the first black plastic bag torn off a large roll Jaki's bought. Most of the contents of the fridge follow. The room's already starting to look more civilised when Jaki and Sandrine re-join us. There are three chairs around the table. Ethan and I stand to drink our tea.

Rory sits across from Sandrine and addresses her with both firmness and subtlety. I taught him neither. "This is how it is. You have a problem and Daniel's paying the price. When social services find out, they're going to take him away and you may never get him back. So what are you willing to do differently to keep him?"

Hopefully the ensuing silence is Sandrine taking it in and considering her response. The first thing she says is "I'm doing my best."

"No. You're not. Where are the drugs coming from? In fact, what drugs are you doing?"

Sandrine's head goes down. She says nothing. The silence lasts until she raises it again. Looks quizzically at each of us in turn. Rory takes this as a cue to explain who we all are. "They can help. But if you'd rather talk to just me, that's okay. We can go into the lounge."

"Yes. That would be better, I think."

Leaving the room, Rory turns to issue an instruction to the rest of us. "Carry on cleaning then." Jaki's reaction is instantaneous. A wet dishcloth hits the kitchen door precisely where his head was only a second or so earlier.

We've moved on to tackle the bedrooms by the time Rory returns. He looks strained. "She's dozing now. On the settee."

"Time for a tea break. Crack open the biscuits." Bundle everybody back into the kitchen. "So Rory, what gives?"

Rory sips from his mug and the reason for his difficulty is quickly apparent in his explanation. "She's drinking. But the main problem is her coke habit. She's getting it free whenever she wants it. She's using everyday. I don't think she even remotely wants to stop. Maybe she doesn't remember what being straight is like. The only way to get her off the stuff is to cut off her supply. But the person who's giving it to her is my Dad."

I may be the one person in the room for whom this comes as no surprise at all. But then again I know more about Tony Lenahan's borderline activities than anyone around the table. I also know the police haven't got enough to take him down. Yet. Or in the near future probably. Waiting for them will simply mean the exponential growth of Sandrine's habit while Daniel's chances of normal family life become non-existent.

Jaki weighs in with an idea. "If we can't stop the supply to her here, couldn't we take her somewhere else. Away from him."

"Will she agree to stay anywhere else? And what about Daniel's school?"

"That wouldn't matter for a few weeks at his age. Anyway they'll be breaking up for Christmas soon. But where would be safe?" She knows the answer of course. It can't be her one-bedroomed flat. I've been set up. I've even got professional minders on tap already.

"Alright, I surrender. We'll put them up at my house. Thanks to Ethan and Jimmy, there's no real need for me to stay at The White Hart any more. You could move in too, Jaki. Play chaperone. And Rory. If you want. We could give Daniel a decent Christmas. Bet he's never had one of those."

"My father will expect me to be at home with them over Christmas. But I could come down some of the time. We could try this. Couldn't we? Yes? Jaki? Is this okay with you?"

A Cheshire Cat smile from my niece. Either because she's engineered it all or because Rory hasn't twigged the extent of her manipulation of the discussion. "Mum will want some time with me when she's off duty. But I'll talk to her."

"No! I'll talk to my sister. If she's not working, she can come over too. We'll make it a proper house party." Enthusiasm's growing in me by the minute. Despite the seriousness of the Sandrine issue, we could turn Trescombe into a great refuge. And have some real fun while we're at it.

"Let's do it then."

***

Finishing Sandrine's flat takes the whole day. Jaki finds a suspicious hoard of powder which gets flushed away. We have to borrow a neighbour's hoover because Sandrine's is bust. We also need hefty portions of fish and chips for lunch. I don't much enjoy cleaning the toilet and bathroom sink but I don't trust any of the others not to skimp given the state they're in. The place looks and smells completely different when we're done. Jaki guides Sandrine through a bag-packing process. She purloins Sandrine's mobile and slips it to me for safekeeping. Sandrine doesn't seem to take in quite why it's necessary for her to come with us but casual acquiescence will do for now. Make a mental note to myself to disconnect my phone and hide it back in the biscuit tin. Remove all chances of Sandrine calling anybody if she takes it into her head she's been kidnapped.

Rory collects Daniel from school. We're out of here.

***

Trescombe is a large family house which doesn't get used as it should. Normally I rattle around in it. It's good to fill it with people for a change. Even if I have to raid the shops to buy more duvets and bedding for them.

One slice of poetic justice. Jaki and Rory can have one of the double bedrooms on the top floor which she seldom bothers to clean properly because she knows I virtually never go up there. On the first floor, apart from my room, there are two smaller bedrooms which Sandrine and Daniel can have. I won't insist Ethan sleep across the threshold like a medieval retainer. He can have the sofa-bed in my study. So everyone's accommodated.

Not so easy to establish a workable daily routine. He may not have school but Daniel rises early. Natural enough for a five year old. Sandrine gets up late, if at all. Jaki's day depends on the timing of her lectures which differs each day. Rory is required for training most days but for varying periods of time. I'm not back coaching or doing any other paid work yet so I'm the flexible lynch pin. Are lynch pins flexible? It doesn't seem likely. Anyway it falls to me to hold things together. Thank goodness for Ethan and Jimmy. Ethan in particular proves brilliant at child care.

I talk on the phone to Gail most days. Sometimes for an hour at a stretch. About everything except why we're not together and the real reasons I had to leave last March. And why I stayed away for eight months. She doesn't ask. I wonder if perhaps she doesn't want to know the answers. Or suspects she knows them already. Anyway she can't drive with the cast on her wrist. Indeed she finds it difficult to do all manner of things. Even getting dressed poses major headaches. And the husband is being particularly awkward and has effectively confined her under house arrest. So I don't get to see her. It's driving me insane.

I'm paying for Jimmy anyway so I let him drive wherever I need to go. I cancelled the instruction to take my own car out of storage. Where it's been since I flew out to Istanbul.

We go shopping most days. Mainly because Jaki keeps giving me lists of appliances, kitchenware and foodstuffs which I never knew were essential when I lived on my own.

Christmas closes in on us. Inexorably. But my most fervent wish is finally realised. Gail manages to plan an afternoon escape. And I get to see her at last.

***

In the car park. Standing waiting in the shelter afforded by the castle wall. It's bitterly cold now. Perhaps we should have arranged to meet in a coffee shop.

Gail comes round the corner. Easy to spot in a bright red woolly hat. Her coat is less stylish; an old black puffa jacket, slit open up the left arm. She's wearing boots. Sensible. A silky grey scarf is wrapped around her throat and she's wearing a single black leather glove. The unprotected fingers protruding from her cast must be frozen.

She stops an arms length away from me. Says nothing at first. Nor do I. Looking at each other is communication enough.

In the end she breaks the silence. "Hello." Just the one word.

I want her in the compass of my arms. But I want her to come to me. If she does I'll have certainty she means it. She takes a step forward and she's very close now. I don't twitch a muscle. The look in her eyes is something strange and wonderful. I take in her perfume; familiar, subtle, a perfect foil for her natural scent. I can't think of anything to say, except her name. And slowly, like a tall tree bending in the wind, she leans into me until her head makes contact with my chest. Which is when my hands come up of their own volition, take her face between them and I get to sample the sheer joy of the first proper kiss from her, from anyone, in too many months.

And then, miracle of miracles, the first falling snowflakes of this winter, eddying down to cold-kiss our foreheads. A blessing of sorts. She says "It's snowing." As though it's the most wonderful thing in the world. She makes me smile. Her almost childlike delight in all manner of things makes me see them afresh. And I know I love her. And I'll always love her. And it's so painfully raw, I can hardly handle how different it is from anything I've ever felt before. Half a lifetime to get to this point and now at last I understand what it's all about.

Chapter VI Then: June

Gail recovers first. A pleading look and a warning shake of her head. I understand her only too clearly. Straighten up. Say, "Sorry." Walk past her. Out of the bar. Across the lobby. In between Sudhir and his colleague. As I reach it, a tall, good-looking girl waltzes in, taking it for granted that I'll hold the door open for her. A voice behind me says "Evening, Sandrine." Don't look back. Cross the car park. Get in my car. I'm going home. I really do need that drink now.

***

Sunday. Wake early. Make a cup of tea. Follow up with a bowl of mixed cereal, chopped fresh fruit and yoghurt topped off with an unnecessary helping of sugar. Fetch the Sunday papers. More tea. Passing time until it's a reasonable hour. Run out of patience. Phone Megan far too early. Not that she sounds anything other than wide awake and breezy when she answers on the third ring.

"Hi. How are things with you?"

"Hard to tell at the moment. Look, I literally bumped into Gail at Rory Lenahan's birthday party last night. She seemed scared as hell to see me."

"I don't think she's scared of you. Only of being seen with you."

"Really? Well I can't go on without seeing her. Have to know what's going on. If you can't give me her phone number..."

"I've said I can't."

"Then let her know I have to talk to her. Get her to call me. Whenever she can. Is that okay?"

"I can ask her."

"That's all I want, Megs."

"How are you doing? Really?"

"Can't comment without swearing."

She laughs. Says her goodbyes. Hangs up.

The day drags. Sundays are often a boring pain. Today is no exception. Gail's on my mind whenever I stop doing any of the household tasks I'm forcing myself to tackle. A month getting used to not having her around and I'm blown away by one glimpse of her at a party. I'd forgotten how beautiful she is. But what on earth makes her so afraid? I hope to hell it's not me. Maybe it's that she knows I don't merely want to talk to her. I want to hold her. And more. And that's what makes me so dangerous to her. That I can't just be a friend. That I want it all.

Dog-tired. Sleep better.

Up, shower and careful shave. All the weekend stubble removed. Re-lather and do it again. Smooth. Practice smiling at the mirror. I'll do.

Second cup of tea in hand when the doorbell rings. Carry it into the hall and open the front door. Nobody there. Look around. Nothing. Close the door. Only then notice the white envelope lying on the tiles under the letterbox. It has my name on it. Very precise handwriting. The letter opener's on the side table. Use it to slit the flap. No letter. Just a business card. For Smith-Ryan Furnishings with an address in Newark and a telephone number. Find I'm breathing raggedly and my pulse is racing. Physiologically normal for shock. Back to the kitchen. Use the phone.

An unfamiliar female voice. "Hello. Smith-Ryan."

"I'd like to speak to Gail Ryan, please."

"I'm afraid she's not in till this afternoon. Can I help you?"

"It's alright, thanks. I'll try again later."

Hang up. It rings again immediately. Except it doesn't. Realise it's the doorbell once more. Open the front door. This time Gail herself is standing on the step. Clipboard at odds with a floaty, green, summer dress.

"Hello," she says. "I'm sorry to bother you on such a lovely day. I represent an interior design company. We're currently working in your area and can therefore offer special discounts to you. On cushions, blinds and upholstery. I understand you may need some new curtains made. Perhaps I could come in to measure up."

"Of course you can." Stand back. But I'm not letting her get past me. Grab her. Hug her.

"Gently." An admonition. She back-heels the door. It slams. And she kisses me. And I forget what time of day it is. Never mind all the things I want to ask her.

***

When we've dis-engaged she accepts a cup of tea and undertakes a tour of my house. Smiles a lot. Admires everything. Comments on various improvements we could effect. Offers to bring me some sample swatches for the lounge. Goes off to work. But not before telling me she won't be needed in the shop on Wednesday. So if I'd like to meet up with her.

"Tell me where and when and I'll be there."

Only when she's gone does it occur to me to question why it's possible for her to turn up at my house now. What's changed.

***

A rich vein of feeling underscores every real happiness. Whether it's possible to put it into words without being mawkish or just downright boring is highly debateable. So I won't. I'm enjoying what's going on too much. In my life there have been quite a few periods of contentment. More often with work than any relationship but, wherever it comes from, if you're wise you grab it and hold on as long as it lasts. This is new though. Consistently wanting to be with the same person. Loving her whatever mood she's in. Looking forward to the insignificantly small pleasures as much as the grander ones. Playing card games together as against concerts or the theatre or planning another holiday together whenever that might turn out to be possible.

Anyway, it's a month of change. Evolution. The creation of an entity called us.

In the early weeks Gail is endlessly careful not to be seen with me. After the first visit she refuses to come to my house. And obviously I can't go to hers. Nor will she let me pick her up from work. So we have to meet away from Lincoln. There are people who enjoy skulduggery. For whom the act of secrecy inflames passion. It would be a lot easier if I was one of them. But I'm not. The constraints of enforced abnormality and distance cause me a lot of frustration. Not when I'm with her. But afterwards. When she's gone home. Or when she can't come to a party or any other kind of social occasion with me. And I go on my own and tell the corrosive little white lies which feed my sense of loss. "Yes, I'm fine." "No, I'm not seeing anybody seriously." "Work's the most important thing in life." "I'm good on my own." I don't even remotely believe what I'm saying. So how plausible my assertions can be is pretty questionable.

***

Gail, playing it safe, opts to travel separately. I drive to Nottingham. She takes the train. I'm there before her. Book a hotel room. Pay cash. The clerk smiles. Guess he's seen it all before. No need to say we'll be vacating early evening because Gail can't stay. Sit in the station buffet to wait for her.

Smile coming back into the hotel foyer, recalling Ellie banging on in Turkey about judging hotels by their carpets. "Never stay in a place with green carpets." No risk of that here. Blue and gold offsetting Scandinavian beech and ash designs.

Speak briefly to the desk clerk while Gail settles down on the settee in the foyer. Isolating herself from the transaction I'm effecting. Take the proffered card-key and cross the floor. Text the room number to Gail. Take the lift up. Have it to myself. I'd rather Gail was in my arms but circumspection is still the primary requirement. Open the door and wait for her to join me. Don't have to wait long for her to emerge into the empty hallway. Self-mockingly, she goes past me on tiptoes and I shut the door behind her.

The room is refreshingly cool. Gail drops her large black handbag at the foot of the bed. The flowers draw the eye. A mass of colour in a silver vase on the coffee table. The florist has risen to the challenge I set her. The French window opens easily and we're leaning on the balustrade, looking out over the city. There's a sense of nervousness about her and I expect her to say something. Instead she simply folds herself into my arms and her mouth locks onto mine. This is what we've both been missing. To be together despite all the obstacles and to know there's a whole afternoon in front of us.

Guide her back inside, an arm around her waist until the bed touches the backs of her knees. She folds gracefully down onto the quilt but I let go.

"Patience". Head to the wine chiller, secreted in the corner, protruding from it the unmistakeable, orange-labelled neck of a champagne bottle. The pop of the cork, a deft juxtaposition of snow-white napkin, bottle and glass and she's got a full flute in her hand. As have I. And settle down next to her, my hip and thigh against hers and our time can begin.

I turn towards her and she shifts onto her side so she can lay her head on my chest with one of my arms around her shoulders and a hand stroking her hair. Her eyes close and there's a sigh in there somewhere but she can't stay still and her fingers find and unfasten the buttons down my shirt until she can burrow in and rest her cheek on my skin.

"Hello there."

This time her sigh is completely unmistakeable for the expression of deep satisfaction it is.

We lie, murmuring endearments, occasionally stirring for a sip of champagne or to steal a kiss. But neither of us will be content to pass too long like this. Not when beneath the passivity, a regular pulsing throb of expectation lurks. It's only a matter of time before my hands must begin their traverse around and over her body. Before long the first groans of her pleasure at my inability to stop touching her. Just as she must touch me as she peels off my clothes, a moot point who will first completely bare the other. And it’s all to come. Making love. Dinner on trays huddled in fleecy dressing gowns. A shared bath, drying each other in enormous soft white towels and curling up together in a bed from which neither of us will willingly rise when I have to take her home.

And so it goes on. Building slowly. Mouths re-learning a myriad ways to come together. The press of lips, the touch of tongues and the deliberate slow scrape of nibbling bites. And the things that four hands can do. Sometimes neutralising each other, clasped so the only thing left is to rub our bodies against each other, divine pressure. But mostly clutching, stroking and caressing exploration of each other. "Nobody spends enough time touching." Realise I've said the thought aloud. "It's the real secret of the universe."

She gasps. And here and now I know she wants me as much as I want her. From her eye a single tear falls as my teeth softly close around her earlobe. And I see it fall, catch it and wipe it away. Recall her doing the same thing for me in Alanya.

"No tears tonight, sweetheart." And her face lights up again and she squeezes me tightly, as though afraid I'll slip away. I know exactly what she's thinking and the words come in absolute sincerity. "Don't be afraid. I love you." At long last the easiest thing in the world to say and to mean.

***

And one day it changes again. Gets even better. With a phone call.

"Invite me to lunch today," she suggests.

"Okay. Where would you like to go? I can offer you a nice little pub in Aubourn or we can drive down to Stamford. There's a great new restaurant there..."

"No. You can cook for me."

"You mean it?"

"Yes."

You don't question luck like this. You just seize the moment. Put the phone down. And rush out to the shops. Come back with beef medallions, salad stuff and the best potatoes I can find to fry into thin, crisp, roundels. And pots of rich chocolate mousse which I'll turn out into little glass bowls as if made from scratch. It's not cheating if you're prepared to own up but don't get asked how you did it.

***

Windows wide in the noonday heat. The air is still and there's music coming from somewhere down the row. A boy is playing with a barking dog on the common, hurling a tennis ball for it to retrieve.

Lean on the bedroom windowsill watching as, some distance removed, Gail picks her way between trip-worthy tussocks of vegetation. Her concentration is deep and total, her brow furrowed in thought. I watch her coming closer and marvel that this amazing woman seems to be in love with me. Not sure how I come to deserve such a blessing. Realise something else too. So ingrained is she in my consciousness I can readily pick her out in a crowd or from a mile away. It's her strolling gait, the shape of her body in motion and the surmounting mop of dark hair.

Go down and open the front door. Leave it wedged ajar for her. Put the coffee pot on so she'll be greeted by enticing aromas. Wonder what on earth her news can be. Put all such thoughts aside as she comes in, slamming the door behind her, wearing the broad smile I fell in love with in Alanya. Take her in my arms and kiss her until our lips are almost too tender to do it anymore.

Much, much later. Lying on the bed. Naked and deeply at ease with each other, our bodies almost over warm wherever they touch. I don't want to spoil anything but now I've reached the point where I absolutely have to ask.

"What's happened? What's different about today? Why are you so suddenly able to be here again?"

Gail's laugh is soft. Contained. She wants to hold on to her secret just a little longer. But her smile is too broad. This is important. She kisses my neck. And my jaw. And my ear. Not a process of procrastination I'd normally object to in the slightest but at this moment..."Tell me. Just tell me."

It bursts out on a wave of happiness.

"He's gone. He's left. I don't believe it. But he has. He's finally gone."

Shrieks of glee. Some of them mine. Hugs and kisses. Floods of them.

It may be early but we've got the best reason ever. Break out the champagne.

***

Saturday afternoon. I'm cooking pastrami lamb over charcoal in the back garden. We're lounging around in deck chairs making sure it doesn't burn.

"What are you doing for your birthday?"

"Not really thought about it. It's ages yet. Probably a few beers with Patrick. Unless you'd like to come somewhere with me."

"We could do that. But I've got a better idea. I'll make you a party. If you'd like one."

"Well. I suppose...That would be great. It's just that I've not done anything like that in a long time."

"Then it's high time you did. It'll be lovely. We can have it in the garden. Or at the front; on the common. We need to get someone to help with the food. I'm not that great a cook. And we'll get a gazebo and we need some more garden chairs."

"Yeah. Of course."

"So just say 'Thank you' and let me do it."

"Thank you, Gail."

"Now we could work out who to invite."

The list isn't that long. It has Patrick, Clare, Jaki and my Mum on it with half a dozen couples I've known for years. The timing looks perfect for introducing Gail's boys into the mix and Gail suggests asking Ellie and her husband, Brian, and Megan. I'd quite like Rory there too. Now he's eighteen and our relationship is no longer just that of coach and trainee. Resolve to talk to him. See if he'd like to. Perhaps bring a girlfriend.

"This is a really good idea, Gail. I've been fretting about you being away. Doesn't seem so difficult to face now."

"Good. We're away for three weeks so I'll have plenty of chance to explain to the boys what's going on. They know he's left of course. They can hardly miss him not being around. But we've skirted round it. Not talked about it. While we're in Bermuda I can find an opportunity to tell them about you. Explain we're friends. And when we get back it's your birthday and we'll all be here."

"Sounds like a plan to me."

Gail reaches into her handbag and pulls out a travel folder. Leafs through it and carefully separates one airline ticket from the others. "This is his." She tears it in half and casually tosses it onto the barbecue. It blackens, flares into flame and is gone. "Now the lamb will taste even better."

She's right. The meat is spectacularly good.

Chapter VII Now: December

Full house. Less one. The most important of all. To me. A strange time. Peace and goodwill to all men. Except Gail's husband. And one or two others like Rory's father, but I'm not going to dwell on any of them. We'll concentrate on the more positive messages carried on the back of Christ's birth.

None of the philosophy or theology has the slightest relevance to a five year old. Daniel takes all his cues from the physical manifestations of the Christmas spirit. Snow and the small army of snowmen we build for him on the common, interrupting our efforts with snowball fights in which Ethan and Jimmy gallantly defend Sandrine from the assaults of Daniel's forces, usually Rory, Jaki and me. The carol singers, breath crisp in the cold night air and melodies drawn from ancient tradition, enthralling us all. The tree, a tall spruce, brought home in the back of Jimmy's pristine Range Rover. The tree travels mesh-netted and wrapped in an old blanket but bet Jimmy'll still be picking out needles from the upholstery in another six months. And then there's making the house Christmas-ready.

Bring my box of decorations down from the attic. Jaki pronounces it grossly deficient and an expensive shopping expedition ensues, much to Daniel's delight. Thought Sandrine would want to come but she doesn't. Leaving her on her own isn't an option but it's the middle of a busy afternoon so we'll be safe enough in town and Ethan can stay with her. Daniel proves to be born to shop. Loves it. And has very firm opinions on colours; red and gold works, blue and green doesn't. He's certain what objects other than balls are appropriate for our tree and how big our stars should be. He's got his heart set on finding a little wooden reindeer and we have to ransack a lot of places to find just the right one for him. Get home and an argument ensues. I win. The tree moves from hall to lounge and Daniel and Jaki use our purchases to make it look magnificent. The finishing touches are the strings of sharp white and soft blue lights.

Sandrine doesn't come down to view the results of Daniel's creativity. She stays in bed. All the signs are that she's finding the withdrawal process long and painful. She lacks energy and spends far too much time lying down. And she's constantly complaining. Of sore throats, a snuffling cold and fluttery stomachs. She also holds that nothing tastes right to her. Don't suppose cocaine's aftermath exactly enhances the taste buds.

Rory too seems abstracted. But in his case suspect it's because he wants to be with Jaki and his Christmas is circumscribed by divided family loyalties. As well as by the reality of celebrations constrained by the imminence of a match on Boxing Day, with two more games following swiftly thereafter.

***

Just before the council closes down for the Christmas holidays I get the call I've been half expecting and definitely hoping will come. From the Chief Executive's secretary. Or personal assistant as she no doubt styles herself. Any chance of squeezing in a meeting? You bet!

Same office. Same suit. Different tie. It seems to me that local government, along with banking, has become the last refuge of collar and tie. The rest of the business community has gone smart-casual. Suits and jackets survive but colourful, open-neck shirts are now key to the modern dress code. Obviously the public sector is still living in the past if it doesn't need to be seen to be putting comfort and style ahead of long-established tradition.

One other difference over last time. The man I've come to see looks less cheerful. Almost harassed. The realities of the job's responsibilities beginning to dawn. Nor is there much room for polite preliminaries. Straight to business.

"We were talking about some residential developments off Tritton Road."

"Yes, we were. Have you dug up something?"

"Questions really. Things that look suspicious. It's arguable that this project should have gone before our full planning committee for approval. It looks uncontentious on the surface but its scale argues for proper public scrutiny of the application. Instead it was given planning consent under officer delegation."

"Meaning what? That council officers gave permission. Not councillors?"

Correct. The Chairman is shown as a consultee but that's all. The other thing that's odd is to do with the land disposal. When the football club agreed to sell the land there were several abstentions among the board members. And the prior consent of the council wasn't sought for disposal of the asset. And a small piece of industrial land was also sold under delegated authority to enhance access to the site and the price paid doesn't look right. It should have had a ransom value because it allows more intensive development of the backland."

"So what do you need from me now?"

He solemnly shakes his head. "Nothing. I just wanted to reassure you that the matter is being taken very seriously and to thank you for raising it."

"Ah. And ...next steps?"

"My conclusion is that there's enough here for a discussion with the police."

"Then if you've not met her yet, the city commander is Chief Superintendent Clare James." Get to my feet to leave, chuckling inwardly. "You can give her my regards."

***

Christmas Eve. Jimmy goes off to his family mid-afternoon, at my insistence. We're not going anywhere much over the holiday week and Ethan, having nobody to be with, has embraced with alacrity the prospect of being paid to stay over, sleep on the sofa-bed in my study, entertain Daniel and enjoy himself. Sandrine takes herself upstairs soon after tea. It helps in getting Daniel to go up too. He's desperately tired, poor mite, but doesn't want to miss out on anything. Jaki puts him to bed with the promise of the true story of Santa Claus. Knowing my niece, her version will be less than orthodox.

***

The remaining crew have plenty to do. As much of the food preparation as possible. Apart from leaving sprouts and such-like to give Patrick something to do tomorrow. We're not letting him subside directly on arrival into an inebriated heap. Lay up the dinner table. My Turkish linen table cloth with the fantastic embroidery. Best napkins, cutlery and glasses. Balloons to be blown up from a helium canister. Jaki produces small tubs of glittery miniature stars and hearts and sprinkles them over everything. When we're done, the dining room door gets locked and the key hidden so none of our guests can get a sneak preview before we're ready for them. Finally the last of the presents to be wrapped. Each of us has got something for Sandrine but we've gone to town over Daniel. I've also bought an assortment of surprises for Gail. Don't know when she'll be able to come here and open them but they get wrapped in distinctive paper anyway and stowed in my desk drawer. Everybody else's packages go under the tree.

It's long after midnight when Ethan, Rory, Jaki and I share a last drink and mince pie. I'd wondered if Rory would go back to his parents tonight but he's made no move to leave and when he says goodnight, it's to follow his girl upstairs. A last look around. It's a nice house but it has never looked so magical. Change the central heating timer. Turn off all the lights. Look in on Daniel. He’s sound asleep. In his hand he’s clutching the wooden reindeer.

Go to bed.

***

The alarm goes off painfully early. Have to get up to put the turkey in the oven. Back to bed. When I next surface it's to find Ethan playing on the floor with an excited little boy and protecting the gifts under the tree from his ravages. Daniel has already torn apart the presents we'd packed into a sawn off leg of an old pair of Jaki's tights and left at the end of his bed and he doesn't seem totally sold on the notion of waiting until after lunch to find out what else is in store. They're both still in pyjamas so it's as well the heating's kicked in.

"Cup of tea, Ethan?"

"Yes, please."

Boil the kettle. Put tea bags in the teapot instead of into mugs. It's a day for doing things properly.

Time to call New Zealand where it's already late afternoon. Ask Simon, my brother, if his seasonal house guest is behaving herself. "You know Mum." He need add nothing more. Talk to her and she's on good form. Probably spoiling her Kiwi grandchildren for all she's worth. Replace the phone on its cradle and find Sandrine in the doorway, watching me.

"Hi. Happy Christmas. I'm making tea if you want one."

She nods. Pulls her dressing gown tighter around herself. Hovers a moment saying nothing. Drifts off to find Daniel.

Disconnect the phone at the jack point on the wall. Ball up the cable. Hide it back in the biscuit tin. Put the tin in the larder. Make the drinks. Text Gail. Tell her I wish she could be here. The thing with clichés is they tend to be true. Usually.

***

We do a breakfast of sorts. No need for much given what we plan to be tucking into later and the scale of the emergency chocolate stockpile in the lounge. The choice is a sticky, honey-coated cereal or grapefruit, with or without sugar and or brandy. Both figure, with Tunis cake and Cidrax to name but two others, among the nostalgic traditions of my own childhood Christmases.

Rory heads home, sketching a wave to me through the kitchen doorway while I'm taking a call on my mobile from Patrick, who's forgotten what time I've told him to come and eat with us. "Lunch is two-ish. But come as soon as you're ready. We've saved some jobs for you. Everybody should be dressed soon. Doesn't much matter if they're not. Just get over here."

"Okay."

Remember one thing I've forgotten. Christmas crackers. They're still on a shelf in the larder. Go to rectify the omission. Find Rory's not gone yet. He and Jaki are in the hall. Snogging. Not a word in common use in my vocabulary. But given their age and lack of inhibition, it’s the only appropriate verb. Edge noiselessly back into the kitchen and busy myself until the front door slams and an ebullient Jaki breezes in.

"What needs doing, Unc?"

Hand her the box of crackers. And the key. "Shame he can't be here for lunch. What time's he back?"

"Six. Perhaps seven o'clock."

"Avoiding the mother-in-law-to-be then."

"No. You don't really think that. Do you? They've met a few times. And get on alright. Anyway she may still be here. And she's not that intimidating."

"I'm telling you, she's the most intimidating younger sister it's possible to have."

"A bit I suppose. But they do like each other. Really." She doesn't seem that sure. Actually it's quite sweet to see her a little uncertain. Normally she's so in control of herself and everything around her. On impulse I give her a hug. She grins and nudges me aside with the cracker box and heads for the dining room.

The next intruder into my domain is a transformed Sandrine. She's made a real effort. A clinging, green jersey dress, heels and a touch of make-up. Tell her she looks good. Get a nervous smile back.

"I want to say thank you. For us being here. For everything for Daniel. But..."

"What is it?"

"I struggle with this." And her next utterance appals me with its complete absence of self-insight. "I'm doing better. Now I need to see Tony. I want my mobile back, please."

Deep breath. Lie. "It's not here. Rory's got it. But I don't think you ought to contact Tony anyway. He got you into the rut you were in. Remember what you're trying to do. Keep Daniel. Don't give them the slightest excuse to take him away. I know it's hard, but you can do this."

"Yes." An unconvinced little voice.

"Go and sit with Daniel and Ethan. Time to play."

She floats away. Light on her feet. Like a ghost of the young woman who swanned into Rory's birthday party. What? Only eighteen months ago.

***

Doorbell. Patrick. Get him a glass of wine and a sharp knife and put him to work in the kitchen.

Hands busy with parboiled potatoes ready for the roasting tray. Another ring of the bell. Ethan in jeans and t-shirt, in direct contrast to his work garb, sticks his head in. "It's the fuzz."

Jaki shouts from the other room. "I'll get it."

A murmur of voices in the hall and large as life and twice as striking in stalks my niece's mother. She's been in to her office. No other reason for her to be in full Chief Superintendent's battle gear on Christmas Day, crowns on the epaulettes and hat under the arm. It's not every day you get to hug a vision of officialdom.

"Don't get stuff on me. I might get called back in."

Patrick gets his own hug.

"Hey you. Back to the carrots." Put an arm round her waist. Steer her into the lounge and introduce her to the others. "This is my sister, Clare."

I like the shocked faces of Sandrine and Ethan. Leave them to get better acquainted.

***

Sometimes a mix of people flung together works. Sometimes it doesn't. And the desire to make Christmas Day a uniquely special occasion adds pressure but my house guests seem too intrigued by each other to do anything but enjoy themselves. With one exception. Sandrine is quiet and keeping herself to herself. Everybody else displays a gratifying appreciation of both the food and the company. Only Clare may have to drive anywhere today so the mood is enhanced by generous consumption of champagne, wine and Armagnac.

Conversation flows easily. Despite being the only child, Daniel is in the middle of most of it. If the last three weeks has revealed an appetite driven by junk food, he nevertheless devours turkey, roast potatoes and all the trimmings. He even tackles a couple of Patrick's sprouts which is more than I do. Once the crackers are pulled, he dictates the adoption by one and all of paper hats. No excuses. A golden crown looks particularly fetching atop Clare's uniform.

Daniel's less impressed with Christmas pudding, even with the added attractions of clotted cream and brandy butter. Luckily ice cream seems a satisfactory alternative.

Nobody wants tea or coffee yet so I'm collapsing on the settee with another brandy. Jaki insists she and Sandrine will clear up and pile things in the dishwasher. Ethan and Daniel revert to toy cars on the carpet. And Clare and Patrick have their heads together in deep conversation. I get the impression Clare's checking out how much Patrick can tell her about the situation with Sandrine. He knows precious little of course so it's inevitable Clare will move on to me.

"Budge up." She settles herself into my space and gets straight to the point. "Daniel's Rory's brother then?"

"Half-brother. Yes."

"What's he doing here?"

Enlighten her.

"I'd lay a lot of things at Tony's door but not drug dealing."

"Don't suppose he sells it. But recreational use? With his contacts he knows how to get hold of anything."

"And he can afford it. Do you think he'll just let Sandrine go."

"When we were at school, he had the reputation of a Rottweiler. Don't suppose he's changed much. So no. My fear is he won't. Anything that's his, he'll hang on to. Whatever the cost."

Clare changes the subject. "I did want to say I'm sorry I got so angry. When you came back from Turkey."

"You're forgiven."

"I thought you'd blow our investigation." Earning her one of my patent glares. "And I was worried for you, of course."

"You got your reassurances in the wrong order."

"Not really. The best way I can protect you is to put Tony Lenahan away. Legitimately."

"I know. But he's clever. He covers his tracks well. Always keeps insulating layers between himself and outright illegality. And lending money isn't criminal in itself."

"His interest rates are pretty criminal."

"And his collection methods."

Another switch of topic. "How's your Gail?"

"Difficult. But worth it."

"Not sorted out then?"

"No." My turn to pull another issue out of the hat. "How do you feel about Jaki and Rory?"

"Well I don't approve of you encouraging them. Letting them sleep together here." This from my liberally authoritarian sister. I'm astonished. It shows. She bursts into laughter. "No. I'm fine about it. It's just that they're both so young. And I want her to get her degree and a job. Not settle for being a trophy soccer wife."

"I don't think your daughter will ever settle for being a trophy anything."

On cue, the young madam herself re-joins us. "We've got a load on. The pans are soaking. Sandrine's making herself coffee. And I'm going to have another drink."

Gesture over my shoulder. "All on the side. With the clean glasses." She helps herself to a white wine and slumps down next to Patrick.

"What's the time?"

Patrick yawns. Checks his watch. "Just gone five o'clock."

"We've missed the Queen's speech."

"No great loss."

"In your opinion."

Chip in. "I'm with Patrick. You're out-voted."

"Not if Mum backs me."

Clare answers before I can. "Sorry. She doesn't. It must be time for presents."

"Yeah! Yeah!" Daniel's suddenly on his feet and full of enthusiasm.

"Will you get your mum in then?"

He does it at a run.

***

By unspoken agreement, we don't open any of the presents Rory's left for us. They can sit there to be dealt with once he's able to get back to us. Everyone seems pleased with the gifts they do open and Daniel's pile of loot is impressive in scale and variety. The one discordant note as time passes is the change in Daniel's mood. Whether it's weariness or something deeper, he becomes irritable and then downright fractious. And the target of his temper isn't Sandrine but Ethan, who's played tirelessly with him all day.

There's no recall to duty for Clare but still no sign of Rory either. Jaki becomes increasingly disconsolate. Understandably. I might feel the same but my mobile vibrates in my pocket and when I answer it, to my delighted surprise, it's Gail. Take the call out of the room. Sit on the stairs and talk for ages. How we're feeling. How much we miss each other. How the day's going. All good stuff.

"How come you could ring me?"

"I'm here on my own. Just me and the boys. I don't know where he's gone or what's upset him. It's been a pretty civilised day. As far as they ever are. He went and had a pint at the pub with his cronies. Came back for dinner. Ate everything I put in front of him. I was just washing up when I heard the front door slam and he'd gone out again. Not a word to me. So it's quiet here. The boys are on the computer. And I can talk to you. Overall it's a real blessing."

"Wish you'd been here though. You'd have loved it. Family and friends. It's been good." Reassure each other we'll speak tomorrow if we can. Go back into the lounge. Smiling. Inside and out.

In my absence the decision's been taken to put Daniel to bed. Sandrine shows no sign of implementing it so Jaki offers but the task falls to an insistent Ethan. "I need to talk to this young man. Come on, Daniel." He takes Daniel's hand. No strong display of reluctance on the boy's part.

They go up.

***

Couple more lazy hours. Turkey and ham sandwiches. Mince pies. Cups of tea. Conversation peters out. Clare and Patrick break out the backgammon set. Shades of long, long ago. When we were all teenagers. Put a film on. Jaki’s choice. Still no Rory. Dozing contentment. Ended by a hammering on the front door.

It’s loudly insistent. And continuous. Until replaced by the repeated thudding of a kicking boot. Clare, Ethan and Jaki are right behind me as I throw the door wide open. Tony Lenahan, mid-swing, staggers, recovers his balance and grabs the doorframe. Starts shouting for Sandrine. His eyes are bloodshot and the alcohol is apparent even without getting up close and personal. Clare slides alongside me. Tony's not coming in however much he yells and threatens.

"Stop. Shouting. Now." Clare says it calmly and very firmly.

Tony blinks. Focuses on Clare's uniform. Swears to himself. Stoops. Takes a few breaths. Straightens. Speaking carefully says, "I've come to fetch Sandrine. She is here." He's not asking. He's stating only what he already thinks is fact.

"You can't carry on like this. Go home and sober up. Sandrine's not here." My sister lies with absolute conviction. "If you keep shouting I'll have to have you arrested. Which will ruin my evening."

Tony glowers. For a moment I think he's going to take her on. If he attacks her, I'm braced to grab the cricket bat from the umbrella stand and bash him with it. Hitting him could be almost as satisfying as seeing him carted away in handcuffs.

He thinks better of it and shuffles down the steps. "I'll be back for her." His parting shot.

No point in arguing the toss. Slam the door shut.

Sandrine must have heard the altercation but she's had the sense to stay in her room. Clare dusts off her hands as for a job well done. "Now I'll have a glass of wine."

***

Clare's nursing a half-empty glass and I'm part way through another Armagnac when a buzzing sound emerges from the capacious depths of the orange handbag on the floor by Jaki's vacated chair.

"She's in the bathroom. I'll get her."

Gladly leave it to her nearest and dearest. Another sip of brandy before the mini whirlwind strikes. The bag is upended and its contents scattered over the carpet. The mobile is seized and checked. "It's Rory. Going to ring him." Jaki disappears again. Returns much more slowly.

"He wanted to warn us. His father had a call from Sandrine and might come here. I told him he was too late and Tony's been and gone already. He's coming back down as soon as he can. Rory I mean."

"Good."

Clare, the most sober of us, picks up the key point. "Did she say Sandrine had called him?"

“She can't have. I've got her mobile...” Realisation strikes. Sandrine wandered into the kitchen earlier. After I'd been talking to Mum and Simon. Before I disconnected the landline and hid the house phone in the larder. Head into the kitchen. It doesn't take an Einstein. The biscuit tin lies empty on the table and the phone's on the work top. Plugged in. Worse still. The back door's unlocked. Ajar. Don't really need to check upstairs. Daniel's asleep in his bed. But Sandrine's gone.

Chapter VIII Then: July to August

Megan and Ellie want to meet because Gail's asked us to discuss the detailed arrangements for the celebration at the end of the month. In no sense is this a surprise party. I'm pleased to say. I don't like secrecy. Notionally it's to be for my birthday. In fact it has much greater symbolic significance.

We meet at Pimento's. One of the best coffee shops in the world. Bar none. You'll gather I'm an enthusiastic patron. Love the rambling nature of the old building with all its nooks and crannies. And it has such a wonderfully broad selection of coffees and teas from all around the world. And it's got these unusual glass tea-pots. They come with a dipper in the middle to hold the tea leaves. Pimento's is also local to Megan's offices. And Ellie adores their coffee cake. Unanimous choice then.

Megan and Ellie arrive together. Greetings. Find a table. Not easy at this or almost any time of day. Order essential munitions. Compare ideas. Impose practical realities.

"My garden's quite small so there's a limit on numbers. We've got about twenty already, including Gail and me. Got room for a few more. Anybody else you think Gail would like me to invite? She's not said but..."

Megan leads for their side of the table. "It's your party so she probably wouldn't want to drag in people you don't even know. Have you met any of her friends? Apart from us."

"No. I haven't even met her sons yet but they're coming."

Ellie makes a note on her pad. Under the ruled-off section headed 'Food'.

"Any other young people invited?"

"Not on my mental list."

"Vegetarians?"

"One couple. Alison and Paul." Ellie records that too.

"We'll pre-prepare as much food as possible and barbecue a few bits once it's underway."

"Burgers and hot dogs for the boys. And my friend Patrick."

"Chicken and lamb for the rest? Salads? Baked potatoes?"

"Sounds good. What about the veggies?"

"Ellie does a superb Mushroom Borek. It always gets devoured. Not little ones. More like a pie."

Ellie blushes.

"Don't be modest, Ellie. You know it's good." Turns to me. "She is so brilliant."

"I do like food."

"So do I but that doesn't make me half the cook you are."

Butt in. "Me neither. You've got the job, Ellie."

"What else do we need?" Megan dragging us back onto the agenda.

"I'll sort the drinks."

"Good." Ellie puts a tick and my initials against another item.

Point out an apparent omission. "We're missing something vital. What about sweets?"

"Leave desserts to us." Megan winks at Ellie. Won't try to guess what that's about. "Gail said something about garden furniture."

"She did. She's condemned my deck chairs to the scrap heap. And told me to get new tables and chairs. And a gazebo in case it rains. I'll go over to Pennell's this weekend." Pennell's is the expensive garden centre down near the Bentley Hotel. A good place to start looking. Another tick on Ellie's checklist.

"Shall I sort out the invites for you?"

"Yes please, Megs."

"You'll need to give me all the names and addresses then. Emails would be better still."

"Okay."

Tick.

"And we're definitely going for the second Saturday in September?"

"Absolutely. It's my actual birthday."

"Perfect. Can we have some fresh tea?"

"And another piece of cake, please."

***

Pennell's is another place where you're guaranteed to bump into people. Second only to Saturday afternoons on Steep Hill in that regard.

Today fate decrees I should bump into my ex-father-in-law, pushing a trolley of compost bags and new plants.

"Hello, Peter."

"What would you be doing here? Not somewhere I usually expect to find you." He knows full well that I'm a reluctant gardener at best.

"Just choosing some new garden furniture. Been tidying up a bit."

"For some special reason?" Have I said he's bright and intuitive?

"A few people coming over for my birthday."

"A party, heh? Do I get an invitation?"

How to say no to him without giving away too much of my personal business. "That's a bit tricky."

"Why?" Now he's playing naive and arch at one and the same time. "Would there be a young lady involved?"

"The father of my ex-wife shouldn't be allowed to ask questions like that."

"So there is then. Good. You shouldn't be on your own. And by the way, if you're looking for garden furniture, there's a sale on. Up that end." He gestures extravagantly in the general direction he's obviously come from. Where I was heading anyway. "Come over for a drink sometime and tell me all about her."

"I'll come for the drink."

He chuckles. Probably thinks he can ferret a lot more out of me than I'm willing to tell. Remind myself to be on my guard and not to let his best malt loosen my wits and my tongue.

Peter's right about the sale. Find a glass topped table with a coated steel frame. Matching chairs. Comfortable and stylish. At a good price reduction. Reckon to take a dozen if they have them in stock. Plus a couple of recliners. Plenty of gazebos to choose from too. Find an assistant. Agree the order and delivery dates. Pay and get out. This sort of gardening is almost enjoyable.

***

"Well I think it's a great idea." Jaki's in total disagreement with Patrick. Not about the notion of the party but the venue. One of Patrick's clients owns a trip boat moored on the Brayford and since he can get it free of charge... Jaki may not yet have met Gail but she's firmly on the same side. They both prefer dry land and my garden in particular. Now it's undergoing a make-over.

As we sit here, road-testing the new furniture, we're watching two employees of All Seasons Horticulture doing their level best to turn my wilderness into a tamed oasis of cultivated greenery. In a minute or two I'm going to break out a six-pack and offer them a beer. They've already earned one several times over. The rambling hedge separating my house from next door has been clipped and squared off to a reduced height of perhaps six feet and looks wonderful. My grass has been strimmed, mowed and edged. The little summer house at the bottom of the garden has been recovered from the overwhelming clutches of the rampant vine covering it. We still have miniature grapes but we can sit down beneath them now. Especially if Patrick and I can spend Sunday as planned, sanding and re-painting the wrought iron frame and the built-in bench it contains. There are still flower beds to demarcate and re-establish and a couple of trees to sort out but...details. Mere details!

"Want a drink now?"

"Is the Pope Catholic?"

"What about you, Jaki? Wine or beer?"

"White wine please. If you've got some open."

"Yeah. There's a bottle in the fridge. What about you guys? A beer?"

Enthusiastic response. "Could murder one." His colleague says nothing. I'm assuming the older gardener speaks for both of them. They collect their stubbies and carry on. Pass one across to Patrick and flip the top off mine. I'm not offering glasses to save the washing-up. Jaki gets one but only because I can't expect her to swig Chablis from the bottle.

Hot sun on our backs. Almost dozing off in the unaccustomed heat. Inane conversation continues.

"I like the new stuff. It's very comfortable. And it looks good."

"So long as Gail approves. She hasn't seen it yet. Obviously."

"She'll like it."

"You seem pretty sure, Jaki."

A laugh. "I am."

Jaki has the annoying habit of being able to take a drink and make it last forever. Useful for a student. Not so good when her companions are politely waiting for a refill. Patrick cracks first and goes to fetch more beers. He doesn't bother to ask Jaki if she wants a top-up. She examines her half-empty glass, flashes me a meaningful grin and takes another careful sip.

"You can't complain. At the rate you're drinking you won't finish that one till the end of the summer."

Another smile. In acknowledgement.

Take the fresh cold bottle I'm passed. Raise it to my mouth. Swallow. Sigh.

"Anything else we need for the party?"

"No, Jaki. There absolutely isn't."

This is the life.

***

Jaki seems to be asleep. Her eyes are closed anyway, her head's drooping and an occasional genteel snort issues from her general direction. She's not a good enough actress to pull off this degree of apparent absence. Good time for other stuff.

"Couple of legal bits we could sort out now if you want." Patrick's idea of entertainment. Not mine. Shake my head.

"I'd rather discuss you and Clare."

"What about Clare?"

"You know what. Are you seeing my sister?"

"No. Not really. Dinner. An occasional coffee. I like her."

"I know you like her. And she's always liked you. She used to follow you around like a little puppy. Mind you she was about three or four at the time."

"It's hard though. We've so much shared history. I don't remember a time when we weren't around each other. Except at university."

"Well consider your position very carefully. She's got a very protective older brother."

"Has she? She doesn't need one. She's tough as old boots, your Clare. But I can't help thinking that if I'd had the sense to chase after her in the first place, I wouldn't be paying maintenance to any ex-wives."

"Yeah. But you and I joke around things a lot. Let me ask you something serious. And I want an answer. Do you love her?"

"Now there's a question…"

I don't get a straight response. Not sure if I really expected one. Why would Patrick change the habits of a lifetime?

***

Gail's three week holiday absence doesn't initially cause any problems at all. The flow of texts back and forth; the evening phone calls, brief but affectionate and convivial; a postcard recording their arrival. All combine to give me whatever reassurance I need. Midway through the second week I can detect a change. The texts still come each day but the tone is subtly different. It's not what she says but what's missing, unsaid. There's a reserve creeping in and it's making me uneasy. Especially since the phone calls have dried up. Console myself that she'll be back soon and nobody can be expected to communicate normally when thousands of miles apart and one of you's under the Bermudan sun while the other's stranded back in grey old Blighty. Where a typically intermittent summer is stuttering along.

She's not the only one on holiday either. Clare's taken ten days leave and gone away. Somewhere she's being mysterious about. I assume it's not for cosmetic surgery in any of its manifestations. But I don't know that for sure. Perhaps the childhood fixation with the shape of her nose has re-surfaced and uttered an implacable siren call to act, given the currently healthy state of her bank balance. In reality she's most likely to be camping in Cornwall or has scurried off to stay in some historic Portuguese quinta or palace.

I could use Patrick's take on life at the moment, blunt as it would likely be, but, staggeringly for a work-aholic, he's away too.

The third vital arm or leg of my support network, my beloved niece, isn't in evidence either. But in her case I know exactly where she is. An ecological peace camp in the West Midlands. Picketing or protesting. Much the same thing probably, given the causes she espouses. I encourage her. Because it gets up her mother's nose. We've always played these games, Clare and me. Anyway Jaki's back in another day or so. Who knows? I might even trust her to help with more of the party planning and arrangements.

***

Summer is the time when it’s too easy to let your fitness slide. If you do, new season training becomes impossibly hard. It seems worse each year as I get older. One of these days I’ll just give up and find an easier way to make a living but that time isn’t here yet. So I pace myself and start early. On the training ground. Usually on my own. Occasionally with a couple of the ancillary staff or an over-keen reserve team member. Laps of the pitch. Short sprints. Sit-ups. Lunges. Squats. On a sun-baked surface. Better than winter mud but harder on the knees and spine. And all without the motivational benefits of a ball at my feet.

Step it up from training alternate days to every day, Monday to Friday. Lighter meals. Better food balance. No more cake or biscuits or chocolate. Sugar withdrawal headaches arrive and are gone. Less carbs. More protein. Plenty of hydration. Water not isotonic drinks. I'm old-fashioned that way. Stamina levels climbing. Calories burning off. Abs tightening. Mood improving. Hey, Gail will get home and life can really start again. Can't wait.

Turn-round Day dawns. Well that's what I call it. The return from their holidays of all the first team squad. So now the work-rate really picks up and it's time for the good stuff again. Skills coaching for Rory, even though he's getting to the point where he runs rings around me. Without even trying too hard.

And Gail must be back anytime now. So where is she?

***

Gail flies home from Bermuda on Sunday. Sun-tanned. Slimmer. She's sitting in the kitchen the following morning. She's not herself. Or not the self I've come to know. She seems withdrawn. Depressed. Unable to begin to say whatever it is she obviously feels she has to tell me. I take her hand between mine across the table. Stroke and caress it. She's silent. Non-responsive to my touch. Eventually I have to break the silence. "How was the holiday?" A fairly mundane question.

She gazes into space. The look in her eyes is haunted. Lost. At last she says "It didn't go as expected."

"Is the family alright?"

"Yes. Up to a point."

"Are you going to tell me what's wrong?"

Hefty sigh. "When we'd been there a few days, their father took a flight out. He arrived out of the blue. No warning." She volunteers nothing further. Lapses into thought.

Have to prompt. "Why did he come? What did he want?"

"He didn't want me to start divorce proceedings. He threatened to take my youngest away from me if I wouldn't let him come home."

"He can't take them away from you. He won't be able to do that. The courts won't let him."

"He can make an enormous amount of trouble for me. And he can hurt me. Badly. And I don't know if I'm strong enough to fight him."

"He convinced you to take him back?"

"Yes."

"Did he tell you he still has feelings for you? That he loves you? That he's made a big mistake? That he's given up whoever he left you to be with?"

Her expression is bleak. "No."

"Do you want him back?"

"No. Not at all."

"But you'll sacrifice yourself because he’s threatening you?"

"I don't have any real choice. For now. Maybe we can get past this."

"Are you prepared to lose me?"

Shake of her head.

"So what do you want me to do."

"Try to understand. Be here for me if you can. But I'm not asking you to wait. You shouldn't have to. You deserve better than anything I can promise you."

"Suppose I don't want anyone else. Can't just walk away from you."

Half smile. "Then I'm really lucky. But it doesn't change where we are."

"What do we do? Wait and see what happens? What his next set of demands looks like? Let him control us?"

"I don't know. I'm going to have to go to work now. Then go home and...deal with him."

I want to ask her when I'll see her again. But she can't give me an answer. And asking won’t help. So I don't ask. She stands to say goodbye. Puts her hand to my cheek. Strokes it. Walks out into the hall. The door clicks softly shut. I'm sitting alone at my table. A cup of tea, I'll never bother to drink, cooling in front of me.

***

I do see her again. Within days. At my house. Dumb misery and incomprehension. Hers not mine. I know absolutely why we've reached this point. With these stymied feelings. Her sense of hopelessness. Or helplessness. I don't like it. That's an understatement. An inability to change anything is the most frustrating part for me. Enforced inactivity the thing I've always hated most. Not to be able to take a problem by the scruff of its neck and solve it. But I can't sort out her issues. The only person who can change anything is Gail herself. Not unless she tells me what she wants to do and allows me to support her in making some decisions. Something she's unwilling or unable to do. For now she's immobile and silent. Metaphorically speaking. Sobs don't count.

After a while she seems calmer. And goes away. Goes home I presume. Takes my heart with her.

The party doesn't happen. My birthday comes and goes with no recognition beyond the note in her card which reads simply 'I'm so sorry.'

Chapter IX Now: December to February

Christmas done, we follow it with the oddest of celebrations. Instead of mourning the ending of another year of our brief lives, we choose to look forward, hoping against hope that the next twelve months will rectify all the unfulfilled dreams of the year shortly to be dead and gone.

New Years Eve. A complete contrast to Christmas. Clare's working. No idea where Sandrine's gone. Jaki and Rory have invites to a party. Insist they go. No chance of seeing Gail. Which leaves Daniel, Ethan and me to entertain ourselves. Pizza all round. Delivered to the door. No cooking or chores. An early night for our five year old. Beer and a crappy film on the television for Ethan and me. We last through till the chimes of midnight. Just. And head for bed.

Don't hear Jaki and Rory return but they're both up and compos mentis by ten in the morning so they can't have over-indulged too late. As well given that Rory has a match to play. Fortunately a home game. So no travelling. Family consultation around the kitchen table makes the key decision. To go and support Lincoln City FC in their first match of the new year. The season can't get much worse and we may yet witness a revival. Or see Rory score.

Daniel has his winter coat but nothing else and it's going to be cold. I find him a woolly scarf which could encircle him four or five times. And the corner shop has magic mitts; stretchy gloves which expand to fit any size of hand. Allegedly. Daniel doesn't need to test the theory very far. Still now he won't freeze. Not so sure about Jaki who never seems dressed for the actual conditions so much as for her hopeful belief in what the weather would be like if she had complete control over it. She's less my responsibility than Daniel so on her own head be it. My grown-up overcoat makes its first appearance of the winter and Ethan has a voluminous quilted jacket. Probably the height of fashion in Eastern Europe and South Lincolnshire. So we're all equipped to our various preferences.

Unsurprisingly, the game isn't up to much. A goalless draw. Not the thriller I'd vaguely hoped would bind Daniel into a life-long love of football. In fairness, for his age, he behaves immaculately. Patiently accepting hugs from Jaki. Watching the vagaries of the crowd's moods, its roar and moans, with apparent interest. Carefully munching pie and chips; the height of county cuisine to be swilled down with orangeade. We're not going to win any quasi-parent of the year awards today but he seems alright. Perhaps too solemnly content to be true. It's not how small boys normally behave in my limited experience.

And Jaki, my scornfully non-sporty niece, seems to like watching Rory charging round the pitch even if he can't single-handedly break the afternoon deadlock.

Wait for Rory to change out of his red and white stripes. Doesn't take too long. He emerges neat in dark blazer over sweater and jeans. Walking normally. Not limping. Result.

One thing boys don't understand is the concept of too much pizza. So tea in a pizza restaurant is a natural result of letting Daniel choose where we'll eat. Ethan mutters something about going back to the gym. Rory orders pasta and salad. The rest of us simply pile on the toppings and to hell with it.

Back home to watch 'Match of the Day' to the accompaniment of Jaki's groans. She's outnumbered tonight but stays with it to the bitter end and lights out.

***

We don't inflict the next home match on Daniel. Better not to ruin all prospects of him taking to the so-called beautiful game. There'll be plenty more opportunities to see his older brother play. It's hard to get Daniel to say what he would like to do. He wasn't exactly effusive when Sandrine was around. But now you have to recognise how withdrawn he is. Trial and error the only solution.

"How about swimming?"

"Dunno."

"Can you swim?"

"Yeah."

We'll give it a try.

He doesn't seem to have trunks among the possessions his mother packed for him so first off we need to buy him some. Ethan hasn't got any either so an adult pair is also required. Luckily I do have plenty of towels. In the sports supplies cupboard.

At the pool an eagerness builds in Daniel and he bullies us to get changed quicker. His fearless running leap into the water calms any concerns I might have had about his basic ability. And his shout is one of pure joy.

Soon we're playing swimmers and sharks. Ethan and Daniel have to evade the jaws of the Great White. Or more accurately the Great-Almost-Brown. My Turkish tan is holding up well through an English winter. In trying to catch one or other of them, the game soon assumes some semblance of a reality known only to small children. Daniel's shrieks of near hysterical excitement betray the extent to which he unconditionally accepts that it is a shark chasing him and grabbing his leg rather than the vaguely adult human I take myself to be.

Afterwards he wants pizza. Again. Decline that suggestion. Tonight I'm cooking chicken and vegetables. A proper meal. Like it or lump it. Daniel likes it. They all eat it.

***

A mid-evening text from Gail. 'May be able to get out for an hour. Can you meet me? Xx'

Reply. 'Surely can. Where? Xx'

We name a pub. I'm there first. Gail walks in a few minutes later, a vision in black. Turquoise scarf excepted. The white cast is less prominent. Toned down by the natural ageing process and the scrawled messages despoiling it.

She looks around carefully before kissing my cheek. She allows my arm round her waist for a brief moment. And moves toward the bar, asking for mineral water. "I'm driving."

"How's that working? With the wrist and all."

"I've borrowed an automatic for a couple of months. One of my husband's friends has a second-hand car business. He offered. I can't drive mine at the moment." Makes sense.

"How was your New Year? Any better than Christmas?"

"I've talked to you most days. It’s in one ear and out the other with you."

"No. I just want you to keep telling me how much you've missed me. You can talk about anything and I'll be happy to just hear your voice. While I look at you."

Smiles. Good.

"What have you been doing over the holiday?"

"I've got a little boy to look after. Half-brother of a friend. It's complicated." Realise belatedly that Rory may not want me to broadcast anything about Daniel even to someone I trust as much as I have to trust Gail.

"Not a relative then?"

"No. But he's fun to have around. Anyway we're drifting from what we should be discussing."

"Which is?"

"Us. How I feel about you. How much I always miss you when I can't see you. What this year means for us."

She reaches into her handbag. "I've got something for you." Pulls out a small rectangular shape wrapped in silver paper. A ribbon around it and a bow on top. Weigh it in my hand. Not heavy. But solid.

"Are you going to open it?"

"I don't know if I should. I've got your presents at home. Waiting for you to come over and open them."

"I don't know how soon I'll be able to do that. Go on. Open this now."

Carefully slip off the ribbon. Put it in my pocket. To keep. Don't have much extrinsic proof that Gail really exists in my day to day life. Not even a good photograph. So I'm hardly going to toss this ribbon away. Slide a finger under the sellotape and pull the wrappings off. A silver box. With a bottle inside. Containing an unusual aftershave. Not familiar with the brand. Spray some on my wrist. Let it settle. Sniff. Glorious smell. I'd guess expensive. Great choice.

"I love it."

"Good. Shopping for it was spectacularly difficult. Had to evade all the family. And I couldn't have wrapped it without Megan's help."

"I'll use it every day."

"It won't get replaced that quickly."

"Every other day then."

"I got you something else too." This one's wrapped in red foil. "Not for now. You can save it and open it when I'm opening my presents." A promise of things to come.

"A plan indeed."

"I have to get back now."

"I know you do."

***

Twelfth night. I always think we should count Christmas Day. Isn't that the first day of Christmas? So really this is thirteenth night but what do I know? Time for the decorations to come down anyhow. Another job for the whole team but we cede the leading role of packing the stuff carefully into boxes to Jaki and her young assistant.

Gail's presents remain in the drawer. A shame she didn't have the opportunity to see the house all tarted up for Christmas. I should have got the camera out and taken some pictures to show her. I didn't. Maybe next year she'll be here.

***

This time an accusatory note in the Chief Executive's voice. "You didn't say that the Chief Superintendent is your sister."

"No, I didn't. Sorry about that. I didn't want you to think this was my family ganging up on you. That we'd got a bee in our collective bonnets and you could ignore it. Clare's taking it seriously though. Isn't she?"

"Yes. I think so."

"Has she kept you posted on how the investigation's going?"

"Just snippets."

"That's more than she'll tell me. Can you put any pressure on her to move things along?"

"Why would I do that?"

Weak response. "Because I'm asking you."

"Hardly a good enough reason."

"Possibly not. But if I tell you I'm between a rock and a hard place on this. The man I'm sure is behind this is going to start making my life rather uncomfortable, if he isn't distracted by having to deal with the realities of police interest in what he's been doing. In fact I'm amazed there's been nothing much yet. I'm taking it seriously though. I'm not being melodramatic when I say I've got two bodyguards waiting downstairs for me. And they may be all that's standing between me and a pair of broken legs."

"So there's a story in this that might be worth hearing. Are you going to tell me any more?"

Think about it for all of five seconds. Before plunging into the edited highlights.

***

We consult. Daniel doesn't get a vote so it's the unanimous decision that he should go back to his school for the new term. Jimmy can take him and one or other of us can pick him up each day. Have to be there early in case Sandrine turns up. We check the flat but there's still no sign of her.

***

I see Gail. Occasionally and fleetingly. Wholly unsatisfactory. But far better than not seeing her at all.

***

Towards the end of the month, in Pimento's, over a prime Brazilian blend frothed to near perfection, things start to seem more promising. Gail rests her cast on the edge of the table. When I fail to comment, she wiggles her fingers and gestures to it with her good hand.

"What?"

"Does this look like an arm which can ski?"

"Not to me. Why?"

"Every year my impossible husband, who doesn't understand the true value of education, books us a trip to the mountains around the end of January because it's cheaper than waiting till half term. And guess who can't go this year?"

"You! But that's great. Why didn't you say anything before now?"

"I wasn't sure he wouldn't insist on me going anyway. But he hasn't. I've played up how miserable not being able to ski will make me...And I'm off the hook."

Surging excitement. "What are we going to do?"

"Anything we want to. Put Boo in kennels. Take me somewhere lovely. Scotland. The Dales. Anywhere."

"The sea. There's nothing like the sea in winter. We could get a cottage in Norfolk."

"Won't it be freezing?"

"That's what winter coats and log fires are for. And hot water bottles. And not getting out of bed in the morning. And well..."

"Enough. I'm persuaded. Let's do it. They go on the morning of the twenty-fourth. For a week."

"I'll book a cottage. On the coast. Rather than a hotel?"

"Definitely. Couldn't we take Boo with us?"

"You're on."

***

Jaki and Rory are fine looking after Daniel for the week. I'll keep Ethan on to stay with them. Gail and I plan to disappear so we won't need the protection squad.

***

Getting away isn't complicated at all for a change. Gail's text says she's checked with East Midlands Airport and the flight has departed on time and she's phoned her husband and his mobile is switched off. Odds are high they're on the plane. So we're good to go. I can come and collect her and the dog as soon as I'm ready.

My car, returned from the garage, is already packed with my bag, a box of foodstuff and enough cold weather equipment to survive the Arctic, never mind Norfolk. Get in. Turn the engine over. Engage gear. Drive up the hill. Eight minutes. Door to door.

Gail's house is a direct insult to my predictive powers. When it and the neighbouring property were being built, a good many years ago, I remember telling friends about surface run-off from the hilltop and how it would wash the foundations away. It didn't. I was wrong. They're still there. Still too modern. And flashy. Obviously not very saleable in the current climate either. An estate agent's board leans upside down against the side wall of the garage. No longer required, presumably.

Gail opens the door. Pulls me inside before kissing me while her Springer Spaniel does what her breed's known for. Leaping around us, barking with excitement, her nose and flailing forelegs head high on me, and her tail wagging like crazy.

“Get down, Boo! Down!”

“She's alright. Expect she'll calm down.” Get on my knees to play with her ears. Earn a hefty canine sigh.

"I can't carry my bag downstairs. I packed it on the landing..."

"Okay. I'll get it."

Dog-gate at the foot of the staircase. Cream walls. Pictures. Familiar style. Can't place the artist. Good use of colour and form. That's what someone who knows about art might well say. Me? I just like them. Grab the blue suitcase. It's heavy. Ease it down, taking care not to graze the wall.

"Then there's a box of stuff for Boo in the kitchen.” Collect it and put it in the car. Finally Gail remembers Boo's sleeping basket. Fetch that too. Gail sets the alarm and only then thinks about her coat; the old puffa jacket with the slit sleeve. Gives me her handbag to hold while she retrieves the keys with her useable hand. Unlock. Re-enter. Find coat. Re-set alarm. Lock outer door. Climb in car. Settle Boo on an old blanket on the back seat. With a chew to keep her otherwise occupied. Set off.

Get onto the main road to Newark and the A1. Into top gear. Put my foot down. Relax. Gail tips her seat back a bit. Puts her right hand into mine. For as much of the journey as possible, I drive one-handed. Don't slow down more than absolutely necessary. Only problem is changing down to negotiate roundabouts and junctions. These prove to have their own appeal. If I have to take my hand back, Gail lets hers rest on my thigh until I pick it up again. Next time I may find a route with lots more gear changes.

***

The cottage is on a low peninsula a mile or two outside Blakeney. One of a row of three by the dunes, with a view out over the sea. The key waits under the mat. Gail heads in to get the kettle on. Tea will be my reward for giving Boo a quick run. There are no signs of sheep or animal husbandry of any sort to be seen so forgo the lead and let her run.

The wind is biting and the sun's dying so even Boo's enthusiasm evaporates quickly and it's no problem to get her back into the cottage. Call her and she races back, ears flapping like the rollers of a car wash in mid-cycle. The promised cup of tea is waiting and a fire is already roaring in the sitting room grate. Gail owns up. "It was already laid. I only had to light it."

Leave the tea a couple of minutes so I can unload the bags and boxes from the car and dump them at the foot of the steep little staircase. Shut and bolt the front door. We're going nowhere else tonight.

The agenda's simple. Unpack. Turn on the electric under blanket. We won't need hot-water bottles after all. Feed Boo. Cook us a meal. Leave the washing up for the morning despite Gail's objections. Put Boo's basket and water bowl in the kitchen. Put her in the yard for a few minutes. Follow Gail up to bed. Near perfect start.

***

The parts of me sticking out from under the duvet are icy-cold. The central heating hasn't come on. Need to check the controls. Gail is snuggled down in the bed, on her left side with her injured arm outstretched for comfort. Cuddle in to her back for a few precious moments. Before my desire to make us our first cuppas of the morning and Boo's need to be let out become the paramount considerations. Get up. Wrap myself in a thick dressing gown. Carefully navigate the narrow stairs. I have a reputation for being able to fall over the lowest curb edge and these steps pose a clear and substantial risk to life and limb.

Boo stretches lazily as I come into the kitchen. Gathers herself together and bounces out the back door. By the time I get the heating back on, boil the kettle, rake out the grate, make the tea and take a mug up to Gail she's whining to come back in for food. It's that cold.

***

Build a fire. Get the little living room toasty warm. Find the frying pan and put some bacon on a low heat. Lay the table. Not just plates, cutlery and condiments but also a rampart of Christmas presents encircling one of the place settings. Mostly small packages.

Kettle back on for a fresh pot of tea. Call Gail. Back in the kitchen to cook the eggs. Using a little shaped bit of plastic I found in a kitchen shop. You break an egg into its confines and as it cooks, it gives it a perfect heart shape. Don't hear Gail come down. The first I know of her presence is the arms around my waist and her upper body scrunched against my back. Rest one of my hands on top of hers, touching skin and the roughness of her cast. Need my other hand for cookery tasks. Tell her so. "Go and sit down. I'll serve up."

Carefully extract the eggs and put the heart-shaped one on Gail's plate with a couple of rashers and a doorstop of lavishly buttered bread. Carry the plates past an over-interested Springer Spaniel. Boo requires a nudge with my knee before she clears my path.

Go back for the tray which bears the teapot, a jug of milk and two mugs. Can't find any sugar at the moment. But it doesn't matter because neither of us take it in tea. Only in coffee perversely enough.

In my brief absence, the table arrangement has changed slightly. Alongside the small present in the red foil gift wrap which Gail gave me before Christmas there's a rather bigger box, also brightly wrapped. It was certainly not there a moment ago.

"What is it?" Daft question. Like she's going to tell me.

"You can open it when we've eaten. And I love the egg. Come on. Sit down while it's all hot. I don't usually have much for breakfast but this is too perfect to waste."

Have to obey. Mind you I'm famished. Must be the cold weather burning off all the calories. It slips down far too easily and I could eat it all over again.

Sipping a second mug of tea. "You have to start first."

No demur. Her delight is very apparent. She dives in, tearing paper with all the alacrity Daniel exhibited on Christmas Day. And if her expressions of delight are marginally more refined than his, they sound equally genuine.

My new present turns out to be a boxed bottle of champagne.

"Me being selfish" she says." I do get to share it, don't I?"

"Course you do. I'll put it in the fridge for tonight."

"Open the other one."

The paper peels away from a presentation box which in turn contains a magnificent sports watch on a waterproof band. It's engraved on the obverse. A message so clear I grin like a lunatic.

"Thought you needed a new one. That tatty old thing you wear looks like it's on it's last legs."

It's just as well my old watch has no sentimental value whatsoever. It makes it easy to whip it off, chuck it in the waste-paper basket and strap the new one on my wrist.

"It's wonderful. You couldn't have got me anything better. I'll always wear it." Inside I'm choking up. I've never been given anything to carry with me everyday to remind me of someone I love. My ex-wife would certainly never have done anything remotely as extravagant. Even in the early days. I don't have the words to tell her how pleased I am. Luckily my face says it all for me. She gets that and glows with pleasure.

"Do you like yours? Did I get some of them right?"

"You did." She moves things around, picking out a pair of earrings and puts them on. Little crescent moons in silver. "I'm going to get dressed." Which is my realisation of a fundamental oversight on my part. She's still in her dressing gown. Let her get halfway upstairs before starting after her. Hearing her squeal. Catch her in the bedroom doorway.

Tumble with her onto the bed. Lots of laughter. Don't emerge for another hour or so.

***

The week takes on its own pattern. Late risings. Leisurely meals. Long walks along the coast until Boo's exhausted. Evenings by the fireside in the cottage or in an atmospheric little pub in the nearest village. Sleeping deeply and peacefully. Waking refreshed to do it all over again. Not to mention the joy of taking her to bed and coming awake to find her beside me or, best of all, cradled spoon-like into my body.

Leaving the cottage on our last day with considerable reluctance. Driving back to Lincoln slowly and carefully. Both of us quiet. Her dog, sensing our mood, lies unmoving on the rug over the backseat. Her head rests solemnly on her fore-paws. She radiates what I feel.

Deliver Gail back to her other life. Help her unpack and put everything away. See the time has come for me to be out of there. A fleeting hug. A last kiss. And gone.

***

I have one simple question. Why isn't life like it was in Norfolk all the time? Or even just more of the time.

***

An accumulation of post is piled on the kitchen table. Jaki's work presumably. Mainly circulars. A few official pieces of mail and underneath most of it, obviously hand delivered a while ago, a white envelope. Just my first name in black ink on the front. Slit it open to discover it's from someone wanting me to disappear.

I expect you to be gone. You told S you needed a couple of days. That was a month ago. My patience is exhausted. I don't make pointless threats. Your time is up.

No signature. Guess who that's from.

Chapter X Then: September to October

Fly to Alanya again. In search of her. Spiritually. Not physically. A daft idea. I know it's just a place. Staying in the same hotel. Swimming from the same beach. Eating the same food. Empty experiences. It won't bring me one jot closer to anything I need. Will just leave me feeling lost. Rudderless and low. But I'm doing it anyway.

Arrive about one thirty in the morning. Local time. Two hours earlier back home. It's hot and sticky even this late. May be in for a week of heat-drugged stupor. Suppose that could work.

The hotel's been refurbished in my absence. Fresh paint. New look foyer and bathrooms. Somebody's been splashing the cash. Presumably in the name of competition for scarce tourist dollars. Or more accurately round here now, for euros and sterling. After all Alanya's within a few hundred miles of the Syrian border. Way too close for Americans to feel comfortable hereabouts.

Manage a couple of hours sleep. Make it up in time to catch breakfast. What's not improved quite as much as the décor is the food. To match the new paint and furnishings it would need to be superb. It isn't yet. But who cares really? It's too hot to eat much. Sitting in a window seat. Looking out over the sea. The giant Galatasary flag is still draped down the front of the Hotel Élysée. All of sixty feet long, it hangs there as a constant dig at the Alaiye Kleopatra's managerial support for the arch-enemy, Fenerbache.

Check in with the rep. Managed to lose a brand new pair of sunglasses in transit. On the plane or in the bus. Not much hope of them turning up but might as well have somebody trying to find them.

Could do with a Turkish bath and a massage. Just not spending time in a minibus or taxi travelling the highway out of Alanya up to the big hamam I went to with Gail. The refurbished hotel spa will do well enough. So no journey to undertake except downstairs into the basement. No Russian entertainment. No company. The suite is empty. Just a relaxing transaction. Pay my sixty lira. Get the exfoliation over and lie on the hot marble slab with water and foam sloshing over me. Go and get my back worked over good and proper. Don't attempt a conscious thought for the better part of two hours. Certainly try hard to put Gail out of my mind. Almost perfect. Tolerable anyway. The sense of well-being lasts a bit. Unfortunately not long enough.

It's hotter than it was in May. Enervatingly so. Beneath the sunshade, I doze a lot, read a little and scrawl a few letters. Some of those I won't send anywhere.

Alanya Kale. The castle and its citadel. Walls and views. And a long trek to get up there. Five kilometres of steady climbing. Seems a lot further but want to be tired. Might sleep better tonight. Hence refusal of the offered taxi. The scenery up here probably merits its magnificent reputation. The old harbour. The beaches. The trip boats hugging the coastline of cliffs and promontories. The totally blue sea. Struggle to appreciate it. It's not a place to be on my own. Not even going to give it a decent interval. Snag a coke from a roadside vendor and walk back down the hill. Easier downhill although my feet are sore. Ignore blandishments to buy scarves, table cloths and jewellery. Or lucky porcelain eyes to ward off evil spirits. Too late for those.

***

Fresh out of the pool. Sit back on the sun lounger. Bring the tail of the towel up between my legs and over my head. Hold it to my face. And, as silently as possible, start to weep. A few heartbeats is all it takes to pass. Almost as though simply allowing myself to do it is enough to banish the need. Mere seconds to feel better. Put my sunglasses on. Pick up my book. A biography of Kevin Keegan found on the hotel bookshelf. In poor condition. Several pages loose. Read. Forget the world.

***

Late one afternoon. Lying on a sun lounger poolside. Idly looking up. Can't help but notice the barrel-chested man. He's standing on a high balcony staring down at the pool. Short cropped grey hair. Wearing a white, sleeveless top. His arms carry a mass of tattoos. His hands are clamped on the balustrade over which colourful beach towels are draped to dry. His stance is wide-legged and still. Almost rigid. I have the oddest notion he's watching me. The puzzling thing is the fixed nature of that stare over several minutes. His gaze doesn't shift. His focus is the same whenever I look up from my book. Normally if somebody is watching you, they won't want to be caught out doing it and they'll look away and pretend to be looking at something else. He doesn’t and it’s making me feel uncomfortable. Even threatened.

Decide to pack up and go back into the hotel. When I check again, he's finally gone. Tell myself I'm imagining things. Maybe I am. It doesn't stop me doing some counting. Fourth floor up. Third on the left from the lift shaft. So room number 420.

Drop my stuff off in my own room. Put on jeans and a shirt. Getting dressed brings a reduced sense of vulnerability. Walk up one flight of stairs and start down the corridor. Before I even reach 420 the door opens and the tattooed man emerges, tailed by a mousey little woman. He's carrying a book and a towel and he walks past me without any sign of recognition at all. Does that make him an innocent stranger or very good at dissimulation? Can’t be sure either way.

Big supermarket in town. Stock up on water and buy some boxes of Turkish Delight. For a couple of friends at home who will actually eat the stuff. Not me.

Can't find a new SD card for my camera. Give up. What do I want to take any photographs for anyway? Get back to the beach and lie down in the sun with my thoughts. Could be a cheap holiday all round.

A week passes. Don't find my missing sunglasses or see the man from room 420 again. So I was imagining a potential menace. Wasn’t I? Go home somewhat browner. Otherwise a waste of time.

***

Immersing myself in work doesn't seem to help much. I feel ridiculous. Obsessed. Unable to think constructively for any length of time about anything other than where she is. What she's doing. Whether she's thinking of me at all. How much I miss her. Stupid. Stupid. Stupid.

***

October comes with a burst of Indian summer. Cloudless skies and balmy days. I don't enjoy them much. They foreshadow a winter I'm dreading.

There does come a point where I have to pull myself together. To the unutterable relief of my family and friends. I can't live on the occasional subsistence text from Gail. Insufficient to offer more than painful reminders of what could or ought to be. But it's a strange reconstruction of myself which gets stitched back together. One harshly devoid of expressed emotion. A mechanical construct which does what it needs to do. Something deep down's in hibernation. Switched off. I know all that of myself but I'm not sure others even notice. They seem to take at face value what I say and do. Perhaps they don't want to or can't deal with my reality. It makes them feel bad that there's nothing they can do to help. I can identify with that.

The one person I don't seem able to fool is Rory. I suppose he's not so far off the early years of teenage angst that he can fail to spot its middle-aged equivalent in someone he spends so many hours with. He doesn't say anything much. But I'm aware of the care with which he watches me. And the occasional touch of a hand on my shoulder, a reversal of the roles we've developed around each other. Saying more than words can.

Time to let go. Not all of it. Just enough to do better than mere survival. Even abject sorrow wears off eventually.

***

Sitting on the bench outside the front door. Jacket on and scarf. Gazing across the common. Not hard to find.

"I've finished cleaning, Unc. Hey, are you alright?"

A wan smile. Can't raise the real thing. Even for Jaki. "Not really. 'Every unworthy thing may look on her but I may not.' It seems grossly unfair."

"I don't follow you."

"The state of modern education! It's the bard. Or an approximation."

"The what?"

"Not what. Who? Shakespeare. Romeo and Juliet. Learned in school over thirty years ago. As relevant today as the day he penned it."

"So you've not seen Gail?"

"Bulls-eye."

"It will be okay." My young niece, in a spectacularly unselfish mood, sits herself down and puts her arm around my shoulders. I'm very touched.

"Thank you. I'm too old for this."

"No, you're not. Nobody's ever too old to love somebody. And you'll never be too old for anything."

"Such blind confidence."

She humours me with a shake of her head. "I know it will be alright. Mum says you were always the one who would see anything through you set your mind to. And if you really want her, you'll go and get her. Or wait until she's ready."

"Yeah, you're right. Let's change the subject. How about I buy you lunch?"

"You certainly can. Where shall we go?"

A decent pub-restaurant is the only possible answer.

The Wig and Mitre. At my expense of course. Not that I begrudge keeping my sister's only child from dropping over the brink of starvation. And as always she's good company. As well as being a hearty eater.

She interrupts my thoughts. "Who's that woman looking at us?"

I've got my back to the rest of the room so I can hardly be expected to provide an intelligent answer to Jaki's question.

"Should I turn round to look?"

"Don't be too obvious about it." Like a 180 degree rotation of the neck and head isn't going to be other than overwhelmingly apparent to whoever the woman might be.

I don't try to hide the movement. Swivel. Observe. Summon her to join us with a wave of the hand. She arrives in a pretty, long-sleeved blue dress, to the undisguised fascination of my niece. "Hello." And I get a quick embrace delivered by the smiling brunette as I'm rising from my chair.

"Are you eating?"

"I think so. Something quick and nutritious."

"Then join us. This is Jaki. My least objectionable niece."

"Thanks, Unc."

"And this is Megan."

"Hi."

Megan settles onto the bench-seat next to me. Jaki's curiosity remains obvious. I suppose in Jaki's experience attractive younger women rarely swan in to accost her uncle and never with the ease with which Megan makes herself comfortable, even steadying herself by laying her hand on my forearm. Jaki can't help herself. "Who are you? How do you know each other?"

Megan feeds her a deliberately misleading line. I presume to wind her up. "Oh. We went on holiday together. A while ago. What are you having? I think I'll have the soup of the day. They do a lovely sundried tomato bread with it. How have you been?"

"I'm okay." Lying through my teeth. "Being pragmatic. Not much point in dwelling on what isn't happening. So just getting on with things. Training. Writing a coaching manual..."

"And eating too much." Not sure from the intonation if Jaki's interruption is accusation or question.

"Not at all. Got to set a good example to the lads I'm training. And the club has a new youngster, Ben, they want me to work with."

"You know what they call your sort of pragmatism?"

"No. Is it something insulting, Megs?"

"Mindfulness. They call it mindfulness. Living in the present."

"Nice one. I'll make it my word of the week and use it at least once in every conversation I have."

"He will too."

"Thanks Jaki. You see, Megan, she just carries on where my meddlesome sister leaves off. Bossing me about. Telling me what to do. Dragging me out to buy her expensive lunches..."

"I'm only having soup. Like Megan."

"You shouldn't complain, you know. I'm an only child and I'd love to be part of a big family. Have brothers and sisters. Nephews and nieces. Cousins. I don't know why there's only me. And my family Catholic too."

"I thought you were Welsh.

"You can be Welsh and Catholic."

"I suppose so. Am I allowed to ask if you've seen Gail recently."

The light dawns with Jaki. "You're a friend of Gail's. You were in Turkey when my uncle was there."

"I am. I was."

Momentary female contemplation. Room for me to press my question again.

Get an answer of sorts. "I've not seen her for a bit. She'll be busy. Can't seem to get her on a girls' night out. We used to go out most weeks. Not lately. But I have spoken to her, on the phone. She says she's alright. She won't talk about you though."

"Is that good or bad? It's not very encouraging from where I'm sitting."

"You know how she keeps things to herself. Mulls them over. Pulls them apart until she has a complete take on whatever the issue is. She won't ask for help even if she's desperate. What I do know is that if she'd decided Alanya was a total mistake and she didn't want to see you again whatever the circumstances, she's honest to a fault and she'd have told you so. If she hasn't done anything like that, then its good news for you. Anyway if she's not around it means you're free to take me out." Her pause is inch perfect as she gauges my reaction. Maximum perplexity. "I am joking!"

"Yeah. Look, Megs. I'm sorry. My sense of humour's shot to hell. But I am grateful for what you said. If anything changes with Gail will you let me know? If you can. If you hear before me. Which you probably will."

"Of course I will. But bribe me anyway. Order me some soup."

"It's a deal."

***

Rory. "Can I talk to you about something?" We're walking off the training pitch together. Perspiring nicely after the afternoon's efforts.

"Sure."

"Not here. Can we get a drink?"

"You want to head for the pub? Or my house?"

"Nowhere public. Your place would be great if you don't mind."

"Not at all. You know where I live don't you?"

He checks the house number. He's never been there before today.

The showers are calling. Needfully. "Meet you there in three quarters of an hour. Okay?"

"Yeah. Thanks."

Make coffee. Take adjacent armchairs in my lounge. Make ourselves comfortable. Sip coffee. Verbally go round the houses. Give Rory enough chances to start in on whatever's bothering him. When he doesn't its time to go for the direct approach.

"So what was it you wanted to talk to me about?"

Rory's response takes the form of another question. "How did you get on with your father?"

"Pretty well overall. He was a quiet, self-contained man. Gentle. Quite shy I came to realise. Didn't find it easy to talk to his children once we grew up. When we were young he used to entertain us with games. He'd play Ludo or Monopoly. Or later on it was chess. If the weather was good we used to go up on the moors for French cricket or to fly kites. He just never quite worked out how to relate to us as adults. He tried though. He's been gone a few years now. He developed Alzheimer's. The one thing I hold onto is that when he started forgetting the names of common objects and it was obvious a problem was coming, he did something surprising. For the first time ever he actually told me that he loved me. I already knew it but he'd never been able to say it before. He was a good man. And a good father I think. I was pretty lucky to have him." Snort to cover up my emotion. "Sorry to go on. Why do you ask?"

"You know my father's not like that at all."

"No. He isn't."

"You were at school with him weren't you?"

Caution rears its head at this point. Monosyllabic answers required in all probability. "Yes. I was." Wait to hear what lies behind the question.

"Would you say you knew him well?"

"Good God, no!"

"But you do. You know he's not an easy man to be around. You know how judgemental he can be. You know how he makes his money. Exploiting other people. And you know he hates you. Don't you?"

"We don't get on. Never have. That's true."

"It's more than that though isn't it?"

"It isn't for me to say. I can't tell you what I think you want to know."

Rory changes direction. "My father's pressing me to do some things that are a problem for me."

"Such as?"

"He doesn't want me to move out."

"And you do?"

"Yes. Living at home's not very pleasant these days. Steve, a friend of mine, is getting a flat and he's asked me to share with him. I've said I'd like to."

"You're old enough. It's your choice. What does your mum say?"

"I suspect she'd like to keep me at home too. But she says I should go if I want to. But I don't think my father wants me to stay because he likes having me there... This is difficult..."

"Why does he want you to stay?"

"I think he wants me to keep an eye on Mum. Not to look after her. More like spy on her. Tell him what she's doing. Where she goes. Who she sees. I'm not really sure what he wants to know. He won't tell me. I think he's afraid she might be having an affair. Which is ridiculous. You'd know that if you knew my mum. We had a pretty strange summer break. He had a lot of business to clear and when he wasn't with us it was fine. But the atmosphere when he came on holiday was dreadful. I had to come back early for pre-season as you know. I've never been so pleased to leave them behind in my life. But it made me very concerned for mum's safety. I don't trust him not to lose his temper and lash out at her."

"I understand why you're worried. But I can put your mind to rest on that score. The Tony Lenahan I know doesn't have a temper to lose. Sorry to say this but he's a cold-blooded bastard. I may be biased but that's how I see him. Whatever he does, he'll think through all the ramifications before he acts. He has never to my knowledge ever just lashed out. He isn't a violent man. He's a calculating individual who never ever does his own dirty work. The one with the temper was your Uncle Mickey. Now if it was him you'd have cause to be worried for your mum. But it isn't. Your father has carefully built up his own little financial empire and he isn't going to mess it up whatever your mum says or does."

"I never knew my uncle."

"Of course not. You must have been...What? Two? Not much more. When he copped it."

"Nobody ever talks about him. Except about his dying for his country."

"No. But then everyone was afraid of him. Like me, they probably all prefer to forget he ever existed."

"What was he like? What did he do?"

"No comment."

I get a look of sheer exasperation but he doesn't press me any further.

"Are you saying mum will be alright if I move out?"

"I think she'll be safe enough. From your father. She'll probably expect you home to feed you up regularly. Aren't Italian and Jewish mothers the worst to their kids on that score? Anyway you can't spend all your time protecting her. She won't want that. She'll want you enjoying your life. Your success. The money that's coming your way. The parties.

Even the girls. Everything. To live it and not miss out. To love what you do. Doesn't that make sense?"

"I suppose so."

"I know so. I bet your mum lives for her children. Putting them first. Fiercely protective. Typically Italian mother."

"She's not typically anything. But you're right about her always putting us first."

"There you are then."

The coffees are cold. Offer to make fresh. Rory follows me into the kitchen. Refills the kettle while I rinse the mugs out. Spoon in instant granules and sugar. Top up with hot water and a splash of milk. Swig and swallow. Settle on high stools beside the central island. The conversation re-starts about where we left off.

"I still can't help having a bad feeling about not being there to look after her."

"It's called guilt. And you've got nothing to feel guilty about. Isn't that a line from a song? She can always phone you if she needs you. And you'll check on her regularly. Go see her at weekends. Keep in touch. She'll be fine."

"You're sure?"

"Sure, I'm sure."

"Okay then."

"Want some dinner?"

"What you got?"

"Steaks. In the fridge. Salad."

Nods of approval or acceptance. Probably both.

Much, much later. Rory long gone. Think about turning in early but can't summon the energy or willpower to get upstairs. The witching hour comes and goes. Wake with a start. Still on the settee. Realise I've been dozing. A vivid dream of Gail fleeting away. Dislodged by the dawn chorus. Peer at the clock. More like the pre-dawn chorus. Bloody birds. Go upstairs to bed. Don't reckon to sleep again. But somehow do.

***

Peter Ross phones. Why haven't I been around to see him? To tell him how everything's going. Presumably because I don't want to. Don't feel it's appropriate. Or useful. Shame I had to ask for his help last year at all. It gives him a renewed hook into me. Put him off. Not easy to do. His curiosity knows no reasonable bounds. Hang up eventually. Irritated. Ruffled. Forgot how easily he does this to me. From the first day Julie took me home to meet him. And still does.

***

No training programmed. A free day. Walk up Steep Hill checking various shops. The art centre. The second hand book store. A jewellers with a large range of novelty earrings in the window. End up buying a few small presents, in plenty of time for Christmas. Although God knows if Gail will be around at all then.

Hide-out with the newspaper in The Prince of Wales. Read it cover to cover. Even do the quick crossword. While downing a pint of bitter shandy. Refreshed, start to retrace my tracks downhill. Don't get far before changing my mind about going home. Pop into Megan's office instead. Find her sitting behind a sea of paperwork at her desk. On her own.

“Hi Megs."

"Hello you. Blooming secretary's gone off sick. And I'm fed up. You?"

"Let's not go there. How about a coffee?"

"Alright." She grabs her handbag. Not as vast as many women carry. Finds her keys. Collects a post-it note on which she scrawls 'Back in half hour' and puts it on the door sign. Now turned to read Closed. Locks up. Takes my arm. Accompanies me all of two hundred yards downhill to Pimento's. Seem to spend a lot of time and money there.

Settle with our drinks. And she starts. "Let's be clear. I do not want to talk about Gail. There's nothing I can say that will help. I can't and won't get her to talk to you. And I can't tell you anything more about how her life's going because she won't want me to. Is that understood?"

"Aye-Aye, Captain Jones.

"And less of the cheek."

"Okay. Want to talk about how things are with you?"

"No. They're wonderful. I've started seeing somebody. Met him on eHarmony. Don't look at me like that."

"Like what?"

"There's nothing wrong with on-line dating."

"Sure there isn't. It's even possible they're not all nerds or axe murderers."

"I accept the odds aren't brilliant and I've had a couple of real duffers. But Ian seems alright. So far anyway. And he's almost local. From Nottingham. So no travelling the length and breadth of the country to see each other."

"You have met him then? In person?"

"Twice. I'm going over for the day on Sunday. He's making me lunch. And I'm meeting his kid."

"How old? Boy or girl?"

"She's thirteen. Esme. She lives with him. His ex works in South Africa."

"We all have baggage. Don't we? I think sometimes girls may be less adaptable than boys where their dads are involved. And early teens are a tricky time."

"You are a bundle of joy, aren't you? Can't you find anything hopeful to offer."

"Course I can. If he's nice, you'll work through it. And Esme'll probably love having you for a new big sister to spoil her."

"That's the spirit. Onward and upwards."

"What does that mean exactly?"

"What?"

"Onward and upwards. Does it mean spiritually?"

"Or sexually?" Megan laughs. A low, dirty rumble. "Haven't a clue. Just something my mum used to say a lot."

"I do love the infinite variety of the English language with all its myriad subtleties.. Most of which we don't get half the time."

"If you think so."

"Yeah I do, Megs. I do.

Chapter XI Now: January to February

It seems Clare has a friend. She may have more than one for all I know. But this one works for the council. As Assistant Director of Children's Services. Has the letters CQSW after her name. Clare thinks it'll be worth my while to talk to her. Mostly I trust her judgement. Do as she suggests. Even if she's partly responsible for my abortive exile in Istanbul.

We meet in a pub near County Hall. It does good enough food and a decent range of guest beers but it's invariably quiet in the daytime. As a direct consequence of its well-earned reputation as a gay haunt. Great for lunchtime discussions when you don't want the risk of being overheard.

Diane Ryder. A tall woman, in her forties, with a mane of blonde hair pulled back into a pony tail. Fresh-faced. Sparing on the make-up. Good jewellery. Good shoes. Cool blue coat. Not exactly social worker camouflage-drab. Genuine smile. Friendly and outgoing. Seemingly willing to help.

Buy the drinks. Mineral water for her. Coke for me. Last of the heavy boozers. Hardly.

"Clare told me a little about what you need to know. What you're dealing with. Do you want to tell me in your own words?"

"This is strictly hypothetical..."

"No. That's not how it works. If I'm concerned about a child's safety, I have to report back. You have to persuade me I don't need to worry. If you do that I'll give you some advice and an open channel back to me if things change. Because they will. Is that alright?"

"Seems fair." No point in holding back now. Launch into explanations. Keep names out of it though. Don't want to give up any hostages to fortune. Otherwise she can have pretty much the whole story so far as I know it. She gets the facts about Sandrine's habit and her abandonment of her son; that he's staying with his half-brother with support from his girlfriend and from me. "The real question is how to regularise the situation so his mother can't just swan back in and take him away again unless she's got herself straight and can look after him properly."

"A few questions. The mother and father aren't married and he's not been involved in parenting the child?"

"That's right."

"Is he likely to take an interest in the child's welfare?"

"Probably not. He hasn't shown much interest so far. I think he'd intervene only to control Sandrine. And the drugs are a much more efficient lever. But he's unpredictable. I can't really say what he'd do or not do. His eldest son, the boy's half-brother, is pretty worried about him sabotaging things just because he takes it into his head to see all this as people interfering with him. Especially me. We have a painful history. In many ways he's a control freak."

Realise I've been lulled into a sense of security by Diane's quiet manner and obvious interest and I've revealed a name to her. Inevitable I suppose. I'll try not to beat myself up over the slip.

"Is he named as the father on the child's birth certificate."

"I don't know. I could find out."

"You should. Now are you going to trust me with some details?" She pulls a pen and a spiral bound reporters' notebook out of her shoulder bag. "If the child stays with you for more than twenty-eight days you'll have to do something to regularise matters anyway."

Decision time. Am I going to trust her? In for a penny... Give her the salient names. Her eyebrows reveal her instant recognition of Tony Lenahan's name.

"You know him?"

"Not personally. But he has his claws into a lot of our clients' benefits payments. He scares a lot of people."

"So I gather. He was a little shit at school. Now he's just a much bigger one."

She laughs. "We never change to the people we grow up with do we?"

"Not much."

"And the half-brother, Rory; how old is he?"

"He's only nineteen. Will that count against him?"

"He's over eighteen. So he could be approved as a kinship carer. Is Rory the only other family he's got?"

"There are grandparents I suppose. Rory's grandmother must be pretty old. Tony's father died when he was still at school. Sandrine's French. She came to England to escape her parents and I don't think she ever contacts them. Rory doesn't think so anyway. They probably don't even know she has a son."

"How long has she been here?"

"I don't know. Daniel's five. So sometime before that."

"Is Rory working? Financially stable? Can he afford to support the boy?"

My turn to laugh. "He makes a good living. One of these days he's going to be well-off. Legally. Not like his own father."

"What does he do?"

"He's a footballer. Plays for City. But he'll move up a division or two when his contract's up or the club see the sense in selling him."

"I'm not into sport. But my husband will know about him. He's a mine of information on sporting trivia."

"Not so trivial. Rory could bring the club an enormous transfer fee when he moves. He's that good."

"We've strayed from the main subject a bit. What sort of housing has he got?"

"Normally he lives with his girlfriend. My niece. She's got a one-bedroom flat. But they're all staying at my house in the West End now. I've got five bedrooms. Loads of space."

"You said the girlfriend's your niece? Does that mean we're talking about Clare's daughter?"

"Indeed we are."

My mobile vibrates. On cue. Jacqueline James in person. "Hi Jaki."

"Where are you? Have you met Mum's friend from social services yet?"

"She's with me now."

"I've finished lectures. Can I join you."

"Wait a minute. I'll check with Diane if it's alright."

It is. Tell her where we are and within a few minutes Jaki's sitting with us, sipping a glass of wine at my expense, sandwiches have been ordered and she and Diane are working out whether, when and where they've met before. Women!

Food arrives and order is restored eventually so we can get back into the important stuff.

"I've got enough background to lay out a couple of things for you."

"Okay. Thank you."

"Right. The first priority is always what's in the best interests of the child. Of Daniel. If there are real concerns we have a duty to investigate. I appreciate you wouldn't be happy to leave him with Sandrine at all in her current situation. But where's the evidence of significant harm?"

"We'd say what we've all seen."

"Not enough."

"If you were brought in...in an official capacity. Would you be likely to take him into care or would you leave him with us?"

"He'd be in care. On the Child Protection Register. Just with an approved care package. Which could be with his half-brother. As kinship carer."

"What's the advantage of getting him recognised as Daniel's carer?"

"The main thing is his mother couldn't just turn up and take him away. The approved arrangements for him would be with Rory. Emergency services have access to the register so if a situation did develop you could ring 999 and the police would check with the duty social worker. If someone was insistent about wanting to take Daniel away, the police would make an Emergency Protection Order on the spot. The order would give Rory's home as the appropriate safe environment for Daniel and they could arrest anyone interfering with that."

"So we really could stop Tony or Sandrine messing up the arrangements?"

"Yes. But I have to emphasise that's only if you do this properly."

"Okay. Jaki, what do you think?"

"How do we go about making the arrangement official? Getting Rory recognised as Daniel's kinship carer."

"The key thing, as I said to you already, is having the evidence of significant harm. Proof of his mother's abandonment and the effects of her cocaine use on the child. Whether the school noticed anything. It would have to be assessed by a case worker and his or her recommendation would go to a senior manager to be ratified and signed off. The care arrangements have to be safe of course. Rory would have to show how he'd look after Daniel. And that he can afford to keep him and how he'd cover school holidays and illness. That sort of thing."

"He's got a whole support network in place back at my uncle's. Perhaps we ought to do this properly. I need to discuss it with Rory."

"Of course you do. Its a big decision and it's his to take. There is another option of course which gets you round some of the evidential issues around significant harm. You could see a solicitor and go to court yourselves. Make an application for a residence order. The advantage of doing that pro-actively is it's then a private law matter and the test for getting an order is less onerous. It's what's in the best interests of the child - on the balance of probabilities."

Jaki and I breath the same name in unison. "Patrick."

"Just one other thing. We should try to contact Sandrine. We could ask her to sign an agreement allowing her child to be looked after by the named kinship carer. She'd be admitting she can't cope with looking after Daniel. It's not legally enforceable but it would be evidence the court could consider if things went wrong. Would she sign an agreement?" The question's aimed at me.

"I'm not sure. We don't even know where she is at the moment. She doesn't seem to have gone home to her flat. Maybe Tony's hidden her away somewhere."

"Well having her signature would definitely help things."

"So we might need to find her?"

Diane shrugs. "Afraid so."

***

The obvious next move is to talk to Clare again. Get Sandrine officially reported missing. I'm well past the stage of being bothered about looking stupid. If she's shacked up with Tony, or anybody else for that matter, then fine. At least we'll know she's alive and well. And yes, I appreciate that anything which agitates Tony Lenahan could be akin to poking a hornet's nest. But so be it. There's nobody else to do this. To express concern over Sandrine's disappearance. Her own parents are somewhere in France. Missing presumed abandoned. Rory's stuck between two stools. Daniel's a child. So it has to be me.

Fill in some paperwork. Plenty of blanks left because there's so much I don't know about Sandrine. Listen to Clare's words of caution. Say "Yah, yah, yah." Or a more polite equivalent. Give her the obligatory sibling hug and quit the police station. Something about these places sets my teeth on edge. And makes me thirsty. Cafe or bar? This time the bar wins.

***

Pubs and bars are great and flexible institutions. They cater for every sort of occasion, providing all the liquid fuel anyone could need. These days including tea and coffee. Many of them do solid food too and make a profit out of it. Not like when I was an under-age drinker.

Our local does service on occasion as a lawyer's office. Patrick indulging his professional skills at us or for our benefit. Meaning Daniel's at home with Ethan and his welfare is up for discussion by Jaki, Rory and me.

In fairness to Patrick if he says he'll do a job, he usually does it thoroughly. And he doesn't just charge in with a pre-set opinion formed in ignorance of the facts. So he wants to know everything Diane Ryder told us. Fortunately between us Jaki and I have pretty good, if not total, recall of the lunchtime session we had with the Assistant Director of Children's Services. What we in turn all want to know is whether Rory should commence legal proceedings to obtain a residence order for Daniel.

If I get the gist of it right, behind the 'On the one hand...but on the other hand' guff, Patrick's saying we could do this and he'd be willing to check out the procedural hoops we'd have to go through but that we definitely need to find Sandrine to raise the chances of success above fifty-fifty.

Okay if that's his view, we'd better take sterner measures to track Sandrine down. Wherever she is.

***

Among his heartbreakingly few personal possessions, Daniel owns a little picture frame sitting on the chest of drawers beside his bed. It contains a photo of his mum, probably taken at least a couple of years ago. Sandrine looks straight at the camera, smiling, long auburn hair loose around her face. No hint of the unkempt air and haggard state of recent times.

Jaki scans it into my desk computer. Works some magic. Checks some details with me. Sends her work to my printer. And flourishes the results in my face. A missing person poster; A5 size. Crisp black lettering on white paper. Incorporating the photo of Sandrine. To my untutored eye, it looks the business. Professional. Attention-grabbing.

"Do you think we should offer a reward? A thousand pounds would seem a fortune to anybody off St Giles'. We'd gain a lot of spying eyes on the estate."

"Okay. For information received leading to...Go on. put it in."

Alright. Now to get it out to all the local shops, notice boards and amenities around Lincoln. And on as many lamp posts as we can get away with.

***

Sandrine's whereabouts are increasingly a puzzle. No mother should be able to just walk away from her child and not look back at all. Actually that's rubbish. I've a friend raised by her father after her mother walked out and left them when she was only six years old. But my bias tells me it doesn't happen very often.

Each day, after dropping Daniel at school, I get Jimmy to drive us onto St Giles' so we can check out Sandrine's flat. There's never a sign anyone's been there at all since we cleaned it.

Walking across the verge one morning to get back to the car where Jimmy's waiting for me, I spot a familiar figure. Sudhir walking in my direction. Concentrating on what his companion is saying. The other man is slim, slightly seedy looking. The polar opposite of Sudhir in most respects. He's wearing a warm tweed coat. The sort cut like a suit jacket. With side pockets and a single vent at the back. As I watch Sudhir hands him a wad of banknotes which he stuffs into a pocket. Sudhir raises his head at that moment, catching my eye. He's a few yards away. Close enough for me to see his sheepish smirk. As though he's been caught out. They walk straight past me and all Sudhir says are two short sentences. "I'm working. You shouldn't be here."

Off balance, I don't respond quickly enough to ask about Sandrine. Call after him. "Sudhir! See you down the market?"

He stops. They both stop and turn round. The little man with the money looks like he's about to say something but Sudhir gets in first. "No. Not possible."

End of conversation. I can see he's going to be no help at all in finding the missing Frenchwoman.

***

Television studios should be large spaces containing a multiplicity of lights and technical equipment. And people to work it all. This is nothing like that. We're in a small room with a single cameraman. A blown up photograph of the west front of Lincoln Cathedral covers one wall as a backdrop for filming. Taken from on top of Exchequer Gate it places the interviewees in an unfamiliar, in real life impossible, relationship with the mass of the actual building.

Jaki and I are equipped with ear-pieces and clip-on microphones and a couple of chairs are in place next to the backdrop for us to use. We can see the clock on the opposite wall ticking silently towards the scheduled time of our live interview.

We're asked to take our seats and the technician does his set-up. Points the camera in the right direction. Asks us to tell him what we had for breakfast so he can check his sound levels and be sure the mics are working properly. Then we just have to sit and wait for the ear-pieces to crackle and the countdown to begin.

In a much larger studio somewhere in Leeds, the presenter shifts into his introduction. "For our next story we're heading over to Lincoln to ask our viewers for help. A lovely young French girl unfortunately went missing over Christmas. Sandrine Desmoullins hasn't been seen since Christmas Day. She lived with her five year old son in Lincoln and the police don't seem to have come up with any leads so far. In our Lincoln studio this morning, we have with us ..." He names us, summarising our supposed friendship with Sandrine. Highly inaccurate in several respects but that doesn't matter much. "Now can you tell us a bit about Sandrine?"

We haven't rehearsed this but it seems natural somehow to defer to Jaki and let her kick off. She makes the story of the young mother who disappeared immediately after having the most wonderful Christmas with her son sound unbearably poignant.

"And how is Daniel coping now?" Not sure he should ask that.

"He's staying with friends. He's alright. But he really misses his mum." Well fielded.

"There is of course unusually another dimension to this story. Isn't it true that the policewoman .." He manages to leer over the gender. "…Who is leading the search for Sandrine is in fact your mother? Your uncle's sister." Nothing like pointing out the bleeding obvious. "Aren't you effectively criticising her for the police failure to bring this case to a speedy and happy conclusion?"

This is what the Yanks call a curve ball. Unexpected and unfair. Jaki starts to speak and dries up. Her anger obvious. Step in fairly seamlessly. "The police are doing everything they can. But as my sister reminds me, a lot of unfortunate people go missing every year and it's always worse after the tensions of the holiday season. They're doing all they can with limited resources. That's why we want to ask all your viewers if they've seen her since she left him." Whew! Back on track.

Time's up. The interviewer does his outro. "So please look out for Sandrine and phone us at YTV or Crimestoppers on these numbers..." He gives them. "Thank you for that and we wish you good luck with your search."

"Thank you." But the ear-pieces, and presumably the mics too, are already dead. Divest ourselves of both and hand the gear back.

The camera operator invites us to have a coffee. Jaki refuses for both of us. "Want to get out of here. It's too claustrophobic." She's right. It is. And she's understandably upset about her mum being dragged into it. Anyway we'll get a much better cappuccino down the road.

***

There are no immediate results from the television coverage. A trickle of sightings across Lincolnshire and Humberside. Clare doesn't seem to think any of them are credible or helpful. I'd expected a greater response. Disappointing. And nobody even tries to claim the reward which doesn't bode well.

I do get another unsigned note through my front door though. More of the same.

This campaign isn't good for your health. Stop it. Or I will.

Short and to the point.

Chapter XII Then: December to January

I don't do Christmas these days. Gave it up years ago. Have no truck with it at all. Call me a Scrooge. But it isn't humbug or meanness. I buy, wrap and deliver presents for my family members. And send a select few cards because people send them to me. But that's it. The box of decorations remains in the roof void. Gathering dust. I don't buy a tree. Nor much else by way of festive purchases. Especially, I don't buy any fresh alcohol because I might be tempted to drink the lot.

I do fill up the fridge but don't expect to find a turkey in there or its crown, whatever that might be, or anything else seasonal. By re-stocking, I mean I buy sausages, eggs, lamb chops, baking potatoes and cream cakes. Vegetables and salad are in very short supply in my house but my concession to five-a-day is an enormous bowl of fruit.

Other essential supplies come in the shape of new compact and digital versatile discs; enough new music and films to last the week and a handful of newspapers and magazines previously unread.

The drawbridge goes up at this point. Jaki's at her Mum's and the only person who might appear at the front door and be undeterred by my failure to answer the bell will be Patrick, who knows he can slip through the unlocked side gate and hammer on the kitchen window. I'll let him in of course and he can drain whatever alcoholic remnants survive unimbibed amongst the glut of mostly empty bottles lingering in the sideboard. But I don't want to talk about Gail so if he mentions her all bets are off and he'll find himself slung out.

He doesn't. So he isn't.

Our Christmas Day, in food terms, is unencumbered in the civilisation stakes. We eat bacon sandwiches, bananas and cake. But it's more cultured as far as entertainment goes. We work through half a box set of classic Hitchcock movies. I insist on starting with 'Rear Window' which somehow speaks to me today. And most days. Patrick gets the next choice and so on. Five films later, it's supper time and Patrick reveals he's brought two bottles of excellent red wine with him. So we empty those and the day's done. Just before falling asleep, I realise two things. No text from Gail and I haven't phoned my mother. Grief and lamentations all round then.

***

Boxing Day. Patrick suggests the pub. I don't want to go. So we don't. At some point the doorbell rings and my treacherous friend allows Clare and Jaki into my abode. Not only is Clare out of uniform but she seems to have had enough time off to do some cooking. She brings a large oven dish of turkey pasta with her, a green salad and a bottle of chilled Chablis. Sometimes sisters are worth having. An interesting re-discovery.

Jaki acts surprised that all yesterday's utensils and crockery are in the dishwasher. Clean. I point out that I don't own enough plates or knives and forks to manage two continuous days of staying alive unless some washing up gets done. By me. I don't trust Patrick with what remains of my grandmother's china. But then I've known him since he moved in next door to my family, when I was six. Time enough to learn his faults. And his strengths.

"Shall I lay the table?"

"Thanks, Jaki." Well she offered.

It turns into a surprisingly pleasant day. Being fed without having to make any effort at all certainly helps. As does the uninvited company. Jaki organises a backgammon tournament after lunch. Not clear if there's an overall winner. Patrick volunteers to make tea. He turns out a batch of halfway decent cheese sandwiches with a side order of crisps. Clare knows better than to ask about the absence of salad stuff in them. Watch the football results to discover the Imps have won away from home. That would have been a worthwhile bet if I was a gambling man. By mid-evening alcohol has taken a toll on our faculties and we've regressed into easier games like draughts. If we hadn't all been so weary we might have fallen so low as to find the Ludo at the bottom of the games chest. Clare reminds us she's on duty in the morning and Patrick offers to detour and walk her and Jaki home. I'm left with an empty house and a sense of a day not entirely wasted.

Which is a lot more than can be said for New Years Eve. Drag myself to a party I don't feel like because I think I should but the savage mood I'm in results in a degree of rudeness to a poor, drunken girl who only wants to dance. Leave early. For the best. And whoever you are, I'm sorry.

Go to the football next day. Not exactly the best start to a new year. We lose. Restoration of condition normal. Don't stay around to commiserate with Rory. Life continues like it always does. I mean the alternatives aren't that great are they? And thinking about Gail doesn't shift the day along with sufficient velocity to mean I'm weary enough to sleep at night. So I do things to fill time. Extra training. More workouts. Start re-decorating the top floor of my house. And although it's against my religion, read a book or two.

Occasionally I get a treasured glimpse of Gail . A virtual presence in a text. Or the actuality of a hurried coffee somewhere in town. Gail's obvious concern over the risks of being seen with me make such pleasures bitter-sweet experiences.

Not that she and I are the only discontented souls in this glorious little city. January stays cold, bringing everybody's spirits down. We all soldier on as best we can but nobody seems to be in great shape. Rory, Patrick, Clare or Jaki. Even the usually cheery Megan stomps past me on Steep Hill one morning with hardly more than a grunt of recognition.

A van manages to clout the Roman arch at the top of Bailgate, doing, in one fell swoop, more damage than umpteen centuries of barbarian warfare. Not sure who picks up the tab for that one. The local conservationists are going nuts but within a fortnight a combined universities archaeological team can be seen carefully teasing material out of the ancient wall's newly exposed foundations. Every disaster is also an opportunity not to be missed for someone.

Other news. Scaffolding is going up again across the cathedral's refurbished west front. Guess they missed a bit last time out. New student residences are being built riverside. Actually that's not news. More an ongoing evolutionary process. The unstoppable expansion of the new intellectual epicentre of Lincoln. I struggle to care about any of it. Even though it's my city and it gives us all something to talk about. Better than silence. A little bit better.

What I do like, and take some degree of reassurance in, are marker days. Annual recurrences. The obvious holidays, anniversaries and birthdays. January would be boringly devoid of causes for celebration except that Patrick happens to have been born at the tail end of the month and he's a man who can usually be relied upon to throw a party with some degree of gusto.

None of us have ever tried the new Mexican restaurant up on the Bail. It's not really new of course. It was new many years ago but change gets accepted fairly slowly in this city. So we'll book the not-so-new Mexican. See if their chimichangas measure up to our appetites.

Patrick's particularly excited because Clare's said she'll come to his party. I'm fairly glum but putting a brave face on things because it seems unlikely Gail will be able to join us. Otherwise it's mostly the usual suspects who've been invited. A couple of local solicitors who were at college with Patrick and who have the gumption to play in a metal band, Jaki, Patrick's secretary Joni, Megan with the new boyfriend, Ian, who turns out to have played rugby with Patrick many years ago and has now renewed his acquaintance through the miracle of the six degrees of separation. You know the theory that everyone can establish a link to anybody else in the world through a chain of no more than six people. Try it. It does work.

One thing about parties in restaurants is they don't take much planning once the booking's made and the invitations are out. Get Jaki to order a birthday cake. The rest will pretty much take care of itself.

***

Bet the former circuit court judge and his wife with their upstairs sitting room overlooking Steep Hill know more about what's going on in Lincoln than they did even before they retired. I mean if you want to maximise your chances of meeting anyone you know in the city without the pre-meditation of an arranged meeting, try walking up or down Steep Hill on a Saturday afternoon. Assuming the people you want to meet aren't habituees of the football.

I still nearly manage to walk past Ellie and her husband, bundled up as they are in winter coats, hats, scarves and gloves. Once spotted, the weather becomes an ally and they're easily tempted out of the cold and into a cafe to catch up. Revival by hot infusion. In Ellie's case this means hot chocolate. We're not in Pimento's so the choices are more limited and Ellie's is a lead we both choose to follow.

"Not seen you in ages."

Could remind her that the last time we talked properly was when we were planning my aborted birthday party. Don't really want that as the starting point for discussion so don't raise it. "No. It's been awhile. So what have you been up to?"

"You tell him, Brian." Ellie's smile is serene and I suddenly twig exactly what he's going to say.

He doesn't mince his words either or have the grace to look abashed. Straightforward happiness giving him the gift of blunt factual-ism. "We're having a baby. In June."

"Congratulations." What else can you say? They want one. They're going to have one. Bully for them.

Ellie, uncorked, gives me chapter and verse. Too much information if truth be told. I don't need to know how long they'd been trying or the details of the eventual conception. Doesn't this constitute cruel and unusual punishment of the childless. Parents-to-be never see it that way but it is.

Eventually Ellie gets to the subject I want to know about. "Have you seen Gail this week? I did catch up with her yesterday."

"Actually I've not seen her for a few days." More like a few weeks but I'm not admitting that. To myself let alone to them. "How is she?"

"Alright I think. So you don't know about the house?"

"No. What about it?"

"It's going on the market. They're selling it. He's found a place he likes in Newark."

Well now that's a facer. What the hell am I supposed to do with this information? Is she moving with him? Is this a fresh start? Or does it signal the beginning of the end? Haven't a clue. Questions I can hardly ask Ellie and won't get answers to until I see Gail. Whenever that turns out to be.

Leave them to it when Ellie decides to order a second hot chocolate. You can have too much of a good thing.

***

Don't want to be in a hospital yet again. Really dislike sick visiting when it feels like an obligation or a duty. Not much choice when it's a call from your former father-in-law and he's very unwell. Even if he's a tough old sod and will probably be right as rain if he'll rest long enough to let the drugs work. Actually that may be a trifle over-optimistic as prognoses go. Thrombosis at his age isn't to be taken lightly. Not at any age.

Find Peter sitting up in bed looking bored at what's on television. I've not bothered to buy him grapes. A selection of newspapers and a book on test cricket seems more likely to cheer him up. A bottle of whisky would do the job even better but I'm not trying to smuggle that past the nurses.

He sees me and starts up right away. "About time you got here. Need to talk to you. Want you to do something for me."

"It's good to see you so relaxed and looking so well."

"Don't be such a daft bugger. This is serious. Sit down over here. I want to get some stuff off my chest. About the council."

Pull a chair closer to his bed and settle down to hear him out. "Alright. I'm listening. What is it, Peter?"

"You know we've got no Town Clerk at the moment. Just a fellow acting up till we can appoint a new one. Though they'll call him a Chief Executive now I suppose..."

"It might be a her."

"Nah. The council won't hire a woman for that. Can't see it. Anyway at the moment there's nobody I can share this sort of stuff with in confidence. And I figured somebody with some brains should know what's going on in case I kick the bucket."

"You're going to be fine."

"Maybe so. But it won't do any harm for you to know what I know. As a back-up. Isn't that what you call it for information you put on your computer?"

"Yes it is."

"Right then. The thing is this. I think we might have a problem in the planning department. Some strange decisions being made which don't marry up with council policy and they're being bulldozed through by the chairman. I've been in this game a long time and the only thing that would make sense of it is if money's changing hands."

"You're talking about corruption."

"I am at that, lad. Now I see there's a new development company on the scene. Only they don't seem to develop anything. They buy up land. Cheap I'd guess. They sort out planning permissions. And they sell it on. The company's called Harrigan Homes. I've been watching what they've got their fingers in. There's a file in my roll-top desk. I want you to take charge of it if anything happens to me. You can take it to that sister of yours. See if she can make anything stick against them that's behind it. We had a good reputation as a clean and fair council in the old days. And I'd like it to stay that way. But if this carries on, someone's going to get their fingers burned."

"So I take the file and give it to Clare if you peg out?"

"That's about the size of it."

"I can do that for you. But I'm sure you'll be talking to her yourself before too long."

"Probably. Good. Anything else you want to talk to me about?"

No idea what he's got in mind. "Well, no. I brought you some reading material. Came to check on you. That's it really. Make sure you're alright."

"I'm doing fine. With any luck I'll be out of here in a few days. Now Julie'll be in to see me soon so if you don't want to bump into her, you'd better bugger off now."

"Fine. I'll do that."

"Good. And thanks a lot."

Duty done. Home with a clear conscience. But something else to think about.

***

After quite a break without seeing Gail, we meet. Period. Better than not meeting at all. Unsatisfactory in most other respects. Precious little physical contact. No discussion of anything important. Strange that I'm the one who used to run a mile not to have to discuss his feelings and am now hoist on my own petard. But I am getting better at the waiting game. Now I know what I want out of life at least I'm saved from charging off down side-tracks and tangents in search of illusory happiness. Doesn't mean I'll get what I want of course. Only that there are no alternative options anymore. Have to wait things out. I do mention Patrick's party to her. And get the non-committal response I expected.

***

Patrick really pulls out all the stops to demonstrate totality of enjoyment of the evening. And the party does go with a swing. We've all ignored instructions and brought presents. And what do you buy for the man who has everything? Ingenuity unleashed. Expensive jokes. Gadgets. Cleaning kit for his shotguns. Bizarre cooking utensils. Anything other than alcohol he doesn't really need to consume and books he'll never read.

The food's pretty good. The wine flows. The atmosphere gets raucous. Patrick's been insistent from the start that he's picking up the bill. But there's someone who isn't quite in the mood however much he tries.

There's an Italian story about two opposing planets. Felona, a place of joy and Sorona a world of sorrow. Time and space shifts and the opposing mirror images see-saw. Felona falls and Sorona rises. It's like that tonight. I came here accepting that nothing could be as I desire it to be. And Patrick was on top of the world. Two contrasting pivotal moments. For me the completely unanticipated arrival of someone to sit beside who stays for most of the evening and let's me walk her home. For Patrick the opposite emotions. Clare pulls an unexpected duty. And can’t get there at all.

Chapter XIII Now: March

At first I don't text Gail. Think she needs time to come to terms with how she feels about me now. Whether it fundamentally changes what's possible between us or not. When she doesn't contact me I wait, increasingly impatiently, to be put out of my misery. Eventually, I send her a text asking how she is. The good news I get a response within the hour. The bad news. All it says is 'Give me more time.'

***

A week passes. A fortnight. Try again. Keep it as light as I can. No hint of the brewing despair in me. Mustn't put pressure on her. Know she can't handle that. Again a quick response. Bleaker. 'I don't know how to deal with anything at home or with you or what I should do. I'm sorry. xx'

Thank God for the 'xx'. Not much else to hang on to. Give myself a strict talking to. If I crave what I can't have and fixate on it, I'm going to sink into a miserable morass. I can't afford to let myself do that. Have to focus on the bright things I do have and should make every effort to enjoy. Easier said than done but I have a party to go to. At my sister's. An engagement party for Jaki and Rory. Coming up fast.

***

Phone call. From Gail.

"I need to see you. I don't know how to carry on. Need to talk to you. Where can we meet? Tomorrow?"

Now I know what being a yo-yo feels like. I'm not going to describe it. You can either picture it. Or you can't.

***

Reality isn't like fiction. Facts can't be dropped in whenever convenient. Unless something actually happens to us, we just have to wait to find out what's going on until somebody thinks to fill us in. So it is with the mugging which Jaki takes in her stride and Rory doesn't. And Rory, not my niece, tells me some hours after the event.

"She had her bag snatched this morning. On her way to lectures. She got punched because she wouldn't let go.

She'll have a nasty black eye tomorrow. It's swelling that fast. I can't help worrying this may be connected to last year. That it could be the start of more warnings from my father."

"Why would he need to do that? He got what he wanted from me. I kept my word. And mugging Jaki? I don't think so."

"I think I ought to talk to him."

"Why? What would that achieve? Have you seen him at all lately?"

"No. I haven't . Not much at all since I moved in with Jaki." Glum sigh. "You think I'm wrong then?"

"Pretty sure you are. Yeah. Just look after her."

"She's right as rain. Already reported the theft. Got onto the accommodation people for new keys. Been to the bank to void her credit cards..."

"Cards? How many has she got?"

"Her own and she's an authorised user for one of mine."

Raised eyebrows.

"It's only money."

"Easy to say that."

Flare of anger from Rory. "I earn it. I'll do what I like with it."

"Okay...okay. I'm not having a go at you. You just need to know Jaki's not great with money."

"Yeah. Well..."

The response of my resident professional, Ethan, to the loss of Jaki's handbag and all her and our keys is to find my toolbox, head into town, buy new locks for my house and fit them, returning my key ring with replacements on it only when he's been back to get the requisite number of new sets cut.

Get to tackle Jaki in private later on. Her reassurance is absolute. "It wasn't the big man who threatened me before. This was a young guy. Bit of a druggie I'd say. It's simply one of those things. I liked that handbag but I'll get a new one. I'm perfectly alright."

"Apart from the eye."

"Well that does hurt. But it could've been a lot worse."

"Of course it could. Will you try and persuade Rory not to take it up with his father?"

Nods. "I will. I have. But he's so protective. And stubborn."

"Keep trying. Better to let sleeping dogs lie. And sharks."

"What?"

Explain my new-found theory that Tony's a reincarnated shark. She laughs. "More like a snake."

"Have you met him yet?"

"Nope."

"Either which way, he's better left unrattled."

***

Don't sleep well. Worrying. Even late to meet Gail.

Find her sitting, waiting patiently. Big smile and then a perceptive observation. "Something's up. What's the matter? Are you alright?"

"Yeah. But I'm rather concerned about my niece, Jaki. She got mugged yesterday. Got a horrible black eye. Just worried that it's no coincidence. It could be a follow on to something vicious that happened to her last year."

She gets straight to the point. "Part of why you went away?"

"Yes."

"Shouldn't you tell me about that now?"

"Gail, I will tell you everything in a month or two. I promise. When things are sorted out. It's a police matter and I'm not supposed to discuss it with anyone at all."

Her disappointment that I'm shutting her out shows but she doesn't say anything else. Her silence compels me to add to what I've said. "It's really difficult because I don't want to have secrets from you. It doesn't just involve Jaki but my sister and my trainee, Rory. Will you trust me to choose the right time to lay it all out for you?"

"I suppose so. I have to really. Don't I?"

"Just trust me." Asking that even though trusting people is pretty hard where I come from. But I'll try if she can too.

"You won't be angry if I raise it again. I'll only be doing it because things are getting on top of me and I have to know."

Not sure I understand where she's coming from but acquiescence is easy enough. "No. I won't get mad. But this will get sorted sooner rather than later." It sounds like a promise I've given her before. Or has she said it to me? Hope to hell it turns out to be true. The one thing in my favour is that I really mean it. Really want it to be so.

***

The call from Istanbul to my mobile comes out of the blue. And from three hours ahead of Greenwich Mean Time. It's tea-time there. Early afternoon for me. A voice obviously Turkish. But not heavily accented. Excellent English subject to the odd use of an incorrect tense. Forgivable lapses. Especially when compared to my execrable Turkish.

"Hello Umit. To what do I owe the pleasure?"

"I plan coming over. Next week. To London. To agree my terms with one of your players of Queens Park Rangers. Out of contract at end of season. I hope we can meet."

"It'd be great. I'm sure I can get down to London..."

"No. You misunderstand me. I plan to come down to Lincoln."

"Up to Lincoln. We say up when we're travelling north. Unless you come from London or you're at Cambridge or Oxford University when anywhere else is down. It's a status thing." Can't help teaching. It's in my blood.

"Yes. Yes. Whatever. I want to be coming up to Lincoln. Could I meet your young man? Lenahan. Rory Lenahan." He pronounces the name 'Roreee.'

The old fox. He doesn't really want to see me. This is a poaching trip. Well I'll ensure Rory is well-briefed before Umit gets here. "Of course you must. Can you stay over? When can you come?"

"Thursday. Is that working for you?"

"It's great. See you then. Just text me the time of your train and I'll meet you at Lincoln Station."

***

An evening with Umit may be boring for Jaki but totally engrossing for the household's male contingent. Even Ethan's so fascinated he forgoes putting Daniel to bed. Apart from an occasional divergence into the subject of food, the beer-fuelled conversation is exclusively football. Tactics, training methods, sports nutrition, performance, recent results, continental developments, players likely to feature in the African Cup of Nations, marketing opportunities in China and stadia crowd control. For starters.

The main course requires a shift into the lounge to use the television. For the last five years I've videoed Rory in training and intercut footage illustrating the application of his growing skills to match situations. The best material comes from television cameras but even the amateur nature of much of the filming can't disguise the progress of raw talent towards something much closer to the finished article. Occasionally I've reviewed the stuff with Rory but never done it comprehensively till now. Even I can't help being amazed at some of what we've captured. Rory is slightly sheepish at being the centre of attention but thaws with Umit's highly specific and expertly informed praise, which is, in every sense, well-deserved. Jaki stays with it, watching and listening in unaccustomed silence. Not so boring an evening for her after all it seems.

Talk turns to the future. The opportunities and temptations Rory will face in the months and years to come. Umit's advice is sound and largely reinforces the stance I've taken with him.

Finally Umit says what he came up from London to be persuaded he'd want to say. "When you're ready for a change from English football, you come to me. I will place you in a Turkish club for say two years. You will earn good money and have good experience. Perhaps even Champions League is not impossible. The time is not yet. But perhaps more soon than you think. My friend here always knows how to reach me if you want to talk. And I will always give you good advice. Even if you not wish to come to play in Turkey."

On that last point Umit is entirely genuine. I'm sure of that.

"So tomorrow we come to see training. Yes is alright?"

"Yes, it is. And thank you for taking such an interest in me." Typical Rory. His modesty means it's sometimes easy to forget just how much talent he has.

Umit rises early. Before Rory and me anyway. Find him in the kitchen laughing with Daniel and Jaki, munching on large wodges of toast and sipping black coffee. I'd wondered if Jaki's relative silence last night indicated a degree of intimidation at the prospects Umit was raising. Plainly not if her ease with him now is anything to go by.

"Your niece. She is a joker. But she will be a tough negotiator if I ever sign her Rory. She tells me this."

"She's a smart cookie. And a fighter. You noticed her black eye." Jaki flushes with pleasure. Couldn't have found anything to say she'd appreciate more just now.

"Are you coming with us to see the training?"

"I'd like to, Umit. But I can't. I have to go to lectures this morning."

"Always the work comes first. Well then I will hope to see you next time I come to England. Or you will come to Istanbul. And I will show you and Rory the sights. There are many of them. As your uncle knows well."

"Thanks. Hope you enjoy the day. And safe journey home."

"I am sure I will."

On impulse she hugs him on the way out. Umit has a way of winning people over. Hear her shout to Rory from the hall and the noise of his dash downstairs to kiss her goodbye.

A good start to the day.

***

I've talked about feeling like a proverbial yo-yo. No fun at all. Not quite true. The highs are fantastic. The lows awful. Overall not good. The recognised pattern looks like this. Absence. Doubts. Meeting needed to resolve doubts. Phone call. Meeting. Discussion. Parting. Reflection. Nothing is resolved. Re-run the cycle. It's exhausting. Emotionally speaking. Going on week after week. Got to break out of it somehow.

Open question. Got any suggestions?

***

Ethan will mind Daniel. Jimmy's driving me to Clare’s. I'm carrying a brightly wrapped package. A beautiful piece of glassware crafted by a local artist which I know Jaki will love. Not so sure about Rory.

Clare's house is a cottage near Bransby, a handful of miles outside Lincoln. It's not in the village proper which is largely in the hands of a single landowner. A trust. People leave it all their worldly goods when they kick the bucket. For the sole purpose of looking after abandoned horses. And donkeys. Not sure why such mammals excite so much more charity than the two-legged poor and desperate. But they do.

I get there fairly early. The drive's not too clogged with cars when Jimmy drops me off with a promise to pick me up in the morning. I've bagged one of the spare bedrooms so I can stay over. A brother gets priority over the forty or fifty other guests for whom the caterer's been working flat out for the last day or so. The enormous table in the conservatory across the back of the house is groaning with goodies.

Clare, calm and collected despite the unaccustomed pink ensemble she's wearing (about as appropriate as a cardigan on a lioness), is overseeing the final touches in the kitchen. Her greeting is perfunctory and accompanied by an instruction to head into the garden and mingle.

It's a mild spring evening but the receding daylight is already under serious competition from the coloured lights placed in the bushes, many of them shaped like small birds. My niece and her fiancée, such an oddly old-fashioned term, are amid a small gaggle of guests. Some of the young men are familiar from the club and other friends are probably either partners or students from the university. They're talking sport. I'd try to deter them if it wasn't such an uphill struggle. Like expecting actors not to talk about roles or barristers their cases. Drift back into the house to help Clare. Pretty soon it's full of people, many of them well known to me. I've had a couple of glasses of wine and am feeling no pain.

Standing in a cluster of friends around Jaki discussing her black eye and the mugging when something extraordinary happens. An arm slides round my waist and when I look round Gail is nestled in beside me. Saying something.

Actually I've no idea what she says. I'm too stunned to take it in. And my reaction is purely physical. I wrap her in my arms and hug her. As if she'll melt away if I don't hold her tightly enough.

"Way to go, Unc." Vaguely heard.

The scent of Gail's hair in my nostrils, so familiar it drives me crazy. Her upturned face and that smile. Her mouth begging to be kissed. But she slides her lips away when I try it. "I think we should behave better in front of my son."

"Your son?"

"Right here, Coach. But don't mind me."

Find we're flanked by both Jaki and Rory. Two grinning souls. So obvious they already knew. Both of them. Seems I'm the only poor sod who's in danger of a seizure from sheer shock. I have a million and one questions...But they all die on my lips. All I really want to do is hold Gail and let the room revolve around us.

It's much, much later before a truth belatedly dawns on me. Gail being Rory's mother makes her husband...Tony Lenahan. Well to misquote Dorothy Parker, I suppose it puts all my enemies in one bastard. Tomorrow soon enough to worry about him.

I'm a bit slow on the uptake on several fronts tonight. Another one is failing to notice that Gail's wrist has regained freedom of movement. Put it down to the after-effects of shock. No more cast. The arm around my waist is unimpeded and flexes with apparent normality at each and every joint. Result.

"Can you stay tonight?" Déjà vu all over again. I've said this to Gail before in another place and time.

She shakes her head. "I have to go home. I've got Liam at look after. And he's too young to understand. Have to take it slowly."

"Are you saying this is going to be alright? Us I mean."

"I think so. I'm not strong enough not to see you. I've tried and it makes me miserable."

"Me too."

"I know. But I can't say now what's going to be possible and what's not. I keep hoping Tony will find someone he really wants to be with permanently. And divorce me. He's had plenty of opportunities; lots of other women. I thought maybe that French girl...But he always comes back. He won't let me go. We have to wait. Be patient."

It's the longest speech I've ever had from her about her life. And I have to look supportive and say I understand when like hell I do. My natural instinct leans towards confrontation and resolution not playing bystander. But she has to be allowed to do it her own way if she's to own the outcomes. I know enough to appreciate that pleading with her to change her mind and come with me now simply won't work. Leave her to it. No other way.

***

Breakfast. In the kitchen. Rory still abed. Clare ditto. Just Jaki and me and a pan of bacon and eggs.

"How long have you known she was my Gail?"

"Rory introduced us weeks ago. But recently she mentioned Turkey. The name thing was puzzling but it had to be her. And she's just your type."

"I don't have a type."

"Yes you do. Well perhaps I mean that she's right for you. Not like that last bimbo you were seeing. The blonde bombshell."

"That was ages ago..." Give up protesting. Not much use telling her Angela had several good qualities. After all stick-ability wasn't one of them.

"So I told her how I was related to you. And her reaction when I mentioned your name... I just knew I was right. I had to talk to Rory because I knew you'd both be coming to the party. And we agreed to just let things happen."

"Well. Thank you for that." Gruffly spoken. Raw emotion clogging my throat.

The sound of a car in the lane. Near simultaneous shriek from a bedroom. Clatter of mules on the stairs. Enter one sister swearing like a trooper. "She's here. She's early. Blast! Bugger! Damn!"

"What? Who?" Jaki, half risen to her feet, looks more alarmed than I do. But then I know Clare's capacity for melodrama at least as well as she does. Better in fact. Based on over forty years co-existence.

"Your grandmother! Shit! Shit!" She's trying to ram a small mountain of stuff into the dishwasher.

"Mum's back from New Zealand? Why didn't you say?"

"It's supposed to be a surprise. It's why I told you to stop around for lunch. Thought we'd have a nice reunion for her. Now she's up from Gatwick hours earlier than she said."

Doorbell. Clare freezes.

"Oh just go and let her in. She'll have to take us as she finds us."

The only tranquil one in the next few moments is the sweet taxi driver; and I mean really sweet. He carries in Mum's bags, fusses over her, finally graciously accepts the fare with a substantial gratuity and leaves her, with some reluctance, to her family's tender mercies.

So. My mother. Not a quiet and gentle soul like my Dad. A person of volcanic emotions all confined in an impossibly small package. Guess where my sister gets her temperament from. Don't be fooled by the little old lady image. That's there for taxi-drivers and other service sector personnel. The word formidable was invented to describe her. Set aside the puff of white hair on her head and her slight stoop. She doesn't need the walking stick she carries. It's a weapon not an aid. In her time she has caused politicians, consultants and lawyers to quail. The only exception for whom she has a soft spot is Patrick. Or is it a blind spot? He came into our house as the new neighbour's son and found himself adopted by my Mum to make up for all the perceived defects in her own sons. And don't get me started on the lethal competition which constitutes her familial relationship with Clare.

"Well Mum. Did you have a good holiday? How are the Kiwis?"

"Never mind that. How did Jaki come by that eye?" One of my mother's talents. She misses nothing. Not the tiniest trace evidence or the most casually discarded clue. It comes from the long years managing the merry dance Simon, Clare and I led her when we were growing up. Face it, we were never the easiest children in the world. In short, she's constitutionally incapable of missing a trick. Let alone something as obvious as Jaki's shiner.

Hence her full-frontal verbal assault.

“I had my handbag stolen, Grandma. I was mugged in the street. It’s nothing serious.”

"If you say so. Now I need a cup of tea. Parched is what I am. All those hours in the plane. Didn't sleep much. They don't make proper tea and coffee on planes you know. It's all powder."

A hovering Jaki takes responsibility for putting the kettle on. "Sit down Grandma." Pulls out a seat for her at the kitchen table. Trying to mollycoddle her into a semblance of submission.

"I've been sitting down enough in the last couple of days." Nevertheless she subsides onto a chair and reduces the tension in the room by fifty per cent in a single stroke. Jaki puts the tea in front of her. It's in a china cup with a matching saucer. The milk's in a small ceramic jug and the sugar lumps are in a bowl. With tongs. We all know Mum's sensibilities and how advantageous it can be to give proper regard to them.

"That's nice, dear. Now then. What's been going on while I've been away?" She seems to take it as a given that we will somehow already know all my brother's antipodean news by the mysterious process of kinship osmosis. Whatever she's heard at first hand, she feels no need to enlighten us about. What matters is what we've been managing to screw up in her absence overseas. The things she hasn't been told yet and is hyper-curious to learn. Which is when I realise and start to grin. The main object of her attention needn't be me and my on-off-on friendship with Gail. On my right hand sits a newly-engaged niece. The perfect trump card. Ready to be thrown to the wolves. Lack of consultation and involvement in such key decisions as Jaki and Rory's betrothal ought to be a great distraction from my own shortcomings. Or Clare's for that matter unless she has to stand proxy for Jaki when the brickbats are flying around.

Oddly my mother takes the news fairly calmly. "Is he a nice boy?" Not sure who that's addressed to. Neither do Clare and Jaki who start to answer it in tandem. Both pause. Start again. Then decide it's Jaki's to field. Hear her say something about Rory being my trainee. Bringing me back into the frame when I'm thinking I'm home and dry. But then again Mum seems quite sanguine about someone dependent on a character reference from me. The three months in New Zealand really has done her the world of good. Perhaps missing the coldly debilitating effects of this English winter accounts for her good mood. Or is she just happy to see us?

"Cat got your tongue?" More like it.

"He's a good lad. Hard-working. Talented. He may be young. He's not twenty yet. But he's pretty mature for his age. And before you ask; I think he really loves your grand-daughter."

"Your father was only nineteen when I met him." My mother revealing her inner romantic edge. Wonders may never cease.

“I didn't know that."

"I was young too. But I knew he was the one. Right from the off."

I've no desire to spoil the moment by mentioning the faint possibility that my Dad may have been the first and only man who'd condone her temper, cater for her every whim and never stop loving her. Perhaps I'm over-stating things. I often do.

***

"What exactly are you doing about Tony Lenahan?"

Clare's office. Storm clouds outside. And in my soul as the song has it.

"Slow progress. But we are getting there. I promise. Is this about Gail?"

"It's about the fact that I don't want to be looking over my shoulder indefinitely. He must know by now that I'm back to stay and won't be pushed out again. I've had a couple of nasty notes pushed through my door already. To cap it all he's going to find out any day now that I'm seeing his wife. If he doesn't already know. And now I come to think of it one of his threats last year was something about my girlfriend. Thought he was just fishing then. But maybe he's known all along. You're holding all the recordings I made of his threats. The last straw would be for something about the investigation to leak and ka-boom. I'm in the nasty brown stuff."

"It won't leak. This is police business. We've kept it tight as a drum."

"Apart from the ever-growing number of cops who've become involved. This is a small city. Something could easily get out accidentally."

Clare ignores that suggestion. "We're not there yet. I can't say better than that. Much as I wish I could. I'll tell you as soon as anything changes."

"If that's all the assurance you can manage..."

"It is. It really is."

***

Go to Newark. At Gail's suggestion. Get to see the showroom and all her favourite fabrics. Meet her other business half, Jenny Smith. Nice woman. Quiet, industrious soul. Says "Hello," but doesn't stop measuring out trim while answering my questions about the shop and its clientele. Gail makes me a coffee in the minuscule kitchenette and settles us on easy chairs in the workroom.

"What do you think?"

"It's great. The whole set-up looks really professional. Are you going to make the new curtains you promised me?"

"I did, didn't I? Yes we will. We'll choose some material and measure up and you can leave a deposit...I'm joking. About the deposit."

"Hoped you were. Anyway I wanted to ask you something else. There's something I don't get at all. I thought Rory's mum was supposed to be Italian. And yet she's you. My Gail."

"But I am Italian. Half Italian. We lived there till I was nine. My parents separated and my mum brought me back to England and went back to using her maiden name even though they never got divorced. She was called Ryan. Lucy

May Ryan. And being Gail started as a joke. At the airport. It was the first time Tony had ever let me go anywhere without him. And the girls said I should be someone different while I was away. I took off my wedding ring and became Gail. It's not so different to my real name."

"Which is...?"

"Galina. My name is Galina Napolitano. Or Lenahan for the last twenty years."

"Do I call you Galina now? Or Lina perhaps."

"I like being Gail. It was my new start and I like it. You don't mind, do you?"

"Why would I mind? I think I'd have a hard time adjusting to calling you anything else really."

"But you never call me Gail. You say 'Sweet Girl' or 'Darling Girl' most of the time."

"Yeah. I suppose I do. Just habit."

"I don't mind. I like it. When you do it."

"And you're using Ryan for the business."

"Jenny and I'd been discussing starting something together for a long time. When I got back from Alanya, I told Tony I was doing it. And I thought Smith-Ryan sounded perfect for soft-furnishings. Solid and English."

"With a touch of the Irish about it too. Is it a good business?"

"It's going to be. It's growing. And we're learning."

"Good. I'm really proud of you."

"Why?" She's smiling.

"Because I am."

"You deserve a kiss for that."

"Okay." No hardship at all.

***

Grab Rory after training.

"I have a bone to pick with you."

"What is it, coach? Sorry. What's up?"

"I think you've been holding out on me. For a pretty long time."

"What?" He manages a look of genuine bafflement. Unfortunately I know it's false.

"When you met Jaki. Did you know she was my niece?"

"Oh that!" Sounds like an admission to me. "No. Not at first. But when you went away. She talked about her uncle being in Istanbul. And I knew that's where you were. I didn't let on to her. And I was only supposed to contact you in emergency. You told me so."

"So it's my own fault. Is that what you're saying?"

"Yes in a way. Is it a problem?"

Shake of the head. "Not really. Except it seems to run in the family. Can I ask you something more?" Don't give him the chance of refusal. Plough right on. "When did your mum find out who I was?"

"She knew the moment she met you. In Turkey. I'd talked about you so much. About working with you and what I'd learned from you. My father would virtually grind his teeth when I mentioned you. So yes. She knew who you were."

"She never let on. Not once. Come to think of it she never even mentioned you by name. Or Liam. She always talked about you both as her boys. You wait till I see her. She's not going to live this down."

"You won't be angry with her, will you?"

"Do you think I could ever be angry with her? About anything?"

"No." He laughs. Think we're straight now.

Mind you. He doesn't know I'm going to ask Gail to marry me. Sooner or later. And I've no intention of pre-warning him.

Chapter XIV Then: February

Sunday. 9.30 am. Just about to set out to join Patrick for a cooked breakfast at a decent cafe in town. Phone rings. It's Rory. Wanting to talk. Simplest thing is telling him to join us. Even footballers have to eat. He agrees to get in the car and met us there.

Walk in to find Patrick the only customer in the whole front half of the cafe. He's commandeered the choicest table in the window with a grand view of all that moves in this part of Lincoln. No call for us to feel other than safer than safe in here though. Around the big table at the back sit about a dozen of Clare's best and finest. Caps and jackets off. Tucking into massive helpings of precisely what you'd expect to find in a fry-up. The quiet pre-shift period I suppose. They might argue they're having a team meeting I suppose. The sergeant's at the head of the table after all. But the conversation's too fragmented and casual in nature. Maybe the formal briefing came earlier. Before we arrived. Let's give them the benefit of the doubt.

A few minutes more and the cops are starting to get up and settle their bills when Rory walks in. One recognises him and says something complimentary to him about his current form.

"I owe it all to my coach here."

Can't let that stand unchallenged. "Like hell you do. I can't take the credit for pure talent."

"Glad you play for us anyway."

Another one butts in. "They'll sell him sooner or later. They always sell off the good ones."

"True, true."

"Good luck son."

"Thank you."

A stocky-hipped, brunette officer waiting at the counter smiles in my direction. So I ask her. "Good breakfast?"

"The best. We always start here on a weekend. Try the herb sausages."

"I will. Hope you have a peaceful day."

"We don't do crises on Sundays. Not often anyway."

Her turn to pay so I lose her attention.

Let her and the last of her colleagues saunter out to begin their day of crime-busting, or whatever else Clare has in store for them, before raising the weighty matter that's on my mind.

"I think the trousers are the problem, Patrick."

"What're you on about?"

"Those new black combat pants they wear these days. The side-pockets bag out. Makes all the women look like they've got wide hips and big..."

"Don't go there. The owner's coming over." And indeed she is. Pad in hand to take our order.

Platefuls of breakfast land on our table. Mainstays plus black pudding, beans and mushrooms. My order differs from the others. We're all having Lincolnshire sausages but I've ordered the herb variety. Following police guidance. The food is accompanied by great big steaming mugs of tea. Dark and strong. The tea not the mugs. They're plain white ceramic uncluttered by logos. Rory wants more milk.

"Wimp."

Shrugs it off. Matter of fact. "Just how I take it."

By silent consent chewing takes priority over conversation. Munching away until the plates are cleared. The odd scrap of bacon rind or egg white may remain for the pig bin but not much else. Actually that's showing my age. They don't collect leftovers for pig-swill anymore. European health regulations rule. Okay! Patrick leans back and belches. I could easily follow suit but hold it in.

"Now. What's happening with you guys?" Patrick's come over all American.

"Precious little except more of the same." Nothing I want to talk about anyway.

"Rory?"

He's thoughtful. Not unusual in itself. But the quality of his sudden stillness and the length of the silence before he says anything tells those of us who know him well that what's coming is significant. Or important. Or both.

"I went to a party last night."

"And?"

"Met somebody."

So laconic. Have to work really hard to drag stuff out of him. Details and the like.

"Male or female?"

Withering glance. "A girl. Really lovely. Great fun. She's a student at the university." University with a definite article always means our university. Other institutions elsewhere may excel academically but they're also-rans in terms of city pride.

"Are you going to see her again?"

"Possibly. I'd like to. I've got her number."

"And is this such a big deal?" Knowing that for him it certainly could be. Not that he's not had girlfriends before but his whole attitude this morning is the polar opposite of casual and carefree.

"I'm not sure if I should ring her or text her today. Perhaps I ought to wait a bit."

"You want my advice? Don't play games. If you want to ring her, do it. Tell her why you feel you wanted to. If you're straight with her she won't see it as you coming across pushy or needy. Its a plus if you're not afraid to be uncool about your emotions. And if she doesn't want to follow your lead, then you'll know where you stand. Won't you?"

"Yes. I suppose I will." He seems happier.

“Now's a good time."

"Later."

We lapse into other subjects. Agree we should do this more often. And go our separate ways.

***

Sometimes I feel like a one-man dating agency or a relationship counsellor. What with Rory agonising over the new girlfriend and Patrick trying to work out whether it's a sane and sensible thing to see my sister. It isn't of course. And I'm not. I can listen and ask an occasionally pertinent question and even proffer the odd suggestion or two. Not too odd or they'd be rejected out of hand. But that's it.

Rory's okay with this level of support and encouragement. Patrick isn't. For some reason he thinks I should be facilitating his designs on Clare and doubts my motives for refraining from doing so are genuinely to protect him from irreparable long term damage.

An excited Rory. Reporting in.

"She's agreed to come out with me."

"Has she indeed? Where do you plan to take her?"

Rory nonplussed. "Not sure really. I don't know what she likes to do. I thought about a club or something but maybe dinner would be better. So we can talk. Find out about each other."

"You said she's a student?"

"Yes."

"We'll if my niece is anything to go by, she'll be sick of university food and she'll sell her soul for a decent meal. Book a table at The Wig and Mitre. Even their veggie stuff's good."

"God. I'd not thought that she might be a vegetarian."

"The Wig and Mitre."

"You're sure?"

"Yes. Spoil her. If you think she's worth it." Slip that last comment in from sheer devilment. If Rory's fussing this much, she must be quite special.

***

Rory in a rush to get away after training. Seems the new GF is becoming a fixture.

"How many times is that this week, Rory?"

"Three." Sheer glee in every line of his face. "Gotta go, Coach."

Matching actions to words. On the run.

***

Sitting in fireside chairs in a pub on Bailgate. Me with a small beer, a steak and ale pie and a side order of chips. Chunky ones. Rory sipping a soda water laced with lime. A plate of ham and eggs sits beside him, waiting to be tackled. Once in awhile somebody who knows us passes on the way to the bar, sometimes stopping for a quick word, sometimes just giving a nodded greeting.

"We need to start forward planning your career. I want you to sit down with somebody who can help."

"In what way?"

"Promotion. Starting to build your image and reputation beyond Lincoln. Raise your potential value in the transfer market. And the wages you can command. You won't be playing for the Imps too much longer whatever happens and we need some leverage so we have more say in who buys your contract. So we have to get you a real profile in the media. Get you noticed." Note the face he pulls. "I know it's not what you're comfortable with but it's important we do this and get it right."

"Well if you're sure."

"Good. The person I have in mind is local. We've an appointment at Stellar Public Relations tomorrow afternoon. With Megan Jones."

Which brings laughter. Lots of it. "I don't mind talking to Auntie Megan."

"She's your aunt?"

"We'll not technically. But she's one of my mum's oldest friends. You didn't know?"

"No I didn't. Why would I?" But I do now. Have to tread carefully.

***

As inner offices go it's a bit small with four people in it. Pending introductions, don't know the second woman, a petite blonde with a hard stare, but somehow feel I ought to recognise her. Even though I don't. Rory and I were expecting to be meeting Megan on her own.

"This is Mary Steiner. She works for the Daily Mirror. She mainly writes football, athletics and tennis. It's fortuitous she's in Lincoln today. She's doing a preliminary article on the Lincoln Road Race. I took the opportunity to ask her in to meet you."

"So the red-tops employ female sports journalists these days?"

"They're not quite the bastions of sexism they used to be. The Sun actually has more women on the sports pages than anybody. Even us."

Like her coming straight back in the face of my sarcasm. "I never knew that. Suppose I tend to read sports pages without paying much attention to the by-lines. And Lincoln City doesn't get a great deal of coverage."

"No. We don't cover the lower divisions as much as we probably should. But then it's all about circulation. We're planning a series of features on up-and-coming young players though and Megan convinces me your lad should be one of them."

Megan intervenes. "Perhaps start the series with you, Rory. So you can say thank you. But don't call me Auntie Megan."

Forestalled, Rory shuts his mouth.

"So where do we start?"

Mary wants a lot of biographical background. To know where he was born, how he came to be discovered . When he started to play first team football. His scoring record. Sit and let her draw Rory out. Slow beginnings becoming a flood of information. Rory seems to be enjoying talking by the end. Conclusion. Mary's good at her job. Probably has to be better than her male peers just to survive. Her pronouncement. "May be able to get you onto Sky Sports too. I do some Sunday morning shows for them. I think you'd come across well."

Rory's grimace says it all but he puts it into words anyway. "Help. What have you got me into, Coach?"

***

Nothing particularly special about this Sunday. It's not like I'm any sort of regular churchgoer. But sometimes there's an imperative to go. Something from the years spent accompanying my father while my anti-clerical mum kept the younger ones, Clare and Simon, at home with her.

The cathedral's nowhere near full. Find an aisle seat halfway back. Lower my head wondering why a God from whom I'm so removed most of the time would want to hear from me. But say a prayer of supplication anyway. Sit back. Look around. And freeze. A surge of excitement and hope. Four rows ahead of me, three women are sitting together on the opposite side of the aisle. I can only see their backs and quarter profiles as their heads turn to and fro in conversation. But I don't need a clearer view to know them. Ellie, Gail and Megan. And if you think I can concentrate on the service now... Responses, hymns, sermon, blessing. All passing in a blur. All my attention is reserved for the olive-skinned neck, the luxuriant raven hair and the dark stuff of a smart wool coat.

At the end, the organist's playing something soft and elegiac. People around me are getting to their feet and squeezing past me to leave. I'm still sitting there when the three of them reach my row of seats. And stop. Stand to acknowledge them. Gail says something I don't catch to her companions and they pass on, leaving us facing each other in a rapidly emptying cathedral. After a moment she takes the chair next to mine and I sit back down too. An older woman passing by gives us a sharp look and then smiles in recognition. I realise she's almost invariably here whenever I come into the cathedral. She moves away, still smiling to herself.

"Who's that?"

"I don't know. I think she must live here. She's always around but I don't actually know her name or what she does."

"Why are you here today? Were you following me?"

"No!" Only slightly indignant. "Just needed to come. I might have followed you if I'd seen you."

"At least that's honest of you."

"Have you ever walked round the cathedral? Properly? Looked at the carvings? Seen the Lincoln Imp?"

"No."

"Come with me." Take her hand in the cavernous emptiness of this place and walk her round the inner circumference of the massive walls. Point out bits of detail my dad showed me so many years ago. And the little carved devil sitting high up on the masonry. He's poised comfortably, one leg crossed over the other knee. Head up. Small horns jutting forward. And a smugly triumphant expression on his face. "He's on the football club badge. That's why they call them the Imps."

"I think he looks a bit lost. As though he's alighted up there but doesn't know where he is. Deep in the spiritual heart from which he was banished. In the fall."

"Evil living in the midst of sanctity."

"Are you referring to my husband?" An interestingly intuitive leap.

"No. Why would you think that?"

"He's a bully but he's not evil. That would be an over-statement. I didn't see it when we met. And when I did, it was too late."

"It's never too late. People can change. Or choose to take a different path. And life goes on."

"Perhaps." Shivers. "Can we get out of here? I have to go home. You could walk me partway down the hill if you like."

"I would like."

"You have to stop when I say so and let me go the rest of the way on my own."

I'd agree any terms she sees fit to set. So I say "Yes." And if we walk in silence, it's neither awkward nor cause for regret. Just the way it is.

***

The article appears the following Monday. Shorter than I'd hoped but making much of the fortuitous timing of Rory's weekend hat-trick. The accompanying picture taken at training is clipped or photo-shopped or whatever they do to remove me from the left hand edge. I'm pleased to say.

It reaches right round the world inside forty-eight hours and I'm called by Umit, among others. He rings to say "Nice one, son." Or the Turkish equivalent.

Rory is pretty phlegmatic. Not much risk of his head being turned by a few column inches and a grainy photograph even in a national paper. Not for a wonder kid who has commanded, not merely once but twice, the whole back page of the Lincolnshire Echo.

***

The club's chairman is delighted with the press coverage. Conversely the manager is apoplectic but can't vent his anger because the chairman's so pleased. But the interest of one is the potential future monetary return on Rory while the other just sees the probability of losing his star player in the next few months and the impossibility of replacing him. Funny thing club management and the diverse interests of its hierarchy. Puts me in mind of certain property transactions.

***

Clare and Patrick. On or off? Who bloody knows? Ask my sister and she ducks the issue. Ask Patrick and he treats the subject as a joke. Like I can't tell the levity is forced. I think he's hurting and doesn't know what to do except lick his wounds and wait. Remind you of anyone else?

***

Sudhir is around. See him in the streets from time to time. Sometimes he says "Hello." Sometimes he blanks me. Can't see any logical pattern so let's assume the determining factor is what's going on in his own life and nothing to do with me.

***

Peter Ross fails to give up the ghost and is sent home to recuperate. Phone to find out if he needs anything but my ex-wife is apparently moving in to look after him. Lets me off the hook completely. Do make one strong suggestion to him. "Give your file to Clare."

"I'll think about it."

Stubborn or what?

***

Catching up with Rory before we start another training session.

"What did your new girlfriend think of the Mirror article?"

"Actually I didn't show it to her. It would have been like boasting to me. If she picks it up for herself that's fine but I don't want to wave a copy under her nose. She's a student. She probably despises tabloids."

"Fair point." But I know that's rationalisation after the fact. The real issue is his discomfort with the limelight. He'll have to learn though. Going where I think he's going.

Chapter XV Now: April to May

I'm pretty wrong about one thing. I thought or hoped that the yo-yo effect was over.

Gail. Sitting in a quiet corner in a wine bar.

"I don't think I can do this. My life's had more than its fair share of problems. And I'm scared to death at the merest thought of confrontation or violence. You know that. Even the mood in crowds outside a football match worries me. I have to have peace. And now...I've found out all about you. And I can't risk it."

Stay calm. Panic isn't going to help. "You're very brave. Coming and saying it straight to me. It took a lot of courage to do that. But what is it you think you know? You've spent a lot of time with me over the last few months. You probably know me better than my own family does. Are you frightened of me? In any way at all? Have I ever done anything to scare you? What have you been told? Why the change? Why can't you trust your own judgement of me?"

She's shaking. Controls herself. Tries to look me in the eyes. Fails. "I found out how you attacked Mickey. How many stitches he needed. Tony showed me a photo. Mickey with that massive scar on his face. He says you meant to kill him."

"And you believe that?"

"He doesn't have any reason to lie."

"Of course he does. He's trying to manipulate your emotions. To control you. Keep you."

What I want to do is retaliate. Tell her the nature of Tony's business dealings. Assuming she doesn't already know, deep down. How people get hurt by his enforcers when they don't pay up. But I know that's just diversion tactics. We have to deal with my history first.

"He was telling the truth though. I know when he's lying to me. He said it wasn't the only time you assaulted someone."

"I suppose he wasn't lying. Just being economical with the truth. For his own ends. This is pretty strange you asking this stuff. You have all these separate boxes you keep people in. And all these things you never talk about and I don't press you on. Your parents. Your marriage. Your children. Your life away from me. But you want me to tell you...to confess all my secrets..."

She sits there dumbstruck. I've never spoken to her like this before. Perhaps I should have. But I can't even be angry with her. She is who she is and you can't really love somebody and wish bits of them different. I have a dreadful choice to make. I can tell her what she wants to know and in all probability lose her. Or I can carry on hiding behind the defences which have served me pretty well all these years. In which case I'll definitely lose her. No option at all really. Except I don't know if I can do it.

Silence. My turn to look away. Wonder how to start. How to face beginning. In the end just do it.

"It all started fairly innocuously. Knocking off my cap. Chucking it over a wall. Name calling. Emptying my satchel. Trampling on my homework. It kept getting worse. Until I was being picked on every day. If I didn't avoid them I got punched. It was a gang of older boys. Led by Mickey Lenahan. He was fourteen. I was nearly twelve. I stopped going out at break times. But it wasn't even safe in the classroom unless there was a teacher there."

Pause to get my nerve together. I've never told anyone what really happened. Apart from the police. And the social worker who sat in as an appropriate adult. Well that's what they call it these days. Because I wouldn't let them bring my own Mum and Dad in. "One Sunday. Just before the summer holidays. I don't know why I was on my own that day. But they cornered me in a play area and dragged me into the bushes." Deep breath. "Two of them held me down. And Mickey unzipped... And he tried. But he couldn't keep an erection. And one of his friends started laughing. And he began kicking me. A lot. When they left, they threw my shorts and pants up a tree. So."

Shrug. The really hard bit's done. Might as well finish the story. "I couldn't tell my parents. I just knew they wouldn't cope with it. The next day I went into school early. Broke into the grounds-man's hut. I was looking for a knife or some secateurs. What I found was a load of beer bottles. He was a closet alcoholic. Took one and waited by the school gates and when Mickey arrived I smashed the bottle against the pillar and rammed it in his face. I told the police most of it and they repeated enough of it to convince Mickey's parents to hush things up. No charges. I had to move to another school. That was that. Except that I was angry with everybody for quite a while. Until I discovered football. Or it discovered me."

Steal a glance at Gail. She's rock-like in stillness. Looks appalled. Gingerly her hand settles upon mine as it grips the table edge. Squeezes. Just a little. "Tony didn't tell me. He didn't know."

Delusion. "Of course he did. Mickey always had his little brother with him. Tony was there. He watched it all. And laughed."

I want to say something else to her. "He's another kind of monster, your husband. The same as his brother. He may not use his fists but he damages you in a thousand and one ways, every day of your life." She doesn't give me the chance to say it. Gets up, speechless. Just a hint of tears. And goes away.

As for me, I can't cry. There are no tears left in me to waste on the Lenahans. Nor on myself.

Sit a bit longer. Pay for the coffee. Ethan's waiting in the bookshop across the street. Sees me come out. Falls into step. Walks home with me. Both of us deep in our own thoughts.

***

A week for shocks. Another one without warning. No foreboding sense of a life ending. Just an unexpected arrival at the front door and my sister coming into the hall in schizophrenic mode. Half uniformed presence, half concerned sibling. Telling me herself with an arm around my shoulder because she thinks she should. How they've found Sandrine. Washed up on the Hessle foreshore.

"Well we think it's Sandrine."

"Do you need me to identify her?" Feel impelled to offer though its nothing I want to have to face.

"No." Bluntly matter of fact. "She's been stuck in the estuary mud long enough for the water and the fish to do their worst. What's left is pretty skeletal. Some rags of clothing. A cash card in her jeans pocket. How we know it's probably her. We'll trace her parents in France and do DNA tests to be sure."

"How do we tell Daniel his Mum's dead?"

"I don't know. You could ask Diane what she'd do. How she'd do it."

"Your social worker friend?"

"Yes. I'm a bit slow though. We can get a swab from Daniel of course."

"He'll be home from school soon. Jimmy's gone to collect him. How did she end up in the water?"

"Jumped. Off the Humber Bridge. A couple of months ago. It usually takes a while before a body comes up. Some never do. There's some CCTV footage of a woman going over towards the middle of January. That was probably her."

"Poor girl." No tears. Just a sense of inevitability now we know what's happened. Hindsight is always right. "Would you like a cup of tea while you're here?"

"Yes please. A quick one."

And that's it. Washed away with Earl Grey. Does that seem callous? Suppose it does. It's just…Well now we know.

***

Council of war after Daniel's bedtime. Around the kitchen table with Rory, Jaki, and Ethan. A very short agenda. Only one item of discussion. We could draw lots of course. In the end we wear Rory down until he volunteers to tell Daniel in the morning. As gently as he's able. It's Saturday tomorrow so no school. The question is whether Daniel will take it in. And over how much time he'll need it clarified and re-explained in the months and years to come. He isn't quite six yet after all.

***

The inquest opens. We're there in the courtroom. We meaning Clare, Ethan and me. Gail's at work. Rory's training.

Jaki's at lectures. Daniel's at school. There's no sign of Tony Lenahan.

The Humberside coroner starts proceedings with a short statement about the finding of a body at Hessle five days earlier and why this triggers the necessity to hold an inquest. Identification evidence is called. An officer explains the difficulties, the state of the body as retrieved, the possessions found on it and the need to await the results of DNA samples taken from her closest relative. The results of the post-mortem are read into the record. Cause of death unknown awaiting further tests. The only other issues raised are the presently unanswerable questions as to when and where the deceased was last seen alive and by whom. Together with the vexed question of how, without a car, she reached the presumed location of her demise, some thirty-nine miles away from the city.

The hearing is adjourned to a date to be fixed. We stand. The coroner leaves the courtroom. We wander outside. The local reporter hurries off to file his copy. I check my watch. The whole thing took eleven minutes. Not a second longer.

***

"Hey Clare. Why didn't the Lenahan connection come up? Or her drug habit?"

"They will. But we don't want to tip the press off too early. Just leave things to us from here on in."

"Okay Sis. Although you said that to me before. When I left for Istanbul."

***

Had to happen sooner or later. Rory would surely have preferred it to be later but you can't always choose for things to happen when it's most convenient. This is completely unexpected. No chance to plan for cushioned approaches and soft landings. Straight into a full-on confrontation. And basically it's all down to Gail. She it is who decides to come to see me. Without any pre-arrangement. No prior phone call. Presume she wanted to see me on the spur of the moment. I hope that's it. She probably thought to catch me ensconced untidily in the mess of the weekend's newspapers and the aftermath of whatever Sunday lunch I'd rustled up for myself. Instead she walks into a more complicated version of happy families than she could ever have anticipated.

An unsuspecting Jaki goes to the door for her. Thinking it's Rory not his mother. She recovers quickly enough and the greetings are effusive and loud enough to give us some fractional warning. Not that you can clear much away in a few seconds. And I certainly can't hide a five year old and all the evidence of his games and cars scattered across the wood-block flooring.

The lounge door swings wider before I can reach it and Gail walks in with Jaki in her wake. I do get a kiss. A fleeting one before the countdown to Armageddon kicks in. Actually it's a very quiet and internalised crisis whose only sign is the swiftly controlled glimpse of shock on Gail's face. And her voice doesn't shake or in any other way reveal anything of either agitation or surprise. It's matter of fact and gentle.

"Who's this then?" And she's down on her hands and knees with Daniel, making brmm-brmm noises and asking "Can I work this one?"

He smiles at her. The big infectious grin - so like his brother. "Of course. Who are you?"

"Do you know Rory?"

"Yes, silly. He's my brother."

Not a hint of a flinch. "Well I'm Rory's mum."

Daniel looks puzzled for a moment. As if he hasn't ever considered the possibility of Rory having a mother of his own. Then accepts it. Hands her an old blue Corgi toy. One of mine I think. And makes room for her beside him. Next to the wooden garage which is currently his favourite thing.

Ethan says nothing. The nuances are probably lost on him. Exchange a glance with Jaki. Take her arm and pull her into the hall. "Coffee and brandy on a tray. We may need them. And phone Rory. Get him over here. Soon as possible".

No arguments. The great thing about Jaki in an emergency situation. She does what she's told.

Gail's lying propped up on one elbow. Consciously or not, mimicking Daniel. Go and sit myself down on the floor cross-legged close behind her. I can still almost manage a lotus position. Maintaining it for long; now that's another story but in short bursts... Stroke her shoulder. She twists her body to look up at me. Smiles.

Keep it to a low murmur. "Are you alright?"

"Yes."

"Good." Simple affirmations. Vitally important.

"Would you like a drink?"

"I'd love a cup of tea."

"Okay. Your command is my wish."

Heave myself to my feet and head back to the kitchen to countermand an element of my previous request to Jaki. The kettle's not boiled yet so tea's as easy as coffee.

At some point Daniel takes Gail by the hand to show her his room. Then downstairs again to tour the garden. Leaving them to it seems the wisest move. They're still out there when Rory arrives. Show him where they are and watch from the kitchen window as he approaches his mum and hugs her. I'd like to be a fly on the garden fence for the huddled conversation which ensues. But I can guess what needs to be said on both sides.

She comes in to find me still in the kitchen. Making up sandwiches with cold roast beef left over from lunch. Straight into my arms. Not before, divining her intent, I've discarded the carving knife. I think this means its going to be alright but it doesn't hurt to check.

"How are you feeling?"

Her reply surprises me. "Angry." She doesn't show it.

"Why angry?"

"With him. With myself for not seeing it clearly enough before. For not having the courage to tackle him. Letting him walk all over me and my boys. And for this last betrayal... The worst of all. When he wouldn't let me have another one..."

"It's not Daniel's fault though."

"No. It's not. He's such a lovely boy. And the spitting image of Rory."

"Yes he is. Does that make it better or worse?"

"A bit easier. It means I can't hide from the facts. And I know I do that quite a lot. Have done. Not going to anymore."

"And you know how I feel about you?"

"Uh-huh. I think...I think I love you too." The words pushed out quickly so she can't retract them.

"That's just as well really."

"Why?"

"Because I don't want anything one-sided. Wouldn't be any point in that."

"No. There wouldn't."

"Do you want Rory to take you home? You can stay for tea. Got loads of food in."

"I'm not going home. It isn't my home anymore. Can I stay here?"

Pretend to consider it carefully. And give in. "Yeah." Lot of enthusiasm vested in one slurred word. Think some more. "What about Liam?"

"He's on a sleepover at a schoolmate's. I'll get him tomorrow. But what do I do with Boo?"

"Bring her down here too. I don't mind. She'll be fine."

"Rory could pick her up and some other stuff I need."

"Not on his own he's not. Ethan and Jimmy can go with him."

"Good. Need a hand with those sandwiches?"

"You make a pot of tea, sweet girl."

"Sure thing."

Shared tasks. The silence of easy companionship. The real thing. Can't fake it. Or beat it.

Sorted.

Never that simple though. Is it?

***

It's like Christmas all over again. The house full of people unused to living under the same roof with each other but striving to accommodate everybody else's funniosities.

First impressions of Liam highly favourable. Tall like his older brother but stockier build and lighter hair. A face you'd call determined rather than handsome. Almost pugnacious but saved by the warmth of a genuine smile, even teeth and eyes sparkling with both mischief and enthusiasm for life. And far less reserved. The sort of person my grandfather might have rewarded with his ultimate accolade of praise. 'He's a man you could steal horses with.' Reserved for the warm-hearted, the strong and the loyal to a fault. A description tailor-made for Liam. He's curious as hell about Daniel but really good with him. Almost conducting an unconscious competition to rival Rory in the young boy's affections. Especially playing with him after school. Although that may owe as much to avoiding having to tackle his own homework.

I'm not particularly aware of being scrutinised and weighed in my turn by Liam but I seem to pass the test because within a few days he's chattering freely to me about all manner of things. From the nonsensical to the deadly serious. Unlike Rory he doesn't ever seem to play his cards close to his chest. What you see is literally what you get.

Liam's espousal of living at Trescombe helps Gail to settle. Calms some of her fears about the future. Enables her to focus on a routine encompassing long days building the business she and Jenny are establishing in Newark, returning to a household run largely by the men in her life. Liam helps me do most things and loves to cook. Exercising Boo is the other shared responsibility in between bouts at school for him and coaching work for me. Jaki notionally still functions and is paid as our cleaner but has a new and able assistant and bosses him mercilessly.

"He might as well get used to it." Her mantra when I question whether its a wise approach before they're even married.

As for me, I feel like all my Christmases have come at once. Having this woman to share my life, my home, my bedroom is simply wonderful. Not easy at times admittedly. But worth every tricky moment we have to navigate together. Finding out what happiness feels like. Prosaic and sublime. Often at one and the same time.

We hear nothing from Tony at all. No kickback. No threats. No contact in any shape or form. Begin to relax although I know it's dangerous to assume too much. Keep Ethan and Jimmy on. I'm not that stupid. Tony will always be a shark with the cold nature of a predatory fish. And very sharp teeth. So Jimmy carries on chauffeuring Daniel to school and now takes Liam too while Ethan covers as many of the other gaps in our security as he can manage.

***

Not that everything is devoid of tension. Today it’s rising like early mist off a lake. Generated by the imminent arrival of my mother for tea. And of course panic's infectious. So Gail, Jaki, Rory, and even Ethan are all on edge. Only Daniel seems his normal happy self. He's down on the floor playing with his cars, uncaring whether the old woman about to come through the door likes him or not. His newfound sense of security is astonishing and a real credit to all of us. Let's not be modest here.

When Mum arrives, go to the door myself and let her in. She hugs me. Prolongs it and without any extrinsic evidence, I realise she's as nervous as I am about the meeting to come. Whether Clare's had words with her or not, she seems to realise how important it is for her to get on with Gail. And with Rory too. That there's a real risk of alienating both her son and her grand-daughter if she doesn't. If she is judged lacking in warmth and empathy by the interlopers in her family's life. The newcomers who have without so much as a by-your-leave stolen our hearts and our capacity to put her first as the matriarch of all she surveys.

"It's alright, Mum. They won't bite."

Her hand presses my arm. In gratitude? Certainly for emotional rather than physical support. And advances bravely towards the doom which never comes.

Fast forward an hour and wonder what all the concern was about. We're on the third cup of tea in an atmosphere of near harmony. Daniel demands and has become the centre of attention, a position yielded by my mother with every sign of good grace. She makes a real fuss of him. Produces chocolate from her handbag. Finds common ground with Gail about the boy's unfortunate circumstances and our shared duty to put things, which remain unspecified, right for him.

That Daniel provides the bridge for Mum to cross and reach accord with Gail and Rory makes things so much easier. Although Rory does his best too. Quiet charm personified, he sits with an arm round Jaki, a very visible demonstration of the strength of his feelings for her. I'd like the same degree of physical contact with Gail but she's opted tactically to share the other settee with Mum and I have to be content with conspiratorial glances and smiles.

Anyway I play bountiful host, declining offers of help, making fresh drinks at regular intervals and laying out the makings of a high tea to remember on the sideboard, covered for the occasion with my fine Turkish linen table cloth. Don't ask. I was bested by a wizened old crone who saw me coming down the road in Alanya. And settled for twice what I'd have paid for it on Amazon or eBay. I can pretend to myself that's it's a hand-sewn heirloom but it isn't. So might as well use it. And it sets off my china plates, laden with jam and cream scones, slices of coca-cola baked ham, a house specialty shown me some years ago by an iconoclastic, lazy chef, Lincolnshire pork pies, beetroot salad, a favourite of Mum's, plenty of healthy green rubbish and slices of Patrick's birthday cake, the size of which so easily defeated the guests at his party that he insisted we take most of the remainder home. To the benefit of our guest who loves a good fruit cake. Even one she hasn't made herself.

My mother has to point out the obvious to Gail. "The dinner service belonged to my mother of course."

"It's lovely." My sweet liar. Know full well she doesn't think that at all. In fact not so long ago she was on at me to get rid of it and buy some modern, plain white crockery and the decision's already been made to pack it away for occasional use like today and let Gail loose to find a new set she likes. I trust her taste. Mine's non-existent on the immaterial minutiae of daily living. I can see when something works. But the process of narrowing down the choices to get there evades me. So I'll leave it to my expert shopper and style guru and just go along for the ride, credit card at the ready.

Anyway before long they're discussing recovering the settees as well as the long-promised replacement curtains. I may turn out to be Smith-Ryan's best ever customer. There's a whole three-storey house to tackle if Gail gets her teeth into the challenge. As I'm sure she will.

Eventually Daniel gets bored and insists on dragging Ethan away from his paperwork. He's been lurking in the study when not unobtrusively helping me in the kitchen. He's not entirely comfortable with the concept or the actuality of mothers but is trying to mask it with activity. Now he has to come in and answer Mum's questions before he's allowed to take up his usual position on the floor playing with Daniel.

It almost seems as though Mum's taxi arrives too soon in the end so successfully has the afternoon gone. Go out to wave her goodbye. As the cab disappears seize my chance and with an arm under her knees and the other round her back, I swing Gail up and carry her, with her arms around my neck, kicking and shrieking, back into the house.

"Gail. You weigh a ton." Of course she doesn't. Only the existence of the clearing up and the unfairness of leaving it to Ethan prevents an early exodus straight upstairs to bed.

She whispers in my ear. "I'll make it up to you later."

"And I'll hold you to that."

"Good."

***

Take Gail to Pimento's again. Becoming our favourite haunt. Find a quiet corner where we can link fingers across the table while consuming good coffee and even better cakes.

Today bringing the other serious conversation I knew we'd have to get to sooner or later. The subject of 'Istanbul' or more precisely 'Why did you go?'

"You must see it from my point of view. I felt completely abandoned. We'd got through some difficult stuff and then you up and left. Left me. No explanation. No proper goodbye. Just the note you left for Megan to give me. And it said nothing. Look. I kept it. Read it for yourself and think how you'd be if I left you with just a note like that."

I don't have to read the smoothed out sheet of white paper Gail puts in front of me to remember exactly what it says. I didn't just write it. I slaved over it. Almost wept with the unfairness of it all. Finished it with a forlorn sense of hopelessness. Added the postscript as a necessary afterthought. Packed my bag. And left it for her to collect.

Dearest Darling Girl,

If I had to say the things I have to write in this letter to you in person, I would falter. I wouldn't have the courage to go through with what I have to do. I have to disappear for now or otherwise three innocent young people are going to be seriously hurt. I don't know how long it'll be. I wish things were different. I wish I could see a way of not going. I love you.

XXXXXXX

PS If you need anything while I'm gone speak to Clare.

“You want me to tell you how it was.”

"Yes. What was going on? Who made you go?”

"I think you already know the answer to that." Gail’s head goes down. I take it she understands I’m talking about Tony, her husband.

Chapter XVI Then: March to April

Just as the best and worst elements of my life are due to people, it's also the case that it's the doorbell which heralds the most and least welcome interruptions into my day. On this occasion to my astonishment it's Sudhir. Brazenly standing on my doorstep as though he has every right to intrude on my space. He earns himself a glare but shrugs it off nonchalantly.

"Got a message from the boss. He wants to see you. Told me to say he's asking politely. But can you come now?"

"What does he want to talk about?"

"Don't know. But he says he'll make it worth your while. Will you come?"

Now I'm truly astounded. The thought of Tony Lenahan giving me anything, even the time of day. Not going to show it though. "Where does he want to meet?"

"He's here. He's come to you."

"Well he's not coming in my house."

"No...no. He's having coffee at the old grandstand." Which places him about three hundred yards from my front door. As the crow flies.

"I'll get my jacket."

"Thank you. I'll go and tell him you're coming."

On principle, it takes me several minutes to track down the right garment. And put some stuff in the inside pocket. Waiting is good for the Lenahan soul.

It's not too damp underfoot so I cut over the common, check the intermittent traffic and cross the main road. A long black car is parked under the refurbished racecourse sign, now bearing a list of dates for council-organised events. Sudhir is leaning on the car's wing with his arms folded. Tony Lenahan is sitting on the grandstand's lower steps holding a cardboard, takeaway coffee cup. He doesn't rise as I get nearer. Merely gestures, a flourish of his fingers, to the young woman with him. She correctly interprets this as a

dismissal, stands carefully on her high heels, wraps her bla fun fur coat around herself and stalks over to Sudhir and the expensive Mercedes.

Tony nods by way of greeting, leaving it to me to speak first. I keep it simple. "Hello."

"Hello. Thank you very much for coming." Oozing attempted charm. He must know it won't wash with me. Perhaps it's becoming habitual. A new front he's trying on as he moves into a new decade of his life.

I could respond with calculated rudeness. Or I could wait until I find out what he wants. The latter seems the wiser course of action. "Too curious to stay away." Minor sarcasm always likely to go over Tony's head.

"Shall we sit? Or would you prefer to walk?"

"It's a nice day. Let's walk."

"Okay." He places his coffee down on the step. Leaves it there for someone else to clear up. Heaves himself to his feet. He'll have a problem with his girth in a few years time if he doesn't watch it. Carefully dusts down his overcoat and falls into step beside me.

"What do you want with me? I'm not the most likely man in Lincoln to do you a favour."

"Of course you aren't. But this is business. And I want to buy something you own."

"At a fair price?"

"Yes. At a generous price."

"What do I have that you'd be prepared to pay for. I'm not selling you my house if that's what you want."

"No!" Slight note of exasperation intruding. "Your shares."

"What shares?"

"Your shares in the club."

"The football club?"

"Yes. Your shares in the football club."

An affirming nod would have done better than this continuation of the repetitive verbal ping pong we seem to have fallen into. I'm not inclined to stop it either because

deep down I hope it's annoying him. "Why do you want to buy my shares in the football club?"

"Just business." And he names a price about double what they're worth. Which isn't that much. I multiply his figure by a factor of ten and he doesn't flinch. Simply counter-offers by halving my suggestion. My suspicions are well and truly roused and screaming now.

"I'm not sure I wish to sell."

He doesn't so much as pause to take a breath. "Alright. I'll match your price."

"It wasn't an offer. Just an exploration of what they're worth to you."

"Why wouldn't you want to sell? The shares aren't worth you hanging on to them as it is."

"Perhaps not. But you're going to make a lot of money or you wouldn't be prepared to pay me so much more than their current value."

I get an admission out of him. "I will make money. But I'm reflecting that in what I'm willing to pay. What will you take for them? And think carefully. I might stop being nice and find another way to persuade you to let me have them."

"I don't think you will. If it's a proper business deal then you need to do this legitimately. Without comebacks. I don't think you can afford to tarnish this by leaning on me. Or anyone else. And anyway you must know who my sister is."

"Of course I know." He sounds offended for a fraction of a second. As though I've questioned whether he has his fingers anywhere but on the pulse of this city. "Look. You're right. I want to do this deal legitimately. So what can I offer you to sell?"

"You can tell me your plan. Be honest with me."

We've run out of grass verge to walk on. Time to cross the road. Back onto the common. Which won't suit his black Italian lace-ups. Set off again.

"Okay. I'll be straight with you."

"Go on."

"The club has some land I'd like to develop."

"Why would the club sell the land to you?"

"Not to me. To a building company I have an interest in."

"Same difference. Are we talking about Harrigan Homes?"

"Yes, we are. You've heard of them then?"

"I have. It came up in passing. But why would the club sell at all? They could build on the land for their own profit."

"They wouldn't get planning permission."

"You're sure of that? And you would?"

"Yes." Staggeringly confident. Wonder how and why.

"Well even if you're right, they might not see it that way. They could just hang onto the land for now."

"I've already bought a stake in the club. And probably enough other shareholders will support me."

"I thought the council owned a block of shares."

"May be." He's obviously not bothered. So what influence has he got at the council?

"Why do you need my shares then? I could just hang onto them and if at the end of the day the club makes a big profit out of a deal with you, I'd get a decent dividend back for a change."

"People listen to you. And I don't want you voting against me."

"Well that sounds like the real truth. As you see it."

"Yes. It is. So will you sell to me?"

"I don't know yet. Where's the land?"

He tells me. The site doesn't ring any alarm bells with me. I doubt it's particularly sensitive. And given government targets for new housing...He might well be able to develop it for a decent return.

"I'll think about it."

"Thank you." There it is again. That careful politeness. "I'll be in touch in a few days time." For a moment it seems like he's going to offer me a handshake. But he thinks better of it and the moment passes. We walk back side by side saying nothing further until he says, "Goodbye then."

I respond in kind. Sudhir opens the rear door of the car. Tony and Sandrine climb in. They drive away. Eventually shake my head and walk home.

***

Rufus Mitchell corners me. Club Secretary. Avuncular. Overweight. Sixtyish. Seldom seen around the training pitch. Must have made a special journey to be here today.

"Glad I've seen you. Needed to ask you something. Not sure when we last updated our CRB checks. If I get a form down to you, can you get it completed and back to me quickly so I can get it in? Should have done it before the start of the season."

My astonishment clearly shows. The football club and the Criminal Records Bureau are at best distantly acquainted. ""Just routine, old man." Which means its not routine at all. Someone's put him up to it. Someone trying to deliver me a prod about something else entirely.

"Okay." What else would you want me to say?

***

Follow on meeting with Tony about the blasted stake in the football club.

Short but less than sweet.

"You do understand that I have to have this sorted, don't you? I need you to sell me your shares. Or I'll have to take them. And I will. Believe me."

Actually I do believe Tony but I'm not admitting that to him yet. Need to tell Clare where I've got to first.

Clare listens to the recordings from my dictaphone and confirms what I already know. The quality is average with plenty of crackles and occasional drop-outs. But the voices are clear enough to transcribe. The main problem is the content which is not explicit enough for certainty of legal process. Clare's words not mine. I'd say not enough to prosecute the bastard. So I need another meeting to draw him out. To Clare's obvious concern. Place the call. Make the arrangements for tomorrow. Go home.

***

The doorbell and the slamming of the flat of a hand on the glazed upper door panel are accompanied by the keening wails of someone in extreme pain or fear or both. All imparting urgency. Tear downstairs and fling the door wide. For a panic-stricken niece. She throws herself into my arms and her tears soak my shirt-front as I try to squeeze the hysteria out of her. And for awhile fail. Slam the door. Manhandle her into the lounge. Would get her a brandy but she won't let go of me so I can reach it. As best I can, I examine what I can see of her. No apparent sign of physical injury. No blood. Or obviously broken bones. No marks on her face or hands. Stroke her hair. Let her cry and babble. Slowly dying away until a degree of coherence emerges.

And she tells me about the man who was waiting outside her flat for her to get back from lectures. A man who pinned her to a wall and gave her a message for me to heed. A man who terrified her beyond imagining with what he said he'd do to her. And clamped her mouth and nose with a large gloved hand until she almost passed out just to prove he was serious. All in broad daylight.

Put her to bed in the room next to mine. And phone her mother. Clare needs to hear this now. The ante has risen dramatically. We both need to be part of the decision. What do I do next?

I have a live recording of the MC5 live at Detroit 1969. I wasn't there. Born yes but still only an infant. But I can imagine Brother JC Crawford at the microphone. Ranting at the crowd. And the words are engraved in my memory as he screams them. 'Brothers and sisters. Let me see your hands. Let me see…see your hands out there...Now is the time for each and every one of you to decide whether you are going to be part of the problem or part of the solution...' Put it another way. For me it's time to wake up and smell the coffee.

***

Sit in St Hugh's Choir in the cathedral to think. It's cool and peaceful. A place which lets you be yourself. Lets your mind travel wherever it needs to go. Solitude and solutions. Get up with a clear sense of what I need to do to provoke Tony into useable admissions. Leaving via the main west door I pass an upright and lovely lady of indeterminate age on her way in. Her white hair is long and immaculately coiled on top of her head and her coat and black trousers are pressed to a fault. I hold the door open and she murmurs her thanks. Her smile stays with me as I turn up my collar and tighten my scarf against the wind outside. Spring has definitely been delayed.

***

Time to see how far Tony can be pushed to go. No walking around this time allowing weather and vehicle background noise to intrude. We're meeting in a quiet hotel corner. Coffee in front of us which he's ordered. I'm determined both that he'll pay for the refreshments and that I won't touch them.

"The answer is no. Do we have anything else to talk about?"

"Are you sure? I feel the ground has shifted and you should reconsider."

"Why would I do that?"

"Two reasons. Either of them should suffice. First some complaints are going to be made about you. In writing. Your employers are going to have to suspend you and somehow the media are going to get hold of the story which will be disastrous. It's going to come out how your sister, such a high-ranking police officer too, has been covering up for you. They'll have to suspend her as well I expect. And the investigation's going to be long and nasty." And he explains exactly how nasty it's going to be and who's going to be dragged into it. Unfortunately the sound on the tape and any transcript will struggle to bear witness to the lip-smacking enthusiasm he displays. Nor the malice in his eyes as he leans over the low table to point an emphasising finger repeatedly at my chest. Forcing me to face the absolute realisation that nobody matters to him. Everyone is disposable if they're standing in his way. I knew I was but not the other lives he's proposing so casually to ruin. What he's saying he'll do is terrifying in its amorality. He's not finished either.

"The other thing you need to bear in mind is that everybody around you's at risk now. Your niece. Your mother. Even your girlfriend." I wonder how he knows about

Gail. "You don't have a choice any more. You sell me your shares. I'm a man of my word. I'll pay you what I agreed to pay. You take the money. But now I want something else from you. I want you to disappear completely. From Lincoln. From this country. For nine months minimum. If you don't then there's a man who will want to get better acquainted with Miss James and your other loved ones." He defines what he means by acquainted with graphic precision. "Your niece has already met him of course. I don't think she'll be keen to see him again. Will she?"

All salesmen try to get you into a position in which you have to agree with them and close the deal. Tony Lenahan's doing exactly the same thing.

"No she won't." My decision's made. "Send the transfer documents and the money over to my solicitor's office in the morning. Patrick Butler at MacFarlanes. I'll sign it straight away. I'll need to make some personal arrangements but I'll be gone by the end of the week."

"That's a good lad." He has the gall to slap me on the back as he gets up to walk out.

Leaving me shaking. With rage and fear. The feelings I remember so clearly from when I was eleven and my only recourse was to a broken beer bottle. But this time the same sense of helplessness is absent. Finger the dictaphone in my pocket. And tell myself "Gotcha."

***

The timing of my arrival at Patrick's office is fortuitous. Sudhir is standing on the steps examining the brass plate. A large brown envelope in his hands.

"You're in the right place."

I get a nod in greeting. This is business. Serious business. He follows me in.

Patrick's secretary, Joni, rises to give me a kiss. She's wearing a bright dress. Bold yellow on blue print. Great with her colouring. Tell her so. Why nobody's snapped her up already I don't know. Apart from her own impeccably high standards. And the long hours she works for Patrick of course. Introduce Sudhir to her.

"He's free if you want to go straight through."

The door is open. But tap on it anyway. For form's sake. Allow him to bellow, "Come in." Master of his own ship and all that. Pretty sure he's never met Sudhir. Formally anyway. So do the necessary honours and they shake hands. Patrick gets more respect from Sudhir than I do. Just for being a solicitor.

The envelope is handed over and Patrick extracts the contents.

"I'll need to check the wording. And I have to talk it though with my client. Can you give us a few minutes please. Joni will make you a coffee if you'd like one."

Monosyllabic acknowledgement. Patrick isn't to know Sudhir doesn't drink coffee. Ever. And tea only in extremis. Or down the market making common cause with the porters. His preference is fruit juice or water. He's got no chance of the former unless he's very lucky. I know the normal contents of the office fridge so unless Joni's got secret supplies...

The door closes behind Sudhir and Patrick leans back in his big swivel chair.

"Are you sure you want to do this?"

"No. But I think I have to."

"In that case let's read the stuff together. Firstly does the cheque have the right number of zeros on it?"

"Don't let me forget. I need you to organise a line of credit for me when we've sorted this deal out."

"Yeah. Yeah. First things first. Now this deed of transfer states..." Lots of boring detail. The legal code. Never use one word when three will suffice. Never used a short word when a longer one will sound more impressive. Never over-punctuate. In fact never use punctuation at all in case it makes things easier to read. Or understand. Never use English when a Latin alternative is available. Never simplify when you can complicate. Or clarify instead of obfuscate. Learned from Day One in law school. Drilled in until it becomes instinctive. And informs every invoice.

Anyway the crux of it all seems okay and the price is what Tony offered. Much more than the shares are worth. Rather less than I asked for. About right really. Patrick gets Joni in to witness my signature. Dictates a letter of acknowledgement and a receipt. Joni produces clean copies for Patrick to sign. Puts them in a fresh envelope with the share certificates from the safe and gives them to Sudhir to take away with the executed deed. Gives him a reminder about registering the transaction and stamp duty.

"Thank you." Another handshake for Patrick. Another nod to me. And gone.

"Now," says Patrick. " What the hell are you up to?"

***

For a fair price, the taxi driver drops me in the heart of the old city. Not too far from the Galata Bridge with its ever present army of anglers, some fishing for sport, some doubtless, by the look of them, for their evening meal. Plenty of affordable hotels in the backstreets. The nearest with vacancies is called The Agan. Not sure what the name signifies. If anything. Not untypical of this part of town though. Small. Comfortably furnished. Decently maintained. Good facilities except in all probability for an intermittent hot water supply, if my experience is anything to go by. Pretty anonymous too. A world away from the Hiltons and the Hyatts on the other side of the river.

Drop my bag in my room with its limited view across the narrow street to the rooms over the restaurant directly opposite the hotel entrance. Organise one of the bank of safety deposit boxes located in the foyer for myself and lock my passport, new iPad, keys and spare credit cards away. Carrying with me only the minimum I need.

What did we do before we had mobile phones? I suppose thinking back we went incommunicado. Seems impossible now that we have texting and an instant ability to be connected to any other phone number in the world from the lump of plastic and circuitry we carry everywhere we go. So my first visit, dodging oncoming trams and cars, is to a little electronics shop I've been before. Last time I came here it was to buy a replacement camera case. Today I want a Turkcell pay-as-you-go SIM card. Stick it in my bombproof smartphone. That's a euphemism. Right? I mean it's shockproof and waterproof. You can drop it in the sea or bounce it off the wall. It won't so much as suffer a functional blink. And it takes two SIM cards. So you can alternate calls to get the lowest cost. No wonder the big UK telecoms companies don't like it much.

What I want to do next is text Gail but I need to think about the implications of that. So I send the new number to a few other important people; Clare, Jaki, Rory, Patrick and Megan for starters.

Realise I'm hungry. Which round here is easily resolved. Plenty of cafes with chairs outside. No differentiation between pavement and road. So long as there's enough room left for a car to squeeze past, all's well. Not feeling adventurous. Want something quick and filling. Kofta fits the bill. That's meatballs to you. With salad and chips. Resist both dessert and a beer. Opt for diet coke and a black Turkish coffee, sugar-sweet and heavy on the taste buds. Reviving after a day's travel.

Walk back round the corner to my hotel. Ignore the temptation of the bar. I'm getting much more disciplined about avoiding late evening alcohol. Take another coffee outside among the smokers. Go to bed. Sleep like a baby. Put it down to emotional exhaustion.

***

For a moment on waking, I'm unsure where I am. A strange bed and alien light penetrating the gap between the curtains. As an Englishman I'm not used to warming rays of sun on a March morning. Then I remember why I set my alarm. So I could breakfast ahead of the rush. Don't feel much like sharing a table or making conversation about who I am or why I'm here. Not yet. Need to get my head straight. Get over the wrench of enforced dislocation. From home. From Gail. From everything I value and love.

Get up. Shower. In cold water. Not from choice. Towel down. Shave and dress. Jeans, t-shirt and a red hoodie I doubt I'll need for much of the day. Just planning to walk around. Re-acclimatise. Consider. After all this is Day One of the week I'm allowing myself. A sort of holiday. After that I'll set about reeling in Umit and my other contacts. Find something to do for the rest of my first ninety days. Ninety days because that's what the tourist visa allows. Ninety days out of a perfect darts score. One hundred and eighty. Have to work out where I'm going next if I have to. If my friends can't get me an extension. Or I can't get the longer work visa

I'll doubtless need. If Clare hasn't engineered Tony's fall from grace by then. So I can go home.

The choice is to turn left at the end of the street towards the Galata Bridge and the cafes and bars beneath it which may well be clogged up with Syrian refugees or to turn right and head past Topkapi and up to the Grand Bazaar. Go for the latter. Lose myself in the crowds buying and selling. When I'm tired of that I find fresh air, silence and a cappuccino in the roof garden of a hotel. Views over a large chunk of the city. Sit until awareness dawns of the changing light and thus the passage of time. Food. A day gone without decisions or any attempt to contact Gail. A wailing sadness in my head. Bed. Eventually sleep.

***

I put a brave face on everything. But the truth is I don't want to be here at all. And certainly not here alone. If Gail was with me there'd be no need for stoicism or sorrow. Anything we could choose to do together would be just fine with me. But her absence creates frustration and worry.

Sit in Hamdi's cafe. Play backgammon. Discuss the causes of the anti-Erdogan riots. Listen to live music over coffee and brandy at Sirena's under the Galata Bridge. Brave residual demonstrators and their dangerous police shadows, to walk uphill into Taksim. Buy brightly coloured socks and an expensive blue shirt of soft paper-cotton. Explore the Arkeoloji Muzeleri and Topkapi collections. Pore over the exhibits in the armoury which would come in useful if you-know-who was here. I could imagine myself taking one of the vicious looking maces or swords to him. Troll around the spice market, the bonjhuk area with all its specialty beads and materials, and the Grand Bazaar itself. Find a useful bookshop. Buy a volume of beautiful photographs of Istanbul for a preposterous three hundred Turkish lira.

Sit with a mixed bunch of ex-patriates in the Irish bar watching rugby, a game I know nothing about. Not that it stops me trying to explain the rules to a Belgian couple who know even less. Argue with a beautiful Italian girl who mistakes me for Top Gear's James May. Look nothing like him except for the bushy hair. For all of ten seconds consider inviting her back to my hotel room. To prove I'm not a television personality. What else would I want with her? Don't bother. Betrayal for momentary pleasure doesn't have any place in my psyche.

That's my week's worth. Time to find some work. Surprisingly easy as it happens in this football-mad country. All Istanbul's teams are sprinkled with European players. Stars-to-be finding their feet or elite names looking at a last payday as their pace, if not their skills, decline. The problem with my experience isn't finding work. It's doing it legally. Proper clubs can't afford to take on black market workers. Meaning queues, interviews and documentation at government ministries. And lots of procrastination. The unofficial mantra here seems to be never to put off till tomorrow what can be put off till the day after tomorrow.

Eventually my patience snaps and I do what I should have done in the first place. Listen to the advice that I should have got myself a work permit before I arrived. It sounds contrary but it may well be easier to get it in the UK than here in Istanbul. Take hand luggage, a letter from my potential employers and proof of residence at the Agan Hotel, the receipt for two months advance rent. Take a taxi to Kemal Ataturk Airport. Fly to London. Book into a central hotel. Camp at the consulate for a couple of days until they agree to sell me the requisite visa for the fat end of three hundred quid. Covering me for the next nine months. Take a flight back. Only another travel day wasted. Produce the new document at passport control. Allowed in. I'm legal. Now get on with it.

So how to waste nine months? Two hundred and seventy-seven days. Not that I'm counting. How to keep my spirits up and write a weekly letter home, addressing each envelope to Megan in the hope that she'll be willing to find the opportunities to smuggle them like illegal samizdat to Gail? Carrying on doing that without getting any reply.

Letting football consume me. Occasionally visiting a kick-boxing class and usually regretting it next day when the muscles are protesting. I should either do it properly and regularly or not at all. Have a drink with Umit once in a while. He does his best to keep me sane. Sometimes I let him take me to his home in the hinterland between the relative poverty of Kasimpasa, where he grew up, and the wealth of Taksim. His wife and children are great but being part of a loving household for a few hours is a painful reminder of what I don't and may now never have.

All my thoughts and sleepless nights are geared to a city nearly 1700 miles away where people I love go on without me. And I know not what they do.

Chapter XVII Now: June

"I don't understand. If you didn't want to sell the shares. How could he force you to leave? You're not afraid of him."

"Not for myself. But something happened to Jaki. She was attacked going home to her flat one afternoon by a man who gave her a message for me. And told her he'd do the vilest things to her if I didn't back off. He said he'd drip acid on her. Dissolve her face drop by drop. And do the same to anybody else I love."

Gail shakes her head in disbelief.

"That's not the whole story. I was told about plans to plant stories about me so the club would have to suspend me. That wouldn't have mattered. Except...what he was going to allege would have dragged in Rory. And Liam too."

"What was he saying?"

Deep breath. Recalling it moves an incurable sense of injustice in me. Stay calm. "He was going to allege that from the time I began training Rory at thirteen, I was grooming him for sex. And that I'd started on his brother too. And that he'd stopped Liam going to football training because he found out and wanted to save him. You remember Liam was offered a trial with the club because of his brother but I was told he didn't want it. Anyway he said he'd make it very convincing, given my history. He also said he'd allege that Clare had used her position to ensure a police cover-up. He'd have dragged everybody into it. He'd have compromised the criminal investigation I knew was on-going. It would have been leaked to the papers. No smoke without fire. I couldn't let that happen to the boys. It would have killed Rory's career stone-dead for starters..."

"But he's Rory and Liam's father."

"Yes. And your point is...?"

"I don't believe it. He wouldn't. Would he?"

"Apparently he would. You should talk to Clare. She'll fill you in. And there are tapes too. Recordings I made of my meetings with Tony." I've stopped referring to him as Gail's husband. He has no status with her anymore as far as I'm concerned. "Hear him for yourself."

"Does Rory know all this?"

"Not all of it. Just enough to know I wasn't abandoning him on a whim to go to Istanbul."

"I need to talk to him. And Clare."

"Yes. You do."

She leaves me sitting there. Not so much as a backward glance. In a funny way I understand how she feels. How do you carry on caring for somebody who brings this sort of shit down on the heads of your family?

***

The adjourned inquest into Sandrine's death re-convenes on a mild Friday in June. None of the morning sunshine penetrates the old courtrooms which feel chilly in every respect. The heating's been switched off since April Fools Day. I'm glad I put a jacket on.

First up. DNA results. A match. Identity confirmed. Sandrine Desmoullins. Aged 24. Place of birth Saint-Nazaire. A Breton then. Another Celt. Impact injuries; displaced pelvis, broken bones in both feet. Cause of death unascertainable. Drowning? Suffocation in the mud of the estuary bottom? Nobody will ever know for certain. No evidence of injury prior to entering the water. CCTV footage showing she was alone on the bridge immediately before jumping. Uncoerced. Apparently.

The finding looks a foregone conclusion. Suicide. But not quite so clear cut actually. The coroner indicates his reservations. Lack of a farewell note. Witness statements indicating a history of hard drug misuse. Of course they do. One of them is mine. Another from Rory. Last persons to see her alive all in my house Christmas night. But her stated intention then was talking to Tony Lenahan. Who has been questioned. Unco-operatively. Nobody sees hide nor hair of her for three solid weeks before she appears on the bridge cameras. And nothing to show how she got there from Lincoln. No taxi or bus driver coming forward despite televised appeals. No motorist admitting to picking up a hitch-hiker that day. A total blank.

The coroner's verdict distinctly equivocal. He cannot rule out the possibility that she was under the influence of narcotics, possibly taken in dangerous proximity to the consumption of alcohol, at the time of her death. She may have been incapable of forming the intention to take her own life. Conclusion. A form of non-determination. An open verdict.

"All rise."

We do. That's over then.

***

Can't leave things there. Of course I can't. Back in asking to see the coroner's officer. Expect a burly ex-policeman, sympathetic up to a point but bored by over familiarity with death in all its many forms. Once more life teaches me not to stereotype. What I get is a smiling woman of middle years, almost casually dressed. Cord skirt, soft blue cardigan and wedge-heeled sandals. Recognise her. She was in the courtroom. Taking notes. Should kick myself for assuming she was just a secretary. In fact, as I discover, Stephanie Cross is the business. The one who makes things happen for the coroner.

She listens patiently to what I have to tell her and then calmly let's me know that my concerns raise nothing she hasn't already thought for herself. She expresses a seemingly genuine interest in Daniel and Rory and trusts me with one new piece of information, asking me to keep it to myself for now.

"Tony Lenahan has managed to avoid answering questions on a voluntary basis. I understand a warrant has now been issued for his arrest on drug charges. He'll be in custody in Lincoln as soon as they track him down. Humberside officers will be taking the opportunity to interview him down there about Sandrine. And the questions you've posed will all be covered. I promise you."

"That's good. Thanks for seeing me. I'll leave you to it."

"You're welcome." That nice smile again. Bet she's a hit with the uniforms.

***

Driving home, two thoughts cross my mind. Stephanie Cross referred to 'Sandrine'. Not 'Ms Desmoullins'. She can't have known her. When did we get to the point of finding it comfortable to refer to complete strangers by their given names rather than their surnames? And why would the police be any more likely to make any headway with Tony now? Need to ask Clare.

***

Tell Gail all about the inquest over dinner. It's been far too many years since I had the privilege of someone to talk to whenever I needed to share something. Love having her here to bounce ideas off, to tell me when I'm being daft, to share each other's concerns and feelings.

A good weekend literally kicks off with Saturday's game. I'd assumed dragging her to the football would be met with resistance, but Gail admits, to my considerable surprise, that she's never seen Rory play a professional match before. Tony always stopped her going. Sport was his domain not hers. Think seeing her son play and win gives her enormous joy. Catch her smiling to herself in quiet moments all weekend and when I suggest travelling with the official supporters bus to the next away game her response is enthusiastic.

Sunday morning brings a long walk along the riverside with all our motley crew, and a late roast dinner, prepared through the medium of excellent teamwork. At last a woman who can bear to share a kitchen without masquerading as a temporary domestic tyrant.

Wave her off to work Monday morning with a strong sense of satisfaction with life, the universe and everything.

***

Obviously nobody's told Tony he's supposed to be in police custody. I discover he's on the loose for myself. Find him lounging against my gatepost early afternoon. No idea how long he's been there. No sign of any escorts or his big car. Just him. Straightens as he spots me. "Wanted to ask you something to your face. Are you going to leave my wife alone? She shouldn't be here with you. She should be in her own home."

What do I say to that? I'm hardly going to open my heart to him. In fact I'm confessing nothing at all to the smiling sociopath. Stonewall.

"It's her decision. What she wants to do." Is that equivocal enough?

Tony lifts and points a finger at me. "When this is over she won't want you anymore. And you certainly won't want her."

"Is that a threat?" Stupid thing to say. Of course it's a threat. What else could it be?

He laughs. Not a pleasant sound. And saunters away.

Phone Gail at work to warn her. She doesn't answer her mobile. Leave her a message. Wait a bit. Try Gail again. No dice. Try the shop phone. It goes straight to ansaphone so she must be busy with customers. Hope that's it. Leave a message. Tell myself my sense of mild anxiety is misplaced. Its just the affect Tony's had.

Now towards the end of the afternoon. Still no response from Gail. Must have tried half a dozen times. Concern building up in me. Becoming more agitated by the hour. And not sure what to do. Maybe nothing I can do. They close the shop at four on Mondays so no point in driving down to Newark. And can't exactly turn up on the doorstep of her old house demanding to know if she's gone over there to talk to her husband.

Mind you I know someone who can. Phone Megan. Of course she will pop across for me. It's in walking distance of her office anyway. She also gives me Jenny Smith's mobile number. So I phone her next. Turns out she's had the afternoon off to attend something at her son's school. But she left Gail busy in the workroom setting up orders for new stock and materials. She obviously decides to pander to my concern because she offers to go to the shop to see if Gail's still there.

"Would you? You are a star. Thank you so much."

Jenny does phone back as promised. From the shop. "There's nobody here. It was all locked up properly and the alarm was on. And her car's gone. She's taken all the normal keys off the pegboard. The only odd thing is she's left her handbag."

“Where was it?”

“Standing in plain sight in the kitchen. On the worktop. Can’t think why she forgot it.”

I can. To leave a message behind. She wouldn’t willingly leave it. It’s normally super-glued to her arm. Don’t say that to Jenny of course. Don’t want to alarm her. “Okay. Thanks. I’ll tell her. Hopefully she’s on her way home.”

More waiting for the phone to ring. Only a few minutes. But feels a lifetime. And then Megan lands in person instead of calling. Saying there's no sign of anybody at Tony’s. No answer to her repeated knocking. No cars on the driveway. Her spare key, originally given her to get in to feed and walk Boo and never handed back, is useless. Because the other deadlock's on.

"What do we do now?" Reinforcing each other's panic.

Only one choice now. To take things to my sister

***

Try Clare. Get put through extraordinarily quickly.

"I was just going to ring you."

"Saved you the bother. I'm rather concerned. Not been able to get hold of Gail."

"When did you last see her?"

"I saw her off to work this morning."

Clare goes silent on me.

"You there still?"

"Look. Come over to my office. We need to talk."

"I need to find Gail."

"Precisely. Come now. Don't worry. I'll send a couple of my people to Tony’s house. We’ll get somebody down to the shop to check it over properly. So give me Jenny Smith’s number. I want Gail here too as much as you do. For her own safety and because we all have to go over some stuff."

"Now you're worrying me."

"Just come." No words of solace. Nor even platitudes.

Hang up. Find my keys. Call Jimmy and Ethan. Make sure Daniel's alright with Jaki. Get in the car. Go the half mile up

West Parade. Revisit the green-painted reception area. Different sergeant. No delay this time. I'm expected apparently. Ushered straight upstairs. Given a comfortable chair in Clare's office. Offered a drink. Asked to wait. Not told.

Despite the coffee, not feeling good. Premonitions lurking around the corners of my mind. Gail's in trouble. Don't know how I feel it with such certainty. But I do. Deep intuition issuing warnings. Watch the clock on the wall. Black hands against a silver face. It doesn't tick. Small print carries the words 'Radio Controlled' and beside them an icon like the wifi symbol on my laptop. Four minutes pass. Five. Six. Seven. Clare bustles in with an armload of papers she shoves into a space on her desk. Gives me a quick hug. Then straight into it.

"The Lenahan house is locked up. No response to doorbell or phone. My officers are pretty sure it's empty. We're escalating things because we're worried about her safety but we will find her."

"It's because of me, isn't it? That she's not safe from him."

"No. You mustn't think like that. It's more likely down to something she chose to do for herself. Nothing to do with you at all. She helped us last week. Gave us information so we could arrest Tony. I wanted her to come in and stay here when we executed the warrant. Protective custody. Or stay at yours with Jimmy and Ethan to guard her. But she wouldn't. Said she'd carry on working as usual. And it's been a cock-up with Humberside. They took Tony off our hands for questioning about Sandrine's death. His solicitors got to a tame magistrate...Anyway they cut him loose without telling us straight away. He's had several hours head start."

"I knew he was out. He came to see me this afternoon. Making threats. I should have phoned you at once. I just didn't think he'd do anything to really harm her. But when I couldn't get hold of her..."

"What time was that?"

"About one I think. I don't always wear a watch around the house. Only if I'm going out or working. As you very well know."

"The neighbours saw Tony with his Indian driver lunchtime-ish."

"Sudhir."

"Yes, Sudhir. There were a lot of comings and goings then. Tony locked up the house soon after. Looks like he drove down the hill to confront you. The timing fits. Nobody's seen him since."

The space-age phone console emits a steady bleeping sound. She picks up the handset. Listens. Says "Put them through." Introduces herself. Listens some more. Asks a couple of questions. Hangs up.

"Well we know where Tony is now. He turned up with his brief at Hull Central volunteering to answer any questions they have for him."

"But where's Gail?"

"Not with him anyway. That's good news. I've asked them to question Tony if he knows the whereabouts of his wife. They'll ring back with the answer."

"You realise he's given himself an unbreakable alibi?"

She sighs.

Twenty minutes before the return call. It's brief. "He said 'I've no idea. Why should I? I don't keep tabs on where she goes and who she sees.' Lying git!"

"Clare. You said Gail helped you. What did she tell you?"

"She came to see me. Here at work. She gave me the location and combination for a hidden wall safe. At Tony's home. Containing documents and money and a quantity of drugs. We executed a search warrant and arrested Tony on the basis of the hard evidence we found. Even if the drugs were for personal use, there were a fair amount. And the money. Probable proceeds of crime. Lot of it. He'd have to try to prove a legitimate source if he wanted it back and I suspect he couldn't. Our people are trawling the documents and coming up with some promising lines of enquiry. We'll finally make a case against him with this and what we already had."

"So she's a witness. You should have looked after her better."

"I know. I'm very sorry."

***

The police station is over-warm and airless. Need to be outside. Tell Clare I'm going home. She frowns. Know she wants me where she can see me. But doesn't try to stop me leaving. Down the steps. Jimmy's waiting patiently in the car with Ethan. Pulls away carefully from the kerb and drives us back into the West End. The mood is sombre. Nothing constructive to do and no way to make it otherwise.

Come in to find Daniel in bed and Liam, Jaki and Rory sipping coffee in the front room. The television's off. Says a lot about their anxiety levels. It's Liam and Rory's mum too of course. It's such a new fact to me that I still overlook it most of the time. Ethan offers to re-boil the kettle for more coffee we probably won't want to drink. He's on his feet when the doorbell goes. Sounding continuously. A finger pressed down on it.

"I'll go."

Seconds later chaos descends. Loud shouts and the crash of a piece of furniture over-turning. Boo going mad. Jimmy out of his chair marginally ahead of Rory and me. Hard to make sense of the scene in the front of us. Twilight gloom enveloping the hall. A dark-complected man, who I don't immediately recognise because I can't see him properly, is struggling to push the umbrella stand off his back and is being prevented from doing so by the weight of Ethan lying across him and it. When he sees me he stops moving and speaks one word. My name. And I realize it's Sudhir.

"Let him up, Ethan. Get the dog off him. What are you doing here? Do you know something? Any news at all? Tell me. Now!"

"I came to help. Think he's done something very bad."

"Tony?"

"Mr Lenahan. Yes. He was so angry. The night he was arrested. When they let him go. He kept saying 'That bitch!' "

"Sandrine?" Clutching at straws.

"No. His wife. He meant his wife. He said if she wanted to leave him, he'd teach her a lesson. He said he'd make sure she didn't come to you. Or go anywhere."

Utter the unthinkable as calmly as I can. "Has he killed her?"

"No. No. He wants to punish her. For even looking at you. The way his mind works, she can't be sorry if she's dead."

"Do you know where she is? Where's he taken her?"

"Two hard men came to the house. Men who enjoy hurting people for the sake of it. He wouldn't do anything himself. Get his hands dirty. And he wouldn't ask me to do it. He knows I wouldn't."

Cranking up another whole notch of panic. Holding things together by sheer effort of will. "So where is she?"

Sudhir shakes his head. "I don't know for sure. There's places we can check. Empty houses he owns on Wragby Road. And he bought some units off Tritton Road next to the football club land."

At last. Something to do. Icy calm settling as the brain clicks into gear. "We'll try the industrial estate first." Thrust Jimmy out the door as Ethan rights the umbrella stand and the others follow close on our heels. Stop to push Liam back into Jaki's grasp. "You have to stay here!"

Into the Range Rover. "Go! Go!" Jimmy doesn't need urging. Pedal to the metal. The beast takes off. Rocket-like. Alarmingly fast. Taking amber lights at speed. Cutting up anybody who gets in our way. Fortunately traffic's light at this time of the evening. Still miraculous we don't cause an accident. Or it's a tribute to whatever advanced driving courses Jimmy's taken.

"There. Stop there!" Sudhir points out a row of low, shed-like structures. Brick foundations surmounted by fabricated steel sectional walls.

"Okay. Sudhir! Take Ethan. That way. You two with me! We'll do the end two."

Waste of time. Nothing to find. Massive padlocks on roller shutters. Locked security doors. No open rear exits. Back to the front of the buildings. No sign of Sudhir or Ethan. Start to walk back towards the car.

When it all happens. Confusingly swiftly. On-rushing footsteps. Nearly barged over. Ethan shouts "Oi! Stop!" No affect. Back view of a running man. All in black. Black t-shirt, jeans and trainers. Disappearing fast.

Turn in the direction he came from. Starting to move as Sudhir and Jimmy come into view. Sudhir's carrying something. No. Someone. A woman. "Oh, no! God!" Gail. Stains on Sudhir's cream shirt. Bloody stains. "Jesus!" Blood. A lot of blood.

Gently take her from Sudhir. Not as heavy as you'd think. Or it's the adrenalin. Jimmy reversing the car at speed towards us. Ethan and Sudhir helping me get her onto the backseat. Lying on her side. Her head in my lap. Rory hopping into the front seat. Helpless distress written large on his face. Blast away, wheels spinning, leaving the other two unlikely allies to make their own way back.

Accident and Emergency. Arguing at reception. Grab a gurney. A nurse, seeing the urgency, helping us get Gail onto it. Only then really taking in the tattered ruins of her dress and how slickly wet the back of it is.

Horrible touch of déjà vu. Standing there in Lincoln County watching them wheel her away. Helpless. Deeply afraid.

***

A taxi brings Ethan and Sudhir to the hospital. They join us in the cafe. Waiting. It's going to be a long night's vigil at Gail's bedside. When they let Rory and me in to see her. She's had a blood transfusion and her wounds have been cleaned, taped or stitched and bandaged. At the moment she's lying flat on her stomach, sedated to the eyeballs. Going nowhere. But not in any danger. They say. So it must be true.

"Well?"

Ethan looks to Sudhir to answer me.

"The one who ran - he got away. The other one. The one who had the whip. I hit him with a piece of four by two. He was still out when we went back in. Ethan kicked him about. Then we called the police. And got out of there."

"And what they did to her ... Tony ordered that?"

Sudhir affirms with a grunt. Clearing his throat to say something more. Doesn't. Rory's slumped beside him on a low chair. Deeply distressed. Shock and fear'll do that to you, however brave you are.

"You're certain?" I don't want to believe the cold malevolence of it. Even of Tony.

"Sure of it."

"Then he's going to pay."

Ethan finds his voice. Speaks for the first time. "This is evil. What was done. But leave it to your sister. If you go after him, you'll kill him. I know that's what you want to do. I would. But if you do this, you'll be in prison. Or on the run. Either way you won't be here to look after her. And she's going to need you like you won't believe." The calm logic of the professional. He even makes sense through the haze of my own fury.

Sudhir takes my arm. Forces me to sit. Says, "Listen to Ethan. He's right. You have to be calm. Do nothing."

Ethan adds "I'm getting you a coffee."

Consider the cup on the table in front of me. Reaching for it signals surrender. She has to come first. Several miles ahead of revenge. Drink the contents of the mug. Phone Clare. Dismiss Ethan and Sudhir. Tell Rory to go home to Jaki. Tell him his mother will be fine. Try saying that with real conviction. A struggle.

Go back onto the ward. Eventually sleep in the chair by Gail's bed. In the morning start to deal with the puzzled look of hurt in her eyes. We're human beings. Healing is never a quick process.

Chapter XVIII Another Year

I don't like loose ends even though life's full of them.

Clare does her job. Multiple charges. Assault. Supply of Class A drugs. Corruption and conspiracy. And you may laugh; breaches of the Consumer Credit Acts. Well it was failing to pay his taxes that did for Al Capone in the end. But nothing relating to Gail. Even if she had wanted to, I wouldn't let her give evidence. She couldn't be expected to relive her ordeal under cross-examination.

Anthony Lenahan is currently lodging at Strangeways. I suspect he's not finding life very comfortable. He may have money and his drug contacts but they don't afford much protection from complete nutters. And there are more than a few of those in there. I don't like that I'm the sort of man to wish ill to another human being so I just view whatever's happening to him as karmic payback. Life's re-balancing. There still remains the issue of a marriage, or rather its ending, to sort out. Guess we'll get to that in the fullness of time but raising the subject of divorce with Gail mostly seems impossible.

Two middle-ranking council planners who shall be nameless also go to prison. Two years apiece on several counts of corruption. No councillors were charged. Odd that.

Oh and the Lenahan hatchet men turn out to be Polish. Stefan Caroli, the one with the whip, gets deported back to his motherland to face trial on several unsavoury grounds involving criminal enterprise, extortion and violence. The other Pole disappears. Nobody's able to trace him. He's probably hiding out in Nottingham or Manchester or London. Somewhere

Haven't needed Ethan or Jimmy's professional services in a long time. They're doubtless off protecting and driving other clients. We still see Ethan though. He comes by to play with Daniel. In a way he's become a substitute for the father that Tony never cared to be.

Daniel remains an unnaturally quiet and self-contained boy. He must miss his mum but bottles it up inside. It'll have to come out eventually but hopefully not in any catastrophic way. He can be drawn out by shared activities but doesn't seem to make friends his own age. He loves his toy cars and we all add to his stock from time to time. And when you hand over a new one you always get a lovely smile and polite thanks.

Sudir doesn't collect debts any longer. He needed a new career and took up gardening. He does two hours a week on ours. It looks vastly better for his efforts.

Rory and Jaki bought a house not far from mine. So Daniel has a real home now. Jaki's got her degree and is looking for a proper job. Easier said than done. It's not that she needs the money. She and Rory are planning their wedding. Rory's playing for Leicester City. We all have season tickets and drive over to watch most Saturday home games. We in this case means Jaki, Liam, Daniel and me and sometimes Gail when she feels up to it.

With all the others gone, Gail and Liam ensure I don't rattle around my house in the way I used to on my own. Liam at fifteen is quite angry. Sometimes he's baffled by his mother's contradictions. He does play football occasionally. But only for fun. With me. He's not looking at sport as a career. He questions everything and his social awareness leads me to predict a future for him in the voluntary sector. Or maybe he'll drift into law and end up a judge. He cares too much on occasion. About all the injustice in the world in which we live. I don't know how much of that is personal. He never mentions his father but I'm ready for the day when he needs to. He likes walking Boo on the common. She's really his dog now. I like having her in the house. I ought to have had a dog of my own years ago.

Clare has been spotted on the odd date with Patrick. I don't want to see her as wife number three but she's battle-hardened and grown up enough to make her own decisions. I suspect if she sees having a criminal solicitor as an impediment to her elevation to the rank of Assistant Chief Constable, she'll opt for the job. Highly ambitious and politically astute, my sister. I keep warning Patrick.

Ellie spends more time with Gail than Megan does. She copes with whatever state she finds her in with much greater aplomb than Megan seems able to. She brings an ease with her which I find restful and suspect that's why Gail likes spending time with her. She often brings her baby son, Joshua. Nearly a year old now. Sweet and calm like his mother. Gail adores holding him. One of the pleasures she most looks forward to.

The other surprisingly constant visitor is my mother who gently cajoles Gail into games of draughts and connect-four over endless cups of tea. In a sweeping moment of clarity it occurs to me that she has the best chance of all of us of stabilising Gail's spirits. Mum's softly firm with her. Can get her to do things the rest of us can't. On occasion persuading her to walk across the common, Mum leaning on her for support in lieu of the stick she will have artfully forgotten to bring with her. There is more than mere affection there now and it brings me hope of restoration on other fronts too. Sure, progress is slow but we will get there. My hope is that one day she'll be strong enough to return to working with Jenny at Smith-Ryan. With the aid of a new assistant Jenny's keeping the thing going. Actually she says the business is growing. Slowly but still…

The physical scars are becoming less pronounced on Gail's back but are unlikely to fade completely. Her skin was too badly flayed for that. She'll bear the branding of her body to remind her for the rest of her life. But what's really troubling is the vulnerability of her spirit. She isn't the woman I met in Alanya. Or the one I kissed behind Castle Hill. This one's harsher and less joyful. Or on other days, softer and eerily compliant. But my feelings just deepen with each passing season. I don't know how I ever managed to lead any sort of life worth having before she was part of it. Such a large and vital part.

On the good days, Gail will come and find me. If I'm working in my study or reading on the settee she'll put herself into my arms and we'll lie for hours hugging and kissing. But then there are the despairing days when she won't leave the bedroom and nothing of the medication or therapy seems to be working. Black dog days.

I go to the cemetery out on Washingborough Road every once in a while. There are always flowers on Sandrine's grave but I've never seen anyone else there. I wonder who leaves them for her.

Other Books By Andrew Sparke

Broken English

Something akin to poetry. A collection of short pieces

"...Will connect directly with many who'd never darken the poetry section of the bookshop...The shapes are varied: lists, memorandums and sequences of prose feature beside the more obvious poems....invariably they find...natural rhythm...Unlike much of the poetry that's offered these days, it's wholly intelligible without losing the depth that encourages the reader back a second time or more." (Amazon review)

Available on Kindle

Indie Publishing: The Journey Made Easy

"The essential guide for anyone who wants to publish a book"

Available on Kindle

Copper, Trance & Motorways

A man severely shaken by a potentially fatal car accident is pushed to change his life. Completely. The results aren't anything he could have expected.

Due in 2014, this is the second in a Lincoln Trilogy. The three works are separate stories loosely connected by place and fringe characters. The third novel, is due in 2015.

If you enjoyed this novel I'd be really grateful if you could review it at the Amazon website.

Further paperback copies of *Abuse, Cocaine & Soft Furnishings* are available on Amazon from the Amazon Market Place retailer SPARKYS or UK purchasers can send a cheque for £6.99 (which includes UK postage and packing) to Andrew Sparke, 4 Oakleigh Road, Stourbridge, West Midlands, DY8 2JX.

A pictorial record of the places in which *Abuse, Cocaine & Soft Furnishings* is set is available online at http://pinterest.com and there is also an Abuse Cocaine & Soft Furnishings Facebook page.

http://www.andrewsparke.com

http://www.amazon.com/author/andrewsparke

email: andrew.sparke@blueyonder.co.uk